A View to Die For

A VOYEUR WITNESSES MURDER

JULIE FREEBUSH

SFD PUBLICATIONS

Contents

CHAPTER ONE

The Observer

E than pushed his empty plate away, his fork creating a sharp note against the ceramic. The lasagna Claire had made—Emma's favorite—sat heavy in his stomach. The wall clock ticked away the seconds, each one bringing him closer to his appointed time. He glanced at his watch. 7:38 PM.

"That was delicious," he said, forcing himself to meet Claire's eyes across the table.

She smiled, though it didn't quite reach her eyes. "You seemed distracted tonight."

"Just work stuff." He tapped his watch. "End-of-quarter projections."

Emma scraped her fork across her plate, collecting the last bits of cheese. "Dad, can we play Monopoly tonight? You promised last week."

"Not tonight, Em." He checked his watch again. 7:40. "Maybe this weekend."

Claire stacked their plates, her movements deliberate. "You've been saying that for three weekends now."

Ethan stood, collecting silverware to help clear the table. His fingers drummed against the countertop while Claire loaded the dishwasher. 7:45.

"I think I'll take my walk now." He stretched his arms overhead, manufacturing a yawn. "Need some fresh air to clear my head."

Claire paused, dishcloth in hand. "I could join you. It's been ages since we walked together."

The suggestion froze him momentarily. This wasn't part of the routine.

"You've been cooped up all day with your lesson plans," he countered, words flowing from a script he'd rehearsed countless times. "Besides, these walks are kind of my thinking time. You know how I get—need to process the day alone."

"Right." Claire's voice flattened. "Your solitude time."

Emma looked up from her homework at the kitchen table. "Why can't Mom go? You're always alone, Dad."

The innocent observation hung in the air between them.

Ethan forced a smile, ruffling Emma's hair as he passed. "Not always, squirt. I'm here now, aren't I?"

He grabbed his jacket from the hook by the door, avoiding Claire's gaze. Her silence felt weighted, a familiar pressure he'd grown adept at ignoring.

"Back in an hour or so," he called, already halfway out the door.

The night air bit at Ethan's face as he closed the front door behind him. He zipped his jacket and set off down the sidewalk, his pace quickening with each step away from his home. The suburban neighborhood transformed around him—no longer rows of family dwellings but a hunting ground of opportunities, windows glowing like invitations.

The familiar anticipation built in his chest as he rounded the corner, that same electric current he'd first felt at seventeen. His mind drifted back to that summer evening, humid and thick with possibility.

Jason's parents had been away for the weekend. The basement rec room had been their sanctuary—video games, smuggled beers, teenage freedom. Ethan had gone upstairs for more chips, returning earlier than expected. The basement door had been cracked open just enough.

Through that sliver of space, he'd seen Jason with Melissa Coleman on the couch. Her shirt was off, Jason's hands exploring with clumsy eagerness. They hadn't heard Ethan on the stairs. Hadn't noticed him frozen there, breath caught in his throat.

He should have walked away. Should have made noise. Should have done anything but stand there, watching.

But he didn't. For seven uninterrupted minutes, Ethan had remained perfectly still, heart hammering against his ribs, a strange heat flooding his body.

Ethan lingered in the shadows, the door's edge a sharp line against the dimly lit hallway. His breath hitched as Melissa's head bobbed in a rhythmic motion, her long hair curtaining the scene from view, only to reveal Jason's flushed face, his eyes squeezed shut in pleasure.

The sounds of their shared intimacy—faint gasps and the rustle of clothing—seeped into the quiet, wrapping around Ethan like a vice. He felt a tightening in his groin, an involuntary response to the voyeuristic spectacle unfolding before him. His hand drifted down, fingers brushing against the growing bulge in his jeans.

Jason's low moan echoed through the room, and Ethan's own breath shallowed in response. He watched, entranced, as Melissa's hand joined her mouth, working in tandem with practiced ease. Jason's hips bucked upward, seeking more, his fingers tangling in her hair.

Ethan's own body responded in kind, his hand moving with increasing urgency. He bit his lower lip, stifling any sound that might betray his presence. The sensations coursing through him were both foreign and familiar, a secret pleasure that left him feeling both powerful and powerless.

As Jason's climax approached, his body tensed, a coiled spring about to release. Ethan's own release followed shortly after, a silent explosion that left him weak-kneed and gasping for air. He leaned against the wall, his heart pounding in his chest, his body flooded with a mix of shame and exhilaration.

The scene before him shifted. Jason lay back, spent, while Melissa sat up, wiping her mouth with the back of her hand. They were oblivious to the silent observer above, their world confined to the couch and the afterglow of their encounter.

Ethan staggered backward, away from the door. His mind raced, a jumble of conflicting emotions. What had he done? He adjusted his clothes, tucking himself back into his pants and tucking his shirt with trembling hands, and wiped away the evidence of his transgression with his sleeve.

He knew he should feel guilty, should be horrified by his own behavior. But as he crept back downstairs, a sense of intoxicating satisfaction washed over him. There was a power in watching, in not being seen. It was a secret thrill, a forbidden fruit that he had tasted and now craved more of.

It wasn't sexual attraction to either of them—it was something different. The forbidden glimpse into raw intimacy. The power of seeing without being seen.

They never knew he was there. He never told them.

That night in his bed, he'd replayed the scene over and over, addicted to the rush of that stolen moment. He'd felt powerful. Invisible. God-like.

Ethan slowed his pace as he entered Willow Creek Lane. Dusk settled around him, painting the sky in fading purple hues—the perfect cover for his activities. Not quite dark enough for blinds to be drawn, not bright enough to expose him. The sweet spot.

He adjusted his posture, shoulders relaxed, hands in pockets. Just another neighbor taking an evening constitutional.

Nothing to see here. He nodded at Mrs. Peterson watering her front garden, mastering the perfect balance of acknowledgment without invitation for conversation.

"Evening," he called, already moving past. Neighborly. Forgettable.

The route was etched into his muscle memory after months of refinement. First stop: the gap between the Sandersons' hedge and their garden shed. He paused to tie his shoelace, glancing around casually before slipping into the narrow passage. The position offered a perfect sightline into their dining room, where Rebecca Sanderson moved between kitchen and table, serving dinner to her husband and teenage son.

Ethan checked his watch. 8:03. Right on schedule. The Sandersons always ate late.

He stayed just long enough to observe their dinner ritual—Rebecca touching her husband's shoulder as she passed, their son hunched over his phone until scolded. Small intimacies, everyday moments they assumed were private.

Moving on, Ethan crossed to Maple Drive, where construction on the Peterson addition had created a convenient blind spot behind a stack of building materials. He slipped behind it, finding the narrow view into the Grants' living room. Television flickering, casting blue light across Jessica Grant's face as she folded laundry on the couch. Her husband entered the frame, handed her a glass of wine. Their fingers brushed during the exchange.

Ethan's breathing quickened slightly. These glimpses into domestic life—these unguarded moments—fed something in him that normal interaction never could.

His third position required more precision. The newly installed streetlight had complicated things, creating a pool of exposure he needed to avoid. He circled the block, approaching from the east side where shadows from the massive oak trees provided cover. The Coleman house—his favorite. Not for any particular attraction to the occupants, but for their carelessness. They rarely closed their blinds completely.

Ethan positioned himself behind the large maple tree in the Colemans' side yard. From this vantage point, he had a clear view into their living room without risk of exposure. The light from inside spilled onto the lawn, creating a golden rectangle on the grass.

Tonight, however, the scene disappointed. Mr. Coleman slouched in his recliner, remote in hand, flipping channels with robotic regularity. Every twelve seconds—Ethan timed it—another flicker as he searched for something to hold his attention. Mrs. Coleman sat at the dining table behind him, laptop open, glasses perched on her nose, completely absorbed in whatever filled her screen.

No conversation. No interaction. No revealing moments.

Ethan shifted his weight, the familiar disappointment settling in his chest. Some nights were like this—mundane, ordinary, devoid of the intimate glimpses he craved. The Colemans might as well have been mannequins arranged in a department store display of suburban living.

He checked his watch. 8:17. He'd wasted nearly ten minutes on this dead end.

The teenage daughter—Lily, he'd heard Mrs. Coleman call her once—wasn't even home tonight. Her absence removed the usual family dynamics that sometimes provided interesting observations: the eye rolls at parental questions, the body language of adolescent defiance, the unguarded expressions when she thought no one was looking.

Mr. Coleman yawned, scratched his stomach, and settled deeper into his chair. Mrs. Coleman's fingers clacked against her keyboard, pausing only to push her glasses back up her nose.

Nothing worth staying for.

Ethan retreated silently, stepping backward until he was fully concealed by darkness before turning to continue his route. The night still held possibilities.

Ethan's frustration with the Colemans' uneventful evening propelled him further, away from the sterile glow of their television. The crunch of leaves underfoot was the only sound that accompanied his quickened stride. He told himself it was the chill of the evening that had him moving so briskly, a poor excuse even in his own mind.

He made his way to the end of the cul-de-sac—to the Alvarez residence. It was always a gamble, a high-stakes toss of the dice every time he approached their property. But tonight, the universe seemed to be tipping the odds in his favor.

Their living room window—a large, single pane of glass—gleamed like a beacon in the night. The blinds, as they so often were, remained open, inviting the night to peer inside. It was almost as if they were asking for it—for the eyes that might linger just beyond their threshold.

Ethan paused behind the cover of a large willow tree in their neighbor's yard, its drooping branches providing the perfect camouflage. He kept still, his breaths shallow and controlled to avoid drawing attention. The scene before him was like a siren's call—irresistible, dangerous, and utterly intoxicating.

Jenny Alvarez reclined on the plush, suede couch, her body bathed in the soft luminescence of the television. The flickering light danced across her skin, casting a warm glow that seemed to make her even more radiant. She was alone—a rare occurrence—and, to Ethan's surprise, completely nude.

Her long, jet-black hair cascaded over her shoulders, a stark contrast to the fairness of her skin. Jenny's eyes were fixed on the screen, where the unmistakable sounds of passion and pleasure filtered out into the night.

Ethan felt the familiar tightening in his chest, the hitch in his breath as his heart rate accelerated. This was what he'd been searching for—this raw, unfiltered moment of vulnerability that was so compellingly forbidden.

Jenny's hand began to drift across her body, tracing paths over the contours of her breasts, down her flat stomach, and lower still. Her touch was slow, exploratory, as if she were discovering her own body anew.

Ethan's gaze was locked on the scene unfolding before him. His own breaths synced with the rhythm of Jenny's movements, his senses heightened to an almost painful degree. He could see the flush of arousal on her cheeks, the way her lips parted slightly, the rise and fall of her chest as her excitement grew.

Jenny's fingers worked with practiced ease, her body arching in response to the images on the screen and her own deft manipulations. The intensity of her pleasure was almost tangible, a palpable energy that seemed to ripple through the air.

Ethan watched, transfixed, as Jenny's movements became more fervent. Her breaths turned to soft moans, the sounds mingling with those emanating from the television—a symphony of desire.

The world around Ethan seemed to fade into the background, leaving only this singular, intimate tableau. He was an outsider looking in, a silent observer to a deeply personal moment that he knew he should not be witnessing—yet he could not tear himself away.

Finally, with a shuddering gasp, Jenny reached her peak. Her body tensed, then relaxed in a series of undulating waves. The sight of her in the throes of such intense pleasure was almost too much for Ethan to bear.

It was a moment of pure, unadulterated release—a moment that Jenny thought was hers and hers alone. But Ethan had seen it all.

His watch's face glowed faintly in the dark, reminding him that time was not standing still. 8:42 PM. The night was far from over, and there were still more windows to pass, more shadows to explore.

With one last lingering look through the Alvarez's window, Ethan pulled away, stepping back into the anonymity that the night provided. His heart pounded in his ears as he walked away, leaving the scene of his latest stolen observation behind.

The hunt, it seemed, was far from over.

CHAPTER TWO

Hunger

The chill of the evening clung to Ethan's skin as he made his way back home, the taste of forbidden fruit still lingering on his palate. His breath came in short, shallow bursts, the thrill of his nocturnal escapade still coursing through his veins like a potent narcotic. The image of Jenny, her body writhing in ecstasy on the suede couch, was indelibly etched into his mind's eye.

He slipped through the front door, careful not to make a sound. The familiar scent of their home greeted him—a blend of Claire's lavender-scented candles and the faint smell of the paint from her latest artwork. The television cast a flickering glow across the living room, illuminating the figure of his wife curled up on the couch, fast asleep.

Ethan paused, his gaze sweeping over Claire. She looked so peaceful in her slumber, her chest rising and falling in a steady rhythm. The resemblance to the scene he had just witnessed was uncanny—a different couch, a different woman, but the essence of the tableau was the same. It was as if the universe was playing a cruel joke on him, presenting him with a mirror image of his voyeuristic fantasy, yet rendering it utterly untouchable.

The sight of Claire, coupled with the memory of Jenny's release, ignited a fire within Ethan. His body responded with an urgency that bordered on desperation. He approached the couch, his shadow falling over Claire's sleeping form. A part of him—the part that was still tethered to the realm of decency and propriety—urged him to retreat, to allow his wife to rest undisturbed. But the compulsion that had driven him into the night was relentless, and it now demanded satisfaction in the most primal way possible.

He reached out, his hand brushing against Claire's shoulder in an attempt to rouse her gently. "Claire," he whispered, his voice barely above a breath. "Wake up, love."

Claire stirred, her eyelids fluttering open to reveal groggy, questioning eyes. She looked up at him, confusion giving way to a faint smile that never quite reached her haunted gaze. "Ethan? What time is it?" Her voice was a soft murmur, tinged with the remnants of sleep.

"It's late," he replied, his tone husky with desire. He moved closer, his hand trailing down her arm, across the curve of her hip. His intentions were clear, his body language betraying his arousal.

Claire's smile faded, replaced by a look of gentle firmness. She sat up, pulling away from his touch. "Not tonight, Ethan," she said, her voice a quiet resolve. "I'm tired."

Ethan felt a surge of frustration, a mixture of rejection and the sting of unfulfilled lust. He withdrew, his mind flashing back to that night years ago—a night that had nothing to do with desire, but everything to do with control and power.

In his mind's eye, he saw Claire as she must have been during her sophomore year of college—young, vibrant, full of life. But that image shattered as he recalled the sparse details she had shared with him in hushed, halting words. The dimly lit frat house room, the laughter and music muffled by the panic rising in her throat, the weight of a stranger pressing down on her, the crushing sense of helplessness as her protests fell on deaf ears.

The memory of her trauma acted like a cold shower, dousing the flames of his desire. Ethan stepped back, a wave of guilt washing over him. He was a man caught between two worlds—one of twisted compulsion, the other of genuine love and commitment.

"I'm sorry," he murmured, turning away from Claire, his gaze fixed on the darkened window. The night outside was still, the world beyond asleep and oblivious to the turmoil within their home.

Claire's voice reached out to him, soft and understanding. "It's okay, Ethan. Let's just go to bed."

Ethan nodded, a silent agreement to the truce she was offering. He watched as Claire rose from the couch, her movements slow and deliberate, a silent testament to her fatigue.

As she walked past him, Ethan reached out, capturing her hand in his. Her fingers were cool to the touch, a stark contrast to the heat that still simmered beneath his skin.

Together, they made their way to the bedroom, the echo of their footsteps a sobering reminder of the distance that lay between them—a distance that Ethan knew he was responsible for creating.

Morning light filtered through the kitchen blinds, casting golden stripes across the breakfast table. Ethan sipped his coffee, scanning the financial section of the newspaper while occasionally glancing at his phone. The familiar rhythm of their morning routine played out with clockwork precision, as if the tension from the previous night had evaporated with the dawn.

Claire stood at the stove, flipping pancakes with practiced ease. Her hair was pulled back in a loose ponytail, a few stray strands framing her face. She hummed softly, a habit that had always endeared her to Ethan.

"Mom, can I have chocolate chips in mine?" Emma's voice piped up from the table where she sat swinging her legs, coloring book spread before her.

"Just a few, sweetheart. Remember what happened last time you had too much sugar before school?" Claire's voice carried its usual warmth when addressing their daughter.

Emma's face scrunched in theatrical horror. "Mrs. Peterson made me sit at the quiet table."

"And we don't want a repeat of that, do we?" Claire winked, sprinkling a modest amount of chocolate chips onto the cooking batter.

Ethan folded his newspaper, setting it aside. "Big presentation today, kiddo?"

"Uh-huh. I'm showing my volcano. Tyler says it won't erupt, but I know it will." Emma's confidence was unwavering as she vigorously colored a purple sky.

"Tyler doesn't know what he's talking about." Ethan reached across to ruffle her hair. "Your volcano is going to be the best in class."

Claire placed a plate of pancakes in front of Emma, then Ethan, before sitting down with her own. Her movements were fluid, natural—betraying none of the hesitation from their nighttime encounter.

"Don't forget, I have art club after school today," Claire mentioned, cutting into her breakfast. "I'll be home around five."

"I can pick up Emma," Ethan offered, his tone casual. "We could stop for ice cream on the way home."

"Ice cream!" Emma bounced in her seat.

Claire shot Ethan a look that was half-admonishment, half-amusement. "On a Tuesday?"

"Special treat for my volcano scientist." He winked at Emma, who beamed back at him.

The three of them ate together, exchanging small talk about the day ahead. Anyone looking in would see nothing but a loving family sharing breakfast—no hint of the secrets that lurked beneath the surface, no trace of the night's rejection or the shadows that haunted their marriage.

* * *

Ethan stood before the conference room, the polished oak table reflecting the glow from his presentation slides. Ten pairs of eyes tracked his movements as he gestured toward the projection screen.

"The key insight isn't what people say they want." He clicked to the next slide showing heat maps of consumer eye-tracking studies. "It's what they're afraid to admit they desire."

Richard leaned forward, his tie dipping dangerously close to his coffee. "But our survey data shows—"

"Survey data only captures what people are willing to tell us." Ethan's voice carried the quiet confidence that had become his trademark. "Nobody admits they buy luxury watches to feel superior to their neighbors, but the subconscious drivers are there in the micro-expressions during our focus groups."

He advanced to a slide showing a middle-aged woman examining a watch display. "Look at subject twenty-three. Her eyes linger on the mid-range models, but there's a micro-expression of longing when she glances at the premium tier. She's calculating whether the status is worth the financial stretch."

Erika, the creative director, shook her head in amazement. "How do you catch these things? I've watched these videos three times and missed all of this."

Ethan offered a modest shrug while his inner voice supplied the truth: *I've spent thousands of hours watching people when they think no one's looking. I know what desire looks like in its rawest form.*

"The campaign needs to acknowledge the stated practical needs while subtly validating the unspoken emotional wants," he continued, outlining a strategy that would speak to both the conscious and unconscious mind.

Richard whistled low. "This is why you're the best in the business, Miller. You read people like books."

The team nodded in agreement, scribbling notes, completely unaware that Ethan's insights came from darkened windows and secret observations—from watching Jenny arch her back in private ecstasy, from noting how the Davidson couple's arguments always ended with passionate reconciliations, from studying the neighbor who practiced dance routines when she thought no one could see.

"We're essentially selling permission," Ethan concluded, clicking to his final slide. "Permission to want what they already desire but feel guilty about pursuing."

Just like I give myself permission every night, he thought, maintaining his professional smile as the room erupted in approving murmurs.

CHAPTER THREE

The Sales Closer

After the presentation, Ethan gathered his materials as the conference room emptied. Through the glass wall, he spotted Erika Jensen escorting two men in expensive suits toward the elevator bank. He recognized them as representatives from Meridian Capital, a potential client worth millions to the firm.

Erika walked between them, her crimson dress perfectly tailored to showcase her figure without crossing into unprofessional territory. Her hand touched the taller man's forearm as she laughed at something he said, the contact lasting three seconds longer than social convention required.

Ethan noticed how she positioned herself. The slight tilt of her head, exposing the elegant line of her neck. The way she stood just inside their personal space, creating an artificial intimacy. These weren't random behaviors—they were calculated moves in a deliberate performance.

He followed at a distance, pretending to study his phone while tracking their progress toward the lobby. Erika's body language shifted subtly as they approached the reception area where others might observe them. Her laughter became more restrained, her posture more professional, yet she maintained the invisible thread of connection with both men.

"We'll have the proposal to you by Thursday," she promised, her voice carrying across the marble floor. "And perhaps we could discuss it over dinner?"

The shorter executive's eyes dropped briefly to her neckline before returning to her face. "I'd like that."

Ethan slipped into the break room, positioning himself by the coffee machine where he could observe without being noticed. Through the doorway, he watched Erika hand each man a business card, her fingers brushing against theirs during the exchange.

Once the elevator doors closed, her entire demeanor transformed. The seductive smile vanished, replaced by the focused expression of a tactician who had successfully executed a maneuver. She checked her watch, straightened her spine, and walked briskly toward her office, nodding professionally at colleagues she passed.

She's like me, Ethan realized with a jolt of recognition. *She watches people too, studies their weaknesses, their desires. But in-*

stead of observing from the shadows, she inserts herself into the equation.

* * *

The late afternoon sun cast long shadows across the financial district as Ethan lingered by his office window, pretending to pore over market analytics on his computer. In truth, he was waiting for the office to clear, for the steady exodus of employees to reach its ebb, leaving only a skeleton crew of workaholics and overachievers.

Erika's office lay directly opposite his, the blinds perpetually half-drawn, affording her a modicum of privacy while allowing her to survey the comings and goings of her colleagues. Ethan's gaze drifted over to her window, a silent sentinel to the performances that unfolded within.

As the hour hand crept toward six, Ethan noticed the soft glow of Erika's desk lamp, a beacon in the dimming light. A man entered the frame, the same tall figure from earlier. They exchanged words, the conversation too distant for Ethan to discern, but the body language was clear—the prelude to a negotiation.

Ethan watched as Erika stood, her movements fluid and deliberate. She circled the desk, her heels clicking against the hardwood floor, a sound that carried through the stillness of the near-empty building. The man took a seat on the edge of the desk, his legs parting to accommodate her approach.

She stepped into the space he offered, her hand resting on his thigh. Even from this distance, Ethan could sense the palpable shift in the room's atmosphere—a potent cocktail of lust and ambition. Erika's other hand reached for a document on the desk, her finger tracing lines of text as she spoke, her tone lost to the ether but her intent crystal clear.

The man's hand covered hers, stopping the pretense of business. She didn't pull away; instead, she leaned closer, her lips grazing his ear as she whispered something that made him smile.

Then, with a swiftness that belied the meticulous planning behind it, she unzipped her dress. It pooled at her feet, leaving her in lingerie that seemed both a reward and a weapon. The man's eyes widened, a reaction that bordered on comical were it not so predictable.

Erika guided him to the leather couch against the far wall, the very picture of control. She straddled him, the movements of her body a dance of seduction and strategy. Every arch of her back, every roll of her hips, was a calculated step in a complex game of power and persuasion.

And Ethan, hidden in the shadows of his own office, watched with a mix of fascination and unease. He understood the language of her body, the silent dialogue between predator and prey. It was a performance, yes, but one with real stakes—a high-wire act without a safety net.

She's not just using her body, Ethan realized. *She's leveraging desire as a tool, turning sex into a transaction.* It was manipulation at its most artful, a quid pro quo that promised pleasure in exchange for profit.

As the scene unfolded, Ethan felt a disquieting kinship with Erika. They were both observers of human nature, but where Ethan remained a passive spectator, Erika was an active participant, shaping outcomes to her advantage.

She's like me, he thought again, the insight settling in with a resonance that was both chilling and compelling. *But she's bolder, braver... or perhaps just more ruthless.*

Ethan's surveillance continued until the act reached its inevitable conclusion, the man leaving with a satisfied smile and a contract signed under the intoxicating spell of Erika's charms. And as the curtains swayed gently in the aftermath, Ethan found himself wondering what it would be like to cross that line—to step out of the shadows and into the fray.

* * *

The drive home was a blur, the city lights smearing into streaks of white and gold against the encroaching darkness. Ethan's thoughts were a tangle of images—Erika's calculated disrobing, the raw need etched on the client's face, the stark contrast between the artifice of his day and the reality of his nights.

He entered the house quietly, the familiar creak of the front door a silent proclamation of his arrival. The living room was bathed in the soft glow of the television, casting flickering shadows across Claire's face as she lay curled on the couch, lost in some late-night drama.

"Hey," he said, his voice low, not wanting to startle her.

Claire looked up, her eyes heavy with sleep. "You're home late."

"Work," he offered, the lie slipping off his tongue with practiced ease. "Big project."

She nodded, accepting the explanation without question. It was a dance they'd done a thousand times, a choreography of half-truths and omissions that kept their world in delicate balance.

Ethan extended a hand, helping Claire to her feet. "Let's go to bed," he suggested, his tone gentle, belying the urgency that simmered beneath the surface.

In their bedroom, the moonlight filtered through the blinds, casting a silver sheen across the duvet. They undressed in silence, the routine familiar and comforting. Ethan's mind raced with the memory of Erika's uninhibited display, the way she'd wielded her body with such precision and power.

As they slid beneath the covers, Ethan reached for Claire, his hands seeking the warmth of her skin. He pulled her close, his body responding to the proximity, the ache of his arousal undeniable.

Claire stiffened at his touch, a reflex born of years of conditioning, a visceral response to the fear and pain that lurked in the shadows of her past.

"Ethan..." Her voice was a whisper, a plea for understanding.

He heard the unspoken words, felt the tension in her body, the invisible barrier she erected between them. "It's okay," he soothed, his hand moving lower, seeking connection, a spark of the passion he'd witnessed hours before.

Claire's hand caught his, stilling his movements. "I can't," she said, the finality in her voice a clear demarcation of her boundaries.

Ethan withdrew, his desire ebbing in the face of her discomfort. He lay back against the pillow, his gaze fixed on the ceiling, the patterns of light and shadow a poor substitute for the intimacy he craved.

Claire's touch, when it came, was tentative, her fingers skimming the length of him with a clinical detachment that spoke of obligation rather than desire. Her movements were efficient, almost perfunctory, a means to an end devoid of the raw intensity that had consumed Erika and her client.

Ethan closed his eyes, letting the physical sensations wash over him as he willed his mind to align with his body. But the disconnect was palpable, the stark contrast between Claire's mechanical ministrations and Erika's unbridled passion a sobering reminder of the chasm that separated them.

As his body succumbed to the inevitable release, Ethan felt a pang of guilt, a sense of betrayal for the thoughts that had consumed him, for the woman he longed to be with, even as he lay beside his wife.

And as the echoes of his climax faded into the quiet of the night, Ethan was left with the haunting realization that the distance between him and Claire was growing, an ever-widening gulf that threatened to swallow them both.

* * *

The rhythmic sound of Ethan's breathing filled the darkened bedroom. Claire lay motionless beside him, counting each inhale and exhale until she was certain he'd fallen into deep sleep. Slowly, she eased herself from beneath the covers, careful not to disturb the mattress.

Her bare feet made no sound against the carpet as she retrieved her laptop from the dresser drawer where she kept it hidden beneath folded sweaters. The weight of it felt like a secret itself—a portal to the parts of herself she couldn't yet share with Ethan.

Claire slipped into the bathroom, closing the door with practiced silence before settling on the edge of the bathtub. The screen's glow illuminated her face in harsh blue light as she opened an incognito browser window and typed: "sexual trauma recovery intimacy exercises."

The search returned dozens of results. She clicked through to a professional therapy resource site she'd bookmarked weeks earlier. Her eyes scanned the page, absorbing information about progressive desensitization techniques.

"Start with non-sexual touch," she read, underlining the phrase in her notebook. "Build tolerance through gradual exposure in safe environments."

Claire's hand trembled slightly as she wrote, but her jaw was set with determination. Three years of therapy had given her tools, language for what she experienced. But the physical intimacy—that remained the final frontier.

She scrolled further, finding a section on communication exercises for partners. Claire paused, pen hovering above paper. Telling Ethan would mean explaining everything—all the details of the assault, not just the sanitized version she had told him in the past, the therapy, the years of secrecy. The thought made her stomach clench.

Instead, she focused on self-directed exercises. "Mirror work," she wrote, noting the recommendation to practice comfort with her own body first. "Mindfulness during physical sensations."

A new article caught her attention: "Reclaiming Sexual Agency After Trauma." Claire clicked, hungry for any wisdom that might bridge the gap between her mind's desire for connection and her body's instinctive recoil.

She filled three pages with notes, diagrams of breathing techniques, and a weekly schedule of progressive exercises. This wasn't just research—it was a battle plan, a roadmap back to herself.

Claire glanced at her watch. Nearly an hour had passed. She closed the laptop, the screen's light vanishing and leaving her in darkness, clutching her notebook to her chest like armor.

CHAPTER FOUR

Office Encounters

The morning at Horizon Financial began like any other. Ethan, with his usual meticulousness, had arrived early, his mind already cataloging the day's tasks. The office was a symphony of keyboard clicks and hushed conversations, a backdrop to his thoughts that hummed with unspoken anticipation.

As he made his way to the men's room, the day's routine was violated by a sound that did not belong—a soft, unmistakable moan, muffled yet arresting. Ethan paused, his hand on the door handle. His heart thudded in his chest, a drumbeat of voyeuristic instinct that had long since become second nature.

He pushed the door open, the sound of his own breathing amplified in the sudden silence. There, in the furthest stall, the sliver of space beneath the door revealed a pair of sleek, black high heels—Erika's signature footwear.

Ethan's pulse quickened. His gaze remained fixed on those heels, his own reflection in the polished tile walls an afterthought. The stall door was slightly ajar, and as he approached, the sounds of hushed urgency grew clearer.

Peering through the narrow opening, Ethan's breath caught. Erika was there, her skirt hiked up, her blouse undone, straddling a man in the confined space of the stall. Her hair cascaded down her back in golden waves as she moved with a practiced grace that was both mesmerizing and transactional.

The man remained a faceless entity, his own trousers pooled around his ankles—a mere accessory to Erika's performance. Ethan recognized the dynamic immediately; he'd seen it before, the way Erika wielded her sexuality like a weapon, a means to an end.

Ethan's mind raced, cataloging every detail—the flush of Erika's cheeks, the way her lips parted with each breath, the grip of her fingers on the stall's metal walls. It was a tableau of raw, unvarnished need, a scene that would fuel his secret fantasies for nights to come.

Yet, as he watched, a part of him recoiled. This was different from his nightly observations; this was a violation of privacy, an intrusion into a realm that was not his to explore. Ethan's compulsion warred with a burgeoning sense of guilt, a reminder that his actions were not without consequence.

Erika's moans grew louder, her movements more frenzied. Ethan knew he should leave, should turn away and allow the pair their moment of illicit connection. But his feet remained rooted to the spot, betrayal and desire twisting together into a knot that was impossible to untangle.

The moment stretched on, a silent testament to Ethan's inner conflict. And then, as abruptly as it had begun, it was over. Erika stilled, her head bowed, chest heaving as she caught her breath. The man behind her was a shadow, his face still obscured by the angle and the dim lighting.

Ethan took a step back, the sound of his own heartbeat thunderous in his ears. He turned and exited the men's room, leaving the aftermath of the encounter behind him. The scene would be etched into his memory, another secret to carry, another line crossed in the silent theater of his voyeurism.

* * *

The cafeteria buzzed with the midday chatter of Horizon Financial employees. Ethan settled at a table with his usual lunch group—Sandra from Compliance, Marcus from IT, and Priya from Accounting. His mind still replayed the bathroom scene, images of Erika's encounter flashing through his consciousness like a fragmented film reel.

"Earth to Ethan," Priya waved her hand in front of his face. "You've been staring at that salad like it contains the secrets of the universe."

Ethan blinked, forcing himself back to the present. "Sorry. Just thinking about the Henderson account."

"Speaking of accounts," Sandra leaned forward, lowering her voice. "Did you hear about the audit? External firm coming in next week."

Marcus groaned. "Another one? We just had the quarterly review."

"This is different," Sandra's eyes gleamed with the excitement of someone privy to valuable information. "They're specifically targeting vendor payments and consulting fees. Word is they found some irregularities in the transactions Richard's been overseeing."

Ethan's fork paused midway to his mouth. "What kind of irregularities?"

"Payments to shell companies, invoices for services never rendered." Sandra stabbed at her pasta. "Typical embezzlement stuff. They're focusing on something called 'Decker Consulting' in particular."

The cafeteria doors swung open, and Richard Langford strode in, his tailored suit a stark contrast to the casual Friday attire of most employees. Ethan's observational instincts kicked in automatically, cataloging details most would miss.

Richard approached the salad bar, his movements precise but with an underlying stiffness. As he reached for the tongs, Ethan noticed his wedding ring—twirling it, a nervous tell he'd observed before during tense board meetings.

"Speak of the devil," Marcus muttered.

Sandra continued, oblivious to Richard's presence. "The audit team is requesting five years of transaction records. If there's something fishy, they'll find it."

Richard's head turned slightly at the word "audit," though he was too far to hear the specifics. His shoulders tensed, a micro-expression of alarm flashing across his face before disappearing behind his practiced corporate mask.

"Wonder if our bonuses will be affected," Priya sighed.

Ethan watched as Richard abandoned the salad bar, his lunch half-assembled, and checked his phone with unusual urgency. The financial director's fingers moved rapidly over the screen, his jaw clenched tight enough that a muscle twitched visibly along his temple.

"He doesn't look happy," Ethan observed quietly.

"Would you be?" Sandra raised an eyebrow. "If the rumors are true, someone's going down for this."

* * *

"Daddy, I picked Encanto!" Emma bounced on the couch, clutching the remote in her small hands. "You promised we'd watch it together last week."

Ethan checked his watch, the familiar itch already crawling beneath his skin. "That's great, sweetie."

Claire entered with a bowl of popcorn, her eyes meeting Ethan's with immediate understanding. "You're going out again."

It wasn't a question.

"Just for a quick walk." Ethan grabbed his jacket from the hook by the door. "Work stress. Need to clear my head."

Emma's smile collapsed. "But it's movie night. You promised."

"I'll be back before it ends." The lie tasted stale on his tongue, recycled from dozens of similar evenings.

"You always say that." Emma's voice had gone small, her eyes dropping to the floor.

Claire set the popcorn down with deliberate care. "Emma picked this movie especially for you. The father-daughter story reminded her of you."

Guilt flared briefly, but the compulsion burned hotter. Ethan was already calculating the route to Erika's apartment, the optimal viewing position, the chances she'd have company tonight.

"Twenty minutes. Thirty tops." He avoided Emma's disappointed gaze. "Save me some popcorn."

The door closed behind him, muffling Emma's response.

Inside, Emma curled against Claire's side as the movie's colorful opening sequence filled the screen.

"Why doesn't Daddy want to stay home anymore?" Her question hung in the air between them. "Is it because of me?"

Claire's heart cracked. "No, baby. Never because of you."

"Then why?" Emma persisted. "He used to watch movies with us all the time."

Claire stroked her daughter's hair, searching for an explanation that wouldn't further damage her child's sense of security. "Sometimes grown-ups get... distracted by things. It doesn't mean they love their families any less."

"What things?"

"I wish I knew," Claire whispered, more to herself than to Emma.

Across town, Ethan positioned himself in his usual spot behind the oak tree with clear sightlines to Erika's window. Her silhouette moved behind the sheer curtains, the familiar thrill of anticipation rushing through him.

Tonight felt different. More urgent. His earlier jealousy had morphed into something darker, more possessive. He'd begun making mental notes, cataloguing her patterns in his mind with the same analytical precision he applied to consumer behavior studies.

8:37 PM: Returns home

8:42 PM: Changes clothes (bathroom light on)

9:15 PM: Phone call (animated gestures suggest important conversation)

The notes helped him make sense of his obsession, transforming it from shameful voyeurism into something that felt almost legitimate. Research. Analysis. Understanding.

Erika's shadow approached the window. Ethan's breath caught.

* * *

The shadow of a police cruiser slid silently along the darkened street. Detective Zoe Marlowe killed the headlights as they approached the neighborhood's entrance, the glow from dashboard instruments casting harsh angles across her face.

"Third report this month," she said, eyes scanning methodically from house to house. "Same description each time. Male, average height, wearing dark clothing, moving between properties after dark."

Her partner, Detective Reyes, nodded. "Could be teenagers. Could be nothing."

"Could be. Isn't." Marlowe tapped her pen against her notepad. "Pattern's too consistent. Same three-block radius. Same time window. Always solo."

She pulled the cruiser to the curb, positioning it where the streetlight shadow would provide cover. "Let's walk the perimeter."

They exited the vehicle, Marlowe immediately noting the layout of the neighborhood – upper-middle class homes, decent spacing between properties, mature trees providing multiple shadow corridors.

"Perfect hunting ground," she murmured.

"For what?" Reyes asked.

"That's what we're here to find out." Marlowe pointed to a house with a basketball hoop. "Start there. Work north. I'll take the south side. Check for security cameras, doorbell cams, anything that might have caught our prowler."

"Most of these look like standard home security setups. Probably not aimed at the street."

Marlowe's eyes narrowed as she spotted movement near an oak tree several houses down. "That's why we need to find every single one. Get addresses, get consent forms ready. By tomorrow, I want footage from every camera in a five-block radius."

"That's dozens of houses."

"Then we better start knocking." Marlowe was already moving, her stride purposeful. "Check garages too. Look for cameras aimed at driveways. And get the techs ready to pull traffic cam footage from the main intersections."

"You think this is more than just some peeping Tom?"

Marlowe paused, her expression hardening. "Twenty years on the job teaches you one thing: people who watch eventually do more than watch."

CHAPTER FIVE

The Hidden Affair

Ethan's breath fogged the cool glass as he peered through the narrow gap in Erika's curtains. The streetlight cast a jaundiced glow over the scene, etching stark shadows across the couple. Richard's imposing frame loomed over Erika, the strain of their coupling visible in his clenched jaw and the veins standing out on his neck.

Erika lay beneath him, her body a canvas of light and shadow, the practiced grace of her movements betraying the transactional nature of the encounter. Her eyes, usually sharp and calculating, remained distant, unfocused. It was as if she was somewhere else entirely, her mind detached from the act.

Ethan watched, his heart pounding a rhythm of voyeuristic guilt and fascination. Richard's hands, typically reserved for aggressive handshakes and authoritative gestures, were now aggressive in an entirely different context, gripping Erika's hips with an almost punitive force.

The contrast between their public personas and the raw, unsettling display of power and submission was jarring. There was no affection here, no gentle caress or shared laughter. It was a meeting of bodies driven by a mutual understanding of leverage and manipulation.

Richard's grunts of exertion punctuated the silence, the sounds muffled by the glass and the distance. Erika's responses were measured, her cries of pleasure carefully modulated to spur Richard onward. It was a performance, and Ethan realized he was watching a dance of dominance and subjugation play out with Erika holding the reins, despite appearances.

The realization sent a shiver through Ethan. He had always sensed the undercurrents of power in the office, but seeing it manifest so physically was unnerving. Richard, the man who commanded boardrooms and dictated the fates of employees with a word, was reduced to a panting, desperate figure under Erika's spell.

Ethan's gaze shifted back to Erika. Her eyes met his through the window, and for a split second, there was a flicker of recognition. It was gone as quickly as it appeared, replaced by the familiar mask of seduction as she guided Richard to his climax.

Ethan stepped back, his mind racing. The encounter was a stark reminder of the power dynamics at play, not just between Erika and Richard, but within the entire office. It was a game of chess, and Erika was several moves ahead, using her body and her wits as pawns in a much larger, more dangerous game.

As Richard dressed, his movements hurried and slightly un-coordinated, Ethan couldn't help but feel a twinge of pity for the man. He was a titan in the financial world, yet here he was, caught in Erika's web, tangled in the very power he sought to wield.

Ethan turned away from the window, his appetite for obser-vation sated, replaced by a gnawing sense of unease. He had seen enough. The image of Richard and Erika, locked in their silent battle, would be etched in his mind for nights to come.

He retraced his steps through the shadows, the streets silent save for the distant hum of traffic. The night had revealed more than he had bargained for, and Ethan couldn't shake the feeling that he had crossed a line, not just as a voyeur, but as a colleague and a husband.

The encounter had exposed the fragile veneer of profession-alism and respectability that he, like everyone else at Horizon Financial, worked so hard to maintain. And as he made his way home, the weight of that knowledge settled heavily on his shoulders.

* * *

The house was dark when Ethan slipped through the front door, save for the dim glow of the reading lamp in the living room. Claire sat rigid on the couch, her hands folded in her lap, eyes tracking his movements like searchlights.

"It's after midnight." Her voice was unnervingly calm.

Ethan shrugged off his jacket. "I lost track of time."

"On your walk?" The question hung between them, weighted with accusation.

"Yes, on my walk." He avoided her gaze, moving toward the kitchen. "I needed to clear my head."

Claire followed him. "For three hours? Every night this week?"

"What are you, my keeper?" The words came out sharper than he intended, the memory of Richard and Erika still raw in his mind.

"No. I'm your wife. The one you barely look at anymore."

Ethan grabbed a glass from the cabinet, filling it with water to busy his hands. "That's not fair."

"Fair?" Claire's laugh was brittle. "You want to talk about fair? I've been seeing a therapist every Wednesday for the past three years, and you never even noticed I was gone."

The glass froze halfway to his lips. "What?"

"Therapy, Ethan. For what happened in college."

"The assault." He set the glass down. "You told me you were over that."

"Over it?" Her voice cracked. "You don't get 'over' something like that. You learn to live with it. I've been trying to... to want you again. To not flinch when you touch me."

"So that's why you can't stand me touching you? And you never thought to tell me?"

"I was ashamed! I thought I could fix it myself, fix us."

"Three years of lying." His voice hardened. "While I've been walking on eggshells, thinking I was doing something wrong."

"You are doing something wrong!" Claire's control slipped. "These walks, the distance, the way you look through me instead of at me."

"Maybe I'm tired of being rejected by my own wife." The cruel words formed before he could stop them. "Maybe I'm tired of living with someone so frigid she can barely stand a goodnight kiss."

Claire recoiled as if slapped. The silence that followed was deafening, broken only by her ragged breathing.

"Is that what you think of me?" she whispered. "That I'm frigid?"

Ethan's jaw tightened. "What else am I supposed to think? You can barely stand my touch. You give me these... mechanical handjobs like you're doing a chore."

"I'm trying!" Claire's voice rose, tears welling in her eyes. "Every single day, I'm fighting against memories you can't even imagine. Do you know what it's like to have your body betray you? To want to be close to someone but have your entire nervous system scream in protest?"

"And I'm supposed to just accept that? Live like a monk while you work through your issues?" Ethan slammed his glass down. "Maybe I have needs too, Claire. Needs you've ignored for years."

"So this is my fault? All of it?" Claire stepped closer, trembling with rage. "What about your part in this? The distance, the secrets, these goddamn walks that are clearly more important than your family?"

"At least I'm honest about needing space!"

"Honest?" Claire laughed bitterly. "You wouldn't know honesty if it slapped you in the face."

"I can't do this right now." Ethan grabbed his jacket from the chair. "I need air."

"Of course you do. Run away. It's what you're best at."

The door slammed behind him with such force that the picture frames rattled on the wall. Claire stood frozen for a moment before grabbing her own coat and following him into the night.

She spotted him at the end of the block, moving with purpose. Not the meandering pace of someone taking a casual walk. Claire kept her distance, following his tall figure through the neighborhood streets. At the corner of Maple and Third, he suddenly changed direction, cutting through the park. Claire quickened her pace, but by the time she reached the other side, he had vanished.

She stood under a streetlight, scanning the empty sidewalks. Gone. Just like that.

The walk home felt longer, each step heavier than the last. Inside their house—their home that increasingly felt like a stage set rather than a sanctuary—Claire sank onto the couch. She traced the wedding band on her finger, wondering when exactly they had become strangers sharing a mortgage.

Was this what marriage was supposed to be? Secret therapy sessions and midnight disappearances? The weight of her failure pressed against her chest. Maybe she was broken beyond repair. Maybe Ethan deserved someone whole.

Across town, Ethan settled into his usual spot behind the hedges with a clear view of Erika's apartment. His argument with Claire had only strengthened his resolve. This was his refuge, the one place where he controlled what happened. Here, watching others live their uncomplicated lives, he could escape the mess of his own.

CHAPTER SIX

Richard's Secret

The next morning, Ethan arrived at work early, needing the comfort of routine after the explosive fight with Claire. The office was nearly empty, just the cleaning staff and a few dedicated early birds. He rounded the corner to the breakroom and froze.

Richard stood at the copier, scanning documents with unusual intensity. His normally immaculate appearance was slightly disheveled—tie loosened, hair mussed. What caught Ethan's attention wasn't Richard's presence but his behavior: he scanned each document, then immediately deleted the job from the copier's history.

Ethan backed away silently, a skill perfected through years of watching unseen. He retreated to his desk, positioning himself with a clear sightline to Richard's office.

An hour later, Richard emerged with a manila folder tucked under his arm. He glanced around furtively before heading to the elevator. The folder had a small label with "Decker Consulting" printed in neat block letters.

"Decker," Ethan whispered to himself. The name had surfaced in conversations over the past few weeks—always hushed, always when Richard thought no one was listening.

Later that day, Ethan lingered outside the conference room where the financial team held their weekly meeting.

"The audit team is requesting additional documentation for the Decker payments," said the comptroller, voice tense. "They're flagging the invoices as potentially irregular."

"Tell them it's proprietary consulting work," Richard snapped. "Sensitive market analysis that can't be disclosed to junior auditors."

"They're asking for proof the company exists beyond a PO box."

"Christ, do I have to do everything myself?" Richard's voice dropped to a dangerous whisper. "Decker is legitimate. So is Orion Partners and Meridian Services. All properly registered LLC's providing essential services."

Ethan's analytical mind began connecting dots. Three companies, all receiving substantial payments, all mentioned with the same defensive tone. He recalled the lunch conversation about suspicious vendor payments—the exact type of transactions the upcoming audit was targeting.

The next day, Ethan deliberately positioned himself near the finance department's cubicles. Two analysts were huddled over spreadsheets.

"Look at these payment patterns," one whispered. "Decker Consulting receives exactly $87,500 quarterly. Just under the threshold requiring executive approval."

"Same with Orion and Meridian," replied the other. "And all three have the same registered agent in the Caymans."

Ethan's pulse quickened. Shell companies. Offshore accounts. Richard's unexplained wealth. The puzzle pieces were falling into place.

* * *

Richard paced the kitchen while Sophia sat at the marble island, court documents spread before her. Her reading glasses perched on the edge of her nose, the gold judicial pin still fastened to her blazer even at home. Always the judge, even in their goddamn kitchen.

"You're still working?" He loosened his tie, irritation building beneath his practiced smile. "It's almost nine."

"I have a sentencing tomorrow." She didn't look up. "Some of us can't delegate our responsibilities."

The barb landed exactly where she intended. Richard's fingers found his wedding ring, twirling it unconsciously.

"What's that supposed to mean?"

Sophia finally looked up, her expression maddeningly calm. "Nothing, Richard. Just that the justice system doesn't run on creative accounting."

His hand clenched around his tumbler of scotch. The amber liquid sloshed dangerously close to the rim.

"Careful with the Macallan." She returned to her papers. "That bottle cost more than your first car."

The memory surfaced unbidden – three years ago, Marcus Whitfield's smug face across the conference table, threatening to expose irregularities in the quarterly reports.

"I'm taking this to the board, Langford," Marcus had said, sliding the incriminating documents into his leather portfolio. "Should've covered your tracks better."

The boardroom had emptied. Just the two of them remained.

"Let's discuss this reasonably." Richard had approached, hands open in a gesture of conciliation.

"Nothing to discuss. You've been skimming for years."

The rage had erupted from somewhere primal. Richard's hands found Marcus's throat, slamming him against the wall. The portfolio scattered papers across the polished floor.

"You fucking snake—"

Marcus's eyes bulged. His fingers clawed uselessly at Richard's grip.

"Richard!"

He'd barely registered the security guard's shout before they pulled him off. Marcus collapsed, gasping, fumbling for his phone.

"I'm pressing charges, you psychopath."

Three hours later, Richard sat in a holding cell. Then Sophia appeared, speaking quietly to the detective. Documents were signed. Charges disappeared.

In the car afterward, she'd been icily precise: "The DA owes me for the Brennan case. Marcus has a history of substance abuse that would have complicated his testimony. This disappears, but it's the last time, Richard."

Now, in their kitchen, Sophia's voice cut through the memory.

"You're twirling your ring again. What are you nervous about?"

Richard forced his hand still. "Nothing. Just a stressful day."

"Hmm." She gathered her papers. "Try not to solve your problems with your fists this time."

* * *

The front door closed with a muted thud, the sound echoing through the silence of the Miller household. Ethan's frustration simmered beneath the surface, a familiar heat that seemed to grow each time Claire turned away from him. The rejection stung more than he cared to admit, the coldness of their bed a stark contrast to the warmth he craved.

He walked briskly, the night air doing little to cool his temper. The streets were quiet, the neighborhood wrapped in the calm of the late hour. But Ethan's mind was anything but calm. The image of Erika, her body entwined with Richard's, played on a loop in his mind, a spectacle of raw desire that he both resented and coveted.

As he neared Erika's apartment, the glow from her windows beckoned him like a moth to a flame. He took his usual position, hidden in the shadows, where he could watch unnoticed. The curtains were open, offering him an unobstructed view of the passionate scene unfolding within.

Erika and Richard moved with a ferocity that bordered on violence. Their coupling was a clash of power and need, a stark departure from the calculated seduction Ethan had witnessed before. Richard's hands gripped Erika with a possessiveness that seemed to leave marks, while her responses were a mix of pleasure and defiance.

The air within the apartment was thick, charged with the kind of electric tension that only came from the dance of power and surrender. Richard's hands were like iron shackles around Erika's wrists, pinning them against the wall as he stood behind her. His body loomed over hers, a tower of raw masculinity and coiled strength.

Erika's sheer negligee hung off her shoulders, a flimsy barrier that Richard's hungry hands tore away with ease. Her skin, flushed with anticipation, pebbled under the cool air and the heat of his gaze. She arched her back, pressing her nakedness against him, a silent invitation that he accepted with a low growl.

Richard's cock, rigid and pulsing with need, strained against the fabric of his trousers, seeking the warmth of her body. With one hand, he freed himself, the length of him springing forth, thick and veined, the head glistening with a drop of precum that betrayed his eagerness.

Erika's pussy, already slick with desire, throbbed in response to the sight of him. She could feel the wetness between her thighs, a testament to the effect he had on her. Richard's hand snaked around her hip, his fingers finding her swollen clit, eliciting a sharp gasp as he began to tease and manipulate her sensitive flesh.

With a suddenness that took her breath away, Richard spun her around, bending her over the arm of the couch. Her ass, round and inviting, was at the perfect height for him to take her from behind. He positioned himself at her entrance, the broad head of his cock nudging against her wet folds before he thrust into her with one powerful stroke.

Erika's cry of pleasure-pain filled the room as Richard's cock filled her completely. He set a relentless pace, each stroke a demand, a claiming that left no doubt as to who was in control. Her pussy clenched around him, the friction exquisite torture as he drove into her again and again.

Their bodies slapped together in a rhythm as old as time, the sound mingling with their ragged breaths and moans of ecstasy. Richard's fingers dug into her hips, using them as leverage to pound into her warmth with increasing intensity. Erika's orgasm built within her, a rising tide that threatened to sweep her away.

But before she could reach her peak, Richard pulled out, his cock slick with her juices. He turned her around to face him, the hunger in his eyes evident as he guided her to her knees. Erika opened her mouth obediently, her eyes never leaving his as he fed his cock between her willing lips.

She took him deep, her throat contracting around the head of his cock as she swallowed. The sensation was too much for Richard, and with a guttural moan, he released himself into her mouth. Erika swallowed every drop of his hot, salty cum, her eyes fluttering closed in satisfaction as she drained him completely.

When it was over, Richard stepped back, tucking himself away with a sense of finality. Erika remained on her knees, her lips swollen and her breath still coming in short gasps, a picture of post-coital serenity and a job well done.

The truce of their shared intimacy was short-lived, however. As their breathing slowed, the argument began.

"You think you really deserve that promotion?" Richard's voice was a low growl, the remnants of his passion now twisted into anger.

Erika's gaze moved up to meet Richards, her eyes flashing with a cool determination. "I've earned it. You know I have."

"You've earned nothing," Richard spat, his face contorting with resentment. "Everything you have is because of me."

Erika's laugh was sharp and bitter. "Is that what you tell yourself?" She stood, unconcerned with her nakedness as she reached for her robe. "I've documented every transaction, every dirty deal you've made. Don't forget who holds the cards."

Richard's face darkened, the threat to his power igniting a dangerous spark in his eyes. But before he could respond, Erika turned her back on him, walking away with a dismissive toss of her hair.

Defeated, Richard snatched his clothes from the floor and stormed out of the apartment, the slam of the door echoing in his wake. Erika waited until the sound of his footsteps had faded before she reached for the sleek, leather-bound journal on her nightstand.

With a fine-tipped pen, she began to write, her handwriting precise and elegant. Each word, each sentence, was a record of events, a narrative that she controlled. The journal was her insurance policy, her safeguard against the volatility of men like Richard.

Ethan watched, his heart pounding in his chest, as Erika methodically documented her manipulations. He realized then that he was not the only one with secrets, not the only one who found pleasure in the silent observation of others.

But the realization did nothing to quell the unease that had begun to take root within him. He was venturing into dangerous territory, a world where the lines between observer and participant were beginning to blur.

CHAPTER SEVEN

Parallel Lives

Monday morning arrived with the steady rhythm of corporate expectation. Ethan stood before the conference room's floor-to-ceiling windows, the skyline providing a dramatic backdrop as he clicked to the next slide in his presentation. Eight executives from Meridian Partners leaned forward in their chairs, captivated.

"Notice how the test subjects responded to this packaging design," Ethan said, gesturing to the heat map on screen. "The eyes track here first, then here. But what's fascinating isn't where they look—it's what they're thinking when they look there."

He paused, scanning the room. The clients' body language told him everything—crossed arms loosening, heads tilting with curiosity.

"Your current design triggers anxiety about price point before they even register the product benefits." Ethan clicked to his proposed redesign. "This version speaks to their desire for status first, making price secondary."

The CMO from Meridian blinked rapidly. "How could you possibly know that's what they're thinking?"

Ethan smiled. "Because when you shifted in your seat just now, you unconsciously touched your watch—a status symbol—while nodding. We all telegraph our true responses, even when we try to hide them."

A murmur rippled through the room. The CMO glanced at his Rolex, then back at Ethan with widened eyes.

From the doorway, Richard Langford observed the scene, having slipped in midway through the presentation. His fingers twirled his wedding ring—once, twice, three times—as he studied Ethan with growing discomfort.

When applause erupted at Ethan's conclusion, Richard stepped forward with practiced corporate charm. "Meridian is lucky to have Ethan on this account. His... insights are unparalleled."

The clients filed out, buzzing with excitement. Richard remained, his smile fading as the room emptied.

"Impressive performance," Richard said, voice flat. "How do you do it?"

Ethan shrugged. "Just observant, I guess."

"No." Richard's eyes narrowed. "It's more than that. You see things others don't."

"Part of the job, isn't it?"

Richard's jaw tightened. "Just wondering what else you might be observing around here."

The question hung between them, loaded with unspoken meaning.

Ethan met Richard's gaze with practiced neutrality. "Only what I'm paid to observe, Mr. Langford."

* * *

Claire knelt beside the bed, vacuum cleaner humming as she reached underneath to catch the dust bunnies that had accumulated. The nozzle bumped against something solid. She clicked off the machine and reached deeper, her fingers closing around a book.

She pulled it out, brushing off the light coating of dust. *"Rekindling Desire: A Guide for Couples Seeking Intimacy."* The cover showed a couple embracing in silhouette. Her chest tightened as she flipped it open.

Dog-eared pages. Highlighted passages. Notes in Ethan's handwriting crowded the margins.

Try touching her shoulders first - non-threatening?

Suggested dialogue: "I miss being close to you"

Patience = key. Don't show frustration.

Claire's hands trembled. She sank onto the edge of the bed, turning pages. Each one revealed more of Ethan's private thoughts, his careful strategizing around her trauma. One passage about sexual trauma survivors was heavily highlighted, with Ethan's note: *This explains so much. How to help her without pushing?*

Her throat constricted. He knew. Not everything, perhaps, but enough to understand her withdrawal wasn't rejection of him. He'd been studying, trying to understand—while she'd been hiding her therapy, thinking he couldn't handle the truth.

A yellow sticky note marked a chapter titled "When Your Partner Has Experienced Sexual Trauma." Claire read Ethan's note: *Ask about therapy? No—might make her defensive. Be patient. Show love without expectation.*

Tears blurred her vision. All this time, she'd imagined him frustrated, resentful, maybe even looking elsewhere—while he'd been educating himself, trying to navigate her healing without pressuring her.

She turned to the most recent page with notes. The date at the top was from three months ago. The writing was different here—angry, pressed hard into the page: *Nothing works. She doesn't want help. She doesn't want me.*

Claire closed the book, pressing it against her chest. The contradiction between his earlier compassionate notes and this final defeated entry struck her like a physical blow. This was when his nightly walks had started becoming more frequent, more urgent.

What had changed in him?

* * *

Rebecca Sanders tapped her pen against the desk, staring through her window at the apartment building across the street.

The evening light caught the glass, turning some windows into mirrors while leaving others transparent. Her gaze fixed on the first floor, second window from the left—Erika Jensen's apartment.

"I need something compelling, Rebecca," her agent's voice crackled through the speaker. "The publisher's getting antsy. True crime is saturated right now—we need a unique angle."

"I know, Diane." Rebecca swiveled in her chair, facing the wall behind her desk. Crime scene photos, newspaper clippings, and handwritten timelines covered nearly every inch. Red string connected key events in her previous cases—all solved, all published, all increasingly distant successes.

"Your last book is two years old now. Readers have short memories."

Rebecca sighed. "I'm working on something. Just need more time."

"You don't have more time. Your advance is spent, and—"

"I'll call you next week with an update." Rebecca ended the call before her agent could protest.

She turned back to her laptop, scrolling through the document titled "Neighborhood Patterns." The spreadsheet detailed comings and goings of various residents in her line of sight. Time stamps, descriptions, behavioral notes. Her writer's instinct told her something interesting was happening, but the story hadn't revealed itself yet.

Her eyes caught movement outside. A man in dark clothing walked purposefully down the street, stopping in the shadows of a large oak tree. Rebecca recognized him immediately—the same man that she's seen walking here before.

She grabbed her notebook, jotting down the time: 9:17 PM.

Rebecca dimmed her lights and moved closer to the window. The man positioned himself with a clear view of Erika's apartment. His face was partially illuminated by the glow of distant streetlights, revealing an expression of intense concentration.

Rebecca added to her notes: *Subject "Unknown" Appears to be a peeping tom. Unaware of secondary observation (me). Have noticed him walking in the neighborhood on other occasions. Target appears to be Apartment 1B (E.J.).*

She glanced at her chapter draft on screen, then back to the man's silhouette. Perhaps her breakthrough story was unfolding right before her eyes.

CHAPTER EIGHT

The Blackmail

E than's exhalation misted the chilly surface of the window as he observed Richard and Erika through the gap in the curtains. The couple moved with a languid, unhurried rhythm, a stark departure from the frenzied passion he had witnessed before.

Richard cradled Erika's face in his hands, their lips meeting in a tender, almost reverent kiss. Each touch, each caress seemed to carry a weight beyond the physical, a silent communication that Ethan could only guess at from his clandestine vantage point. Richard's movements were deliberate, worshipful even, as he traced the contours of Erika's body with a reverence that belied his usual dominance.

Erika's response was a dance of both surrender and control. She arched into Richard's touch, her fingers interlacing with his as they moved together in a harmony that spoke of a connection deeper than mere lust. The intimacy of the moment was almost tangible, a private ballet performed under the cloak of night.

As the couple reached the crescendo of their lovemaking, Ethan felt an intruder's guilt gnawing at him. There was something sacred in the vulnerability they shared, a stark contrast to the calculated manipulations of their daytime personas.

The tender aftermath was a tableau Ethan had not anticipated. Richard lay spent, his head resting on Erika's chest, listening to the softening rhythm of her breath. It was in this quietude that Erika chose to strike.

"Richard," she began, her voice barely above a whisper, yet it sliced through the silence with precision. "We need to talk about the embezzlement."

Richard stiffened, his body instantly transforming from sated to guarded. He propped himself up on one elbow, his eyes searching her face for the angle of her attack.

"What are you talking about, Erika?" His tone was dismissive, but the telltale twitch of his hand betraying him as it reached for his discarded trousers, the wedding ring catching a stray beam of light.

Erika sat up, unperturbed by her nakedness, her expression resolute. "I've been keeping track, Richard. I know all about the shell companies, the offshore accounts—'Decker' isn't as clever as you think."

Richard's face hardened, the tenderness of moments ago replaced by a practiced mask of indifference. "You don't know shit

Erika. Actually not true, you do know how to fuck and you suck a mean cock. Outside of that, you should just keep your fucking mouth shut."

Erika reached into the bedside drawer, producing a sheaf of documents. "I know I lot more than how to fuck Richard. These transactions, consulting fees for non-existent services? Diverting company funds into your personal slush fund?" She held them out to him. "Explain these."

Richard's gaze flickered between Erika and the papers. He took them, his hands betraying a slight tremor as he scanned the lines of damning evidence. His mind raced, calculating the implications, the potential fallout.

For a moment, he said nothing, the weight of the documents in his hands seeming to anchor him to the reality of his situation. Erika watched him, her eyes sharp, her posture rigid with anticipation.

Finally, Richard spoke, his voice low and controlled. "What do you want, Erika?"

She leaned forward, her voice dropping to a conspiratorial whisper. "I want in, Richard. I want a cut. I want a nice payday from what you've already taken and from now on we're in this together."

Richard's eyes narrowed, the machinations within his mind almost visible as he weighed his options. He knew he was cornered, the game of cat and mouse they'd been playing taking a sudden and unexpected turn.

Erika stared at Richard with a smug grin on her face. The power had shifted between them, a delicious reversal that reminded her of her father's lessons. Watching Richard's face contort with barely contained rage gave her the same rush she'd felt during her first successful con.

"You know, my father taught me that everyone has a weakness," she said, running a finger along the edge of the incriminating documents. "Yours was just so predictable."

Richard's jaw clenched. "This is blackmail."

"I prefer to call it a business negotiation."

The familiar words transported her back to the cramped apartment of her childhood, her father's voice echoing across fifteen years of memory.

"Remember, Erika, men like him think with what's between their legs, not with what's between their ears."

"Why'd Mom leave?" she asked, the question that had haunted her for years.

Her father's expression hardened. "Because she was weak. Wouldn't do what needed to be done." He sat beside her, his voice softening. "But you're not weak, are you, princess?"

She shook her head.

Erika's father leaned against the kitchen counter, cigarette dangling from his lips as he counted the day's take. She was fourteen, watching him sort bills with nimble fingers that never seemed to stop moving.

"Come here, kitten," he beckoned, patting the stool beside him. "Time for another lesson."

Erika sat down, her gangly teenage frame still awkward, but already drawing the wrong kind of attention from men. Her father's eyes—calculating blue, just like hers—assessed her with the detachment of an investor appraising property.

"You're growing up pretty," he said, tapping ash into an empty beer can. "That's capital. Smart men invest their capital."

He spread photographs across the counter—pictures of the wealthy men and women he'd conned that month. Each photo had notes scribbled on the back: weaknesses, vices, pressure points.

"See this one?" He tapped a photo of a silver-haired businessman. "Worth millions, but he can't stop gambling. And this one—" a well-dressed woman with diamonds at her throat "—daddy issues. Seeks validation from older men."

Erika studied the faces, absorbing the methodology behind her father's success.

"Everyone has a weakness," he continued. "Find it, exploit it, control it. That's how you survive in this world."

Her mother had left when Erika was eight, tired of the cons, the constant moving, the inevitable midnight escapes when marks caught on. Her parting words still echoed: "He'll use you too, baby. Just like everyone else."

"You've got something special," her father said, brushing a strand of blonde hair from her face. "Men will want you. And that means you can make them do anything."

He poured himself another whiskey. "Sex is just a transaction, kitten. No different than money changing hands. Learn to use it right, you'll never work a day in your life."

Later that night, Erika lay awake listening to her father charm another mark on the phone, his voice shifting into whatever persona was required. She remembered watching him seduce a wealthy widow the previous month—how he'd transformed before her eyes into exactly what the woman needed.

"Always be what they want," he'd instructed afterward. "But never give them everything they need. Keep them hungry."

By sixteen, she was helping with the cons. By eighteen, she was running her own. When her father was finally arrested, she visited him once in prison.

"Proud of you, kitten," he'd said through the glass partition. "Remember, powerful men have the most to lose. That makes them the easiest to control."

Now, watching Richard's composure crack, Erika felt a familiar satisfaction. Her father would be proud. She'd identified Richard's weakness months ago—his need for control, his financial desperation, his attraction to her—and exploited each one methodically.

"So," she said, leaning back against the headboard, "shall we discuss percentages?"

From his shadowed observation point, Ethan watched the drama unfold, the gears of his own mind turning as he processed the implications of what he'd just witnessed. This was no longer just about voyeurism or the illicit thrill of watching others—this was a high-stakes game that Ethan was now inexorably drawn into.

* * *

The quarterly financial review meeting filled Horizon Financial's main conference room to capacity. Ethan slid into a seat along the back wall, notebook open but mind elsewhere. The events he'd witnessed between Richard and Erika played on repeat in his head.

Chief Financial Officer Melinda Cox stood at the front of the room, laser pointer in hand. "As you all know, our external audit begins next week. The audit team will be conducting a comprehensive review of all financial transactions from the past fiscal year."

Richard sat near the head of the table, posture relaxed, legs crossed at the ankles. His navy suit looked freshly pressed, his silver tie clip catching the fluorescent light. Nothing in his demeanor suggested concern.

"They'll be focusing particularly on vendor relationships and consulting fees," Cox continued, clicking to the next slide. "The SEC has increased scrutiny on financial services firms, so we need to ensure all documentation is in perfect order."

Ethan's gaze fixed on Richard's hands. While his face remained a mask of professional interest, his thumb had begun to rotate his wedding band in small, rhythmic circles. The gold ring spun against his skin, around and around.

"Each department head will need to prepare detailed justifications for any consulting expenditures over fifty thousand dollars," Cox said, her voice fading into background noise as Ethan focused on Richard's tell.

The ring twirled faster as Cox mentioned specific areas of review. "They'll be examining our offshore payment structures and conducting random sampling of vendor contracts, particularly those established within the last eighteen months."

Richard's expression never changed—perfect corporate placidity—but his thumb worked the ring with increasing urgency. Ethan had observed this behavior before, always when Richard faced pressure. The day the quarterly numbers missed projections. The moment before terminating a long-time employee. When the CEO unexpectedly joined their strategy meeting.

"Richard, your team will need to provide complete documentation for the Decker consulting arrangement," Cox said directly.

"Of course," Richard replied smoothly. "Everything's in order."

But his thumb betrayed him, spinning the gold band so vigorously it nearly slipped off his finger.

Chapter Nine

Witness to a Murder

The sunset painted the parking lot in shades of amber and gold. Ethan sat in his car, unwrapping a double cheeseburger with mechanical precision. He hadn't planned to eat fast food tonight—Claire had prepared chicken marsala—but the meeting had triggered an urgent need to witness what would happen between Richard and Erika.

He checked his watch. Still too light for proper concealment. The shadows weren't deep enough yet to hide his presence. Patience had become second nature over the years; rushing led to mistakes, to being seen.

Ethan methodically worked through his fries, each one a timer counting down to darkness. His phone buzzed with a text from Claire: *Where are you?*

He typed back: *Working late. Don't wait up.* The lie came easily now, practiced and smooth.

Another hour passed before true darkness settled. Ethan drove the familiar route to Erika's neighborhood, parking three blocks away in the spot he'd claimed as his own—beneath a broken streetlight, between two large SUVs. He moved with practiced efficiency, keeping his head down as he approached her building.

The small park across from Erika's apartment offered perfect cover—dense shrubbery with gaps that provided unobstructed views of her living room windows. Ethan slipped between the bushes, finding his usual spot. Her curtains were partially open, the interior lights revealing her pacing nervously in a tight black dress.

Twenty minutes later, Richard's silver BMW pulled up to the curb. He emerged clutching a manila envelope, glancing furtively over both shoulders before entering the building.

Ethan shifted position, finding the optimal angle as Richard appeared in Erika's doorway. She greeted him with a cold smile, arms crossed.

"You brought what I asked for?" Her voice carried faintly through the partially open window.

Richard thrust the envelope toward her. "Fifty thousand. That's all you get."

Erika laughed, the sound sharp and cutting. "That's the down payment, Richard. You know the terms."

She opened the envelope, rifling through the cash bundles with practiced fingers.

* * *

Across the street, Rebecca Sanders lowered her binoculars and reached for her notebook. This was the third night in a row she'd spotted the same man lurking in the bushes across from the blonde woman's apartment. Her writer's instinct had been triggered the first night—something about his deliberate movements seemed off.

"Subject appears male, approximately 6'1", lean build," she murmured as she wrote. "Business casual attire—gray slacks, navy button-down, no tie. Same clothing style as previous nights, suggesting coming directly from office job."

Rebecca glanced at her watch and noted the time: 9:17 PM. She flipped back through her previous entries.

"Arrives consistently between 9:10-9:20 PM. Maintains position for 30-45 minutes." She tapped her pen against her lips. "Methodical in approach—parks away from location, uses same path through park, selects identical concealment spot each night."

Through her window, Rebecca had a perfect vantage point. Her apartment directly faced both Erika's windows and the small park where the man positioned himself. She'd set up her writing desk to take advantage of this view weeks ago when researching neighborhood patterns for background material.

"Subject displays professional-level surveillance techniques," she continued writing. "Minimizes movement, utilizes natural cover effectively, maintains awareness of sightlines."

She raised her camera with telephoto lens, capturing several clear shots of his profile. The man's face was partially visible in the ambient light from the street lamps. Rebecca studied the images on her digital display.

"Facial expression intense, focused. Not sexually aroused—appears to be gathering information rather than seeking gratification."

She added a final note: "Possible private investigator? Corporate espionage? Requires further observation."

Rebecca set down her pen and reached for her coffee. After months of writer's block, her instincts were screaming that something significant was unfolding across the street. Whether it would become material for her book remained to be seen, but the methodical observer had become the observed.

* * *

Back at Erika's apartment, Richard paced across her living room, his Italian leather shoes making sharp clicks against the hardwood floor. The stack of cash he'd brought sat on her glass coffee table—fifty thousand dollars in neat bundles.

Erika picked up one stack, riffled through it with her thumb, then tossed it back dismissively. "This is a down payment, Richard. Not the full amount."

"We agreed on fifty." Richard's voice dropped to a dangerous register. He twisted his wedding ring—a nervous habit that betrayed his composure.

"That was before I found the Decker account." Erika's red lips curved into a smile as she watched his face pale. "Two million in an offshore account? You've been busy."

Richard lunged forward, gripping the edge of the table. "How the fuck did you—"

"I'm not just a pretty face." She stood, smoothing her silk robe against her body. "I want half."

"You're insane."

"Am I?" Erika laughed, the sound like breaking glass. "Let's see what the board thinks. Or better yet, your wife. How's Judge Sophia these days? Still oblivious to what a pathetic excuse for a man she married?"

Richard's face flushed crimson. "Watch your mouth."

"Or what?" Erika stepped closer, her perfume filling the space between them. "You'll fuck me into submission? We both know you can't even manage that properly." She trailed a finger down his chest. "Even that pathetic Ethan could probably satisfy me better than you."

Richard froze. "What?"

"Ethan Miller. Your little marketing analyst who's been watching me through my window for weeks." Erika's eyes glittered with malice. "At least he has the decency to look hungry when he sees me naked."

Something snapped in Richard's expression. His hands shot out, wrapping around Erika's throat with sudden, brutal force. Her eyes widened in genuine surprise as he shoved her backward against the wall.

Outside, Ethan watched in horror, his body rigid with shock. Richard's thumbs pressed deeper into Erika's windpipe. Her manicured nails clawed at his wrists, drawing blood that he didn't seem to feel. Her mouth opened and closed like a fish, desperate for air that wouldn't come.

Rebecca Sanders froze at her window, coffee mug suspended halfway to her lips. Through the viewfinder of her camera—positioned on a tripod for her nightly documentation of neighborhood patterns—she watched the scene unfold with horrifying clarity. The telephoto lens captured every detail: Richard's hands locked around Erika's throat, the woman's face contorting as she fought for air.

"Jesus Christ," Rebecca whispered, her writer's mind automatically cataloging details even as her stomach clenched. The expensive art on Erika's walls. The scattered cash. The way Richard's wedding ring caught the light as his fingers tightened.

Movement below caught her eye. Rebecca shifted her gaze downward to the shadowy figure standing rigid on the sidewalk. The man—medium height, unremarkable—staring up at Erika's window. His face, illuminated by the spillover of street light, registered pure shock.

Rebecca grabbed her phone, fingers trembling as she zoomed in to capture his image. The voyeur. The watcher she'd been documenting for days.

Across the street, Ethan's world narrowed to the brutal tableau framed in Erika's window. The wet, desperate sounds of her struggle carried through the partially open window. Each ragged gasp sent electric jolts down his spine. He should move. Call someone. Do something. But his limbs refused to obey, locked in place by a paralyzing cocktail of terror and disbelief.

The metallic taste of fear flooded his mouth. Sweat trickled cold down his back, soaking through his shirt. His heart hammered so violently he felt it might crack his ribs.

Inside the apartment, Erika's struggles weakened. Her arms, which had been flailing against Richard's chest, dropped limply to her sides. Her eyes, bulging with terror, found Ethan's through the window. Recognition flickered there—a final connection that seared itself into his consciousness.

Ethan's lungs burned. He realized he'd been holding his breath, unconsciously mirroring Erika's suffocation. When he finally inhaled, the night air felt like razor blades in his throat.

He should run. He knew he should run. But his feet remained rooted to the concrete as Richard lowered Erika's lifeless body to the floor.

CHAPTER TEN

The Fatal Slip

R ichard stood over Erika's body, his breath coming in ragged gasps. The rage that had consumed him moments ago receded like a tide, leaving cold clarity in its wake. He stared at his hands—they looked foreign to him, like tools that had acted without his permission.

"Erika?" His voice sounded distant to his own ears.

She didn't move. Her eyes remained fixed on the ceiling, unseeing. The perfect blonde hair she'd been so proud of fanned out beneath her head like a halo. The silk robe had fallen open, revealing the body he'd both desired and resented.

Richard dropped to his knees beside her. His fingers trembled as he pressed them against her neck, searching for a pulse. The skin felt warm but unnaturally still. No flutter of life met his touch.

"Fuck. Fuck. FUCK!" He slammed his fist against the hardwood floor.

Outside, Ethan's paralysis finally broke. The sight of Richard kneeling over Erika's body jolted him into action. He stumbled backward, nearly falling as his foot caught on an exposed tree root. His breath came in shallow, panicked bursts as he turned and crashed through the ornamental bushes that had concealed him.

Branches tore at his face and clothes. His heart pounded so violently he could hear nothing but its thundering in his ears. He had to get away. Had to run. Had to—

His company lapel pin caught on a branch, the pin pulling the fabric of his shirt before snapping free. Ethan froze for a split second, his hand reaching instinctively toward it, before self-preservation kicked in. He abandoned it and sprinted down the darkened street.

Inside the apartment, Richard's head snapped up at the sound of breaking branches. He moved to the window, peering out into the darkness. Movement caught his eye—a figure running away from the building, disappearing around the corner.

"Shit," Richard hissed, squinting to make out details. The streetlight revealed only a glimpse—average height, dark jacket, moving fast. Too fast to identify.

Someone had seen. Someone had witnessed everything.

Richard's gaze dropped to the bushes below the window. Something reflective caught the light—a small object on the ground near the disturbed foliage.

Across the street, Rebecca Sanders leaned forward in her desk chair, fingers gripping the edge of her notebook. The scene unfolding through her telephoto lens had sent adrenaline coursing through her body. What had started as routine surveillance had just transformed into something extraordinary.

"Holy shit," she whispered, her voice barely audible even in her empty apartment.

She'd witnessed it all—Richard's arrival, the argument, the violence that followed. The voyeur below had seen it too. The same man she'd been tracking for days, the one who consistently appeared beneath Erika's window.

When he bolted from the bushes, Rebecca grabbed her pen and scribbled frantically:

Subject fled 10:42 PM. Med build, dark jacket (navy?). Possibly left something behind in bushes? Caught on branch? Panicked flight pattern, no attempt at stealth. Heading east on Maple.

She sketched a quick diagram of his escape route, noting the streetlights he passed under and approximate time markers. Her hand moved with practiced efficiency—this wasn't her first time documenting human behavior under duress.

Rebecca glanced back at her camera, adjusting the focus to capture Richard's movements inside the apartment. He was pacing now, running hands through his hair, stopping occasionally to look at Erika's body. The perfect picture of a man unraveling.

She wrote: *Murderer remained at scene. Initial shock reaction consistent with unplanned homicide. No immediate attempt to conceal body or evidence.*

Her mind raced through the narrative implications. Two witnesses to a murder—one hidden in the shadows, one hidden across the street. The voyeur had fled, but she'd remained, documenting everything.

Rebecca flipped back through her notebook, scanning her previous entries about the lurker. Three consecutive nights watching the same window. Always arriving after dark. Always alone. Always watching.

She added: *Possible connection between victim and male observer? Sexual fixation? Need to ID man ASAP.*

Her fingers hovered over her phone. The responsible action would be to call the police immediately. But the writer in her hesitated. This wasn't just a crime—this was the story she'd been waiting for.

* * *

Ethan slammed his car door, nearly missing his fingers. His hands shook so badly he dropped his keys twice before managing to lock the vehicle. The porch light cast grotesque shadows across the lawn as he staggered toward his front door.

He fumbled with his house key, jamming it against the lock plate several times before finding the keyhole. The door swung open, revealing the quiet sanctuary of his home—a place that now felt alien and unsafe.

"Ethan?" Claire's voice floated from the living room. "Is that you?"

He couldn't answer. His throat had closed up, his tongue thick and useless in his mouth. He heard her footsteps approaching as he shrugged off his jacket with jerky movements.

"You're back early," she said, appearing in the hallway. "I thought you'd be out for at least another hour."

His fingers moved automatically to straighten his lapel—a habitual gesture to check his company pin—when his stomach dropped. The pin was gone. The small golden H of Horizon Financial that he'd worn every day for seven years was missing.

"Ethan?" Claire stepped closer, her brow furrowed. "Are you okay? You look like you've seen a ghost."

The pin. At the scene. His DNA. His fingerprints.

"Bathroom," he managed to choke out, pushing past her.

He barely made it to the toilet before violent dry heaves wracked his body. Nothing came up—he hadn't eaten since the fast food hours earlier—but his body convulsed with the effort. Cold sweat beaded on his forehead as he gripped the porcelain bowl.

A witness to murder. The thought pounded in his head with each heave. He'd watched a woman die. Watched Richard kill her. And left evidence behind.

Soft knocking interrupted his spiral.

"Ethan? What's wrong?" Claire's voice came through the door, concern evident despite the barrier between them. "Should I call someone?"

He splashed cold water on his face, staring at his reflection. A stranger looked back—pale, haunted, guilty.

"Food poisoning," he called back, his voice cracking. "Must have been that takeout."

"Can I get you anything? Pepto? Water?"

"No," he said too sharply, then softened his tone. "No, thanks. Just need to get it out of my system."

"Okay." Her voice sounded uncertain. "I'll be in the bedroom if you need me."

* * *

Rebecca hunched over her laptop, the blue glow illuminating her face in the darkened apartment. Her fingers hovered above the keyboard, frozen in indecision. On her screen, the cursor blinked at the end of a sentence: "Subject appears to flee scene after witnessing murder."

She reached for her phone, then pulled her hand back. The detective in her brain—the one that had researched and written three true crime books—screamed that she needed to call the police. But the struggling author in her whispered something else entirely.

"This could be it," she murmured, rubbing her tired eyes. "The book that puts me back on the map."

Her agent's voice echoed in her memory from their last conversation: "Publishers don't want recycled cold cases, Beck. They want something fresh, something you've got unique access to."

And now she had exactly that—a front-row seat to a murder
and its aftermath, unfolding in real time.

Rebecca opened a new document and typed: "WORKING
TITLE: WINDOW OF OPPORTUNITY."

She paused, then began bullet-pointing an outline:

• Beautiful female executive (Erika) - document lifestyle, sexual history, professional climb

• Corporate setting - research Horizon Financial where she
worked, history, recent scandals?

• The murderer - middle-aged executive (need name), motive
appears financial/blackmail

• The watcher - younger man, regular presence outside victim's window, potential second suspect?

• The witness (me) - ethical considerations, involvement vs.
observation

Her fingers flew across the keyboard as she added notes beneath each heading:

"Need to establish timeline of relationship between victim
and killer. Sexual relationship clearly predates murder. Financial connection? Blackmail material observed night of murder -
documents shown."

Rebecca leaned back, conflict etched across her face. She'd
spent years documenting crimes after they'd gone cold, piecing
together fragmented evidence and contradictory testimonies.
Now she had the unprecedented opportunity to chronicle a
murder from day one—to witness the investigation unfold, to
observe suspects in their natural habitat.

She glanced at her phone again. One call would fulfill her civic duty. One call would also potentially shut her out from the story of her career.

"I can always call tomorrow," she whispered, turning back to her outline. "After I've documented everything I saw tonight."

CHAPTER ELEVEN

Richard Finds the Clue

Richard stared at Erika's lifeless body, his hands still trembling from the violence they'd just committed. Her eyes remained open, accusing him from beyond death. The documents she'd threatened him with lay scattered across the coffee table—evidence of his embezzlement from Horizon Financial.

"Fuck, fuck, fuck." His mind raced through a chaotic inventory of what he'd touched in her apartment. The doorknob. The glass she'd handed him. The papers. Her neck.

Richard yanked his handkerchief from his pocket and began wiping surfaces frantically. The doorknob. The glass. The edge of the table. He snatched the documents and stuffed them into his case.

He paused at her body, his breath coming in ragged gasps. He'd never planned this. One moment they were arguing, the next his hands were around her throat, squeezing until the light left her eyes.

Something scratched at his memory—a noise from outside during the struggle. A rustling in the bushes. Someone watching.

Richard rushed to the window and peered down at the shadowy area below. Someone had been there. Someone had seen.

He needed to check. Now.

After one final frenzied sweep of the apartment, wiping anything he might have touched, Richard slipped out the back entrance. He circled around to the front of the building, heart hammering against his ribs.

The bushes beneath Erika's window stood dark and still. Richard dropped to his knees, pawing through the foliage, his expensive suit collecting dirt and leaves. His fingers brushed something metal. He pulled it out, holding it up to catch the dim light from a nearby streetlamp.

A company pin. The same gold-plated Horizon Financial logo every employee received on their five-year anniversary.

Richard turned it over, studying the back where a name should be engraved. The surface was scratched, making it difficult to read in the darkness. He angled it again, squinting.

"Ethan Miller," he whispered, the name sending a chill through him.

The quiet marketing analyst. The one who watched everything. The one who'd impressed clients earlier that week with his uncanny insights.

Richard closed his fist around the pin, the edges digging into his palm. He knew exactly who had been watching him kill Erika.

* * *

Detective Zoe Marlowe ducked under the yellow crime scene tape stretched across Erika Jensen's apartment doorway. The forensics team already swarmed the space, photographing and cataloging evidence with mechanical precision. She took in the scene with narrowed eyes—the body sprawled on the floor, the disarray of papers, the open window.

"So what's the working theory?" Marlowe asked the first officer on scene, a rookie named Diaz who looked slightly green around the gills.

"Robbery gone wrong, Detective. Neighbor heard a commotion, called it in. Perp ransacked the place looking for valuables."

Marlowe's gaze swept the apartment. Designer furniture. Expensive artwork. A Rolex watch still sitting on the bathroom counter. Her attention fixed on the victim's neck, the deep bruising unmistakable.

"If this was a robbery, why didn't they take the watch? Or the laptop?" She pointed to the MacBook sitting untouched on the desk. "And look at those marks. That's personal. Someone wanted her dead."

She crouched beside the body, studying Erika's face. "No defensive wounds on her hands. She knew her killer."

Marlowe stood and walked to the window, pushing the curtain aside. Perfect view of the street. Perfect view for anyone looking in.

"Was anything actually taken?"

"We're still cataloging, but—"

"This wasn't a robbery." Marlowe cut him off. "This was staged to look like one."

She turned to her partner, Detective Rodriguez. "I want all security footage from the building's entrances and exits. Check the traffic cameras at both intersections. And get me footage from any ATMs or stores within a three-block radius."

Rodriguez nodded, already making notes.

"Timeframe?" he asked.

"Six hours before the estimated time of death until two hours after the neighbor's 911 call."

Marlowe stepped closer to the window again, eyes scanning the bushes below. "And have someone check those shrubs for evidence. Perfect hiding spot for someone watching the apartment."

She pulled on latex gloves and carefully moved aside papers on the coffee table, revealing faint smudges.

"Someone wiped this clean. Get prints anyway. They always miss something."

* * *

Richard slammed his front door, hands still trembling. He leaned against it, breathing heavily, before crossing to the bar cart in his study. The scotch burned his throat as he downed it in one gulp.

His wife's voice called from upstairs. "Richard? Is that you?"

"Just finishing some paperwork, Sophia. I'll be up shortly."

He pulled Ethan's company pin from his pocket, examining the silver corporate logo glinting under the desk lamp. Such a small thing to have such immense power. Richard unconsciously twirled his wedding ring.

The home safe was hidden behind a framed Harvard MBA diploma. Richard spun the dial with practiced precision, the soft clicks almost soothing. Inside lay offshore account documents, a second passport, and a USB drive containing blackmail material on two board members. He placed the pin in a small velvet bag and tucked it in the back corner.

"Insurance," he whispered, closing the safe with a satisfying thunk.

At his computer, Richard pulled up the company directory. Ethan Miller. Marketing analyst. Nondescript photo and a brief company approved bio. He opened a new browser window and typed Ethan's name into the search bar.

The results painted a picture of boring suburban normalcy. LinkedIn profile highlighting marketing achievements. Facebook page showing a pretty wife and young daughter. Instagram with occasional family photos and marketing conferences.

"What were you doing outside her window, Ethan?" Richard muttered, scrolling through Ethan's sparse Twitter feed.

He opened the company personnel file next. Employee reviews described Ethan as "exceptionally observant" and "insightful about human behavior." Richard's eyes narrowed. The quiet ones always noticed too much.

Richard created a new folder on his encrypted hard drive labeled "Miller" and began downloading Ethan's social media profiles. He studied a family photo—Ethan, his wife Claire, and their daughter at some beach vacation. They looked happy, normal.

"Perfect," Richard whispered, leaning back in his chair. The pin wasn't evidence to turn over to police. It was leverage. If Ethan went to the authorities about what he saw, Richard would simply claim Ethan himself was the killer, planting his pin at the scene.

But first, he needed to understand exactly what Ethan had seen, and more importantly, what kind of man he was dealing with.

CHAPTER TWELVE

Withdrawal

E than tore through his car, fingers frantically searching under seats and floor mats. The morning sun beat through the windshield as sweat beaded on his forehead. He emptied the glove compartment, scattering insurance papers and receipts across the passenger seat.

"Come on, come on," he muttered, checking the same crevices for the third time.

He knew it was pointless. The silver company pin with its distinctive horizon logo wasn't here. It was lying in the mulch beneath Erika's window, next to crushed azalea bushes where he'd crouched to watch her die.

Inside the house, Ethan methodically searched coat pockets, dresser drawers, and laundry baskets. He retraced every step since returning home that night, checking behind furniture and under rugs. The frantic energy of his search contrasted with the quiet certainty in his gut – the pin was gone, lost at the scene.

Claire found him on his hands and knees in the bedroom closet, pushing aside shoe boxes.

"What are you looking for?" she asked, leaning against the doorframe.

"My company pin. The silver one." His voice sounded strained even to his own ears. "Annual review is next week. Shows company loyalty."

"I'll help you look," Claire offered, kneeling beside him.

Her nearness startled him. It had been months since they'd been this close without tension between them. Her fingers brushed his as they moved shoes aside, and he felt an unexpected surge of emotion.

"Thanks," he whispered.

They worked in companionable silence for several minutes. When their eyes met, something shifted in Claire's expression – a softness he hadn't seen in years.

"Ethan, are you okay? You've seemed... different lately."

The gentleness in her voice cracked something inside him. For a dizzying moment, he imagined telling her everything – the voyeurism, Erika, the murder he'd witnessed.

"I—" The words caught in his throat. Images flashed through his mind: police cars, handcuffs, Emma's tears, Claire's disgust. "I'm just stressed about work."

Claire's hand rested on his arm, her eyes searching his face. "You know you can tell me anything, right?"

The irony of her statement hit him like a physical blow. He nodded, unable to speak past the knot in his throat.

"We'll find your pin," she said, misinterpreting his silence. "Don't worry."

But Ethan knew exactly where it was. And the thought terrified him.

* * *

Rebecca spread her notes across her dining table, creating a physical timeline of the night Erika Jensen died. She'd covered the wall with index cards, but needed to see everything laid out chronologically. The dining table offered a fresh perspective—and she desperately needed one.

"Subject approaches building, appears agitated," she read aloud, fingertips tracing the handwritten notes. "Subject takes position in northeast corner of landscaping beneath target's window."

She glanced at her laptop where she'd downloaded the police scanner recording from that night. According to the timestamp, the first report of a disturbance at Erika's address came in at 10:53 PM. The medical examiner's preliminary report—obtained through a contact at the morgue—estimated time of death between 10:30 and 11:00 PM.

Rebecca picked up her camera and scrolled through photos she'd taken that night. She'd been documenting the voyeur's pattern for potential background research, never expecting to capture evidence of a murder. The timestamp on her first photo of the figure by the bushes read 10:17 PM. The last photo, showing the same figure running from the scene, was taken at 10:42 PM.

"He was there before the murderer arrived," she muttered, "and fled immediately after Erika collapsed."

She positioned these photos alongside her timeline, creating a visual sequence. The mystery man had arrived before the murderer, watched the entire confrontation, and fled only after Erika was dead. Rebecca studied the blurry image of the running figure. Though the distance and darkness obscured details, she could make out a man of average build wearing dark clothing.

Rebecca pulled out her notebook containing observations of neighborhood patterns. For three consecutive nights prior to the murder, she'd noted the same figure lurking near Erika's building. Each time, he'd positioned himself with a clear view into her apartment.

"Not a random witness," Rebecca concluded. "Someone who watched her regularly."

She aligned these previous sightings with her murder timeline. The pattern was clear—this wasn't someone who happened to witness a crime. This was someone whose obsession with Erika had placed him at the perfect vantage point to see her murder.

* * *

Detective Marlowe rapped on Rebecca's door at precisely 9:00 AM, her knock crisp and authoritative. Rebecca had been expecting her—the detective had been methodically working her way through the apartment complex all morning.

"Ms. Sanders? Detective Zoe Marlowe, homicide." She flashed her badge with practiced efficiency. "I understand you have a direct view of the Jensen apartment."

Rebecca nodded, gesturing toward her living room windows. "I do. Please, come in."

Marlowe stepped inside, her gaze immediately cataloging details of Rebecca's apartment—the wall of index cards, the laptop open to a document titled "Chapter Outline," the camera on the coffee table.

"Writer?" Marlowe asked, nodding toward the notes.

"True crime. Working on a new book." Rebecca kept her tone casual. "Though I'm stuck in research phase."

Marlowe's eyes narrowed slightly. "Convenient timing."

"Not for Ms. Jensen."

The detective didn't smile. "Did you know the victim?"

"Just casually. I met her at a neighborhood block party a couple of years ago. We'd wave at each other occasionally, you know, coming and going."

Marlowe pulled out a small notebook. "Notice anything unusual in the days leading up to her death? Visitors, disturbances, patterns changing?"

Rebecca hesitated, carefully selecting what to share. "She had a regular male visitor. Well-dressed, expensive watch. They argued the night she died."

"Argued how?"

"Animated gestures. Couldn't hear anything, but body language was hostile."

"What time was this?"

"Around ten-thirty."

Marlowe made a note. "Anything else unusual that night? Or previous nights?"

Rebecca's mind flashed to her photos of the voyeur—the figure who'd watched the murder unfold. The man who might be her ticket to a breakthrough book. She tapped her fingers against her thigh.

"The neighborhood's been on edge about a prowler. I've noticed unusual shadows occasionally, but nothing I could definitively identify as a person." A careful half-truth.

"You have quite the view here." Marlowe stepped closer to the window. "Perfect for observing."

"Occupational hazard. I people-watch for character studies."

"With that camera?" Marlowe nodded toward Rebecca's equipment.

"Sometimes. For description details."

Marlowe's expression remained neutral, but her eyes sharpened. "I'd be interested in any photos you might have taken that night."

"Just neighborhood atmosphere shots. Nothing useful, I'm afraid." Rebecca kept her voice steady. "But I'll check my files."

Marlowe held Rebecca's gaze for a beat longer than comfortable, then reached into her jacket pocket. She produced a crisp business card with the police department logo and her contact details.

"Well if you recall anything further that might be helpful, you can reach me at this number." Marlowe handed Rebecca her card. "Especially if you remember more about that prowler. We are particularly interested in anyone who might have been in the vicinity that night."

Rebecca accepted the card, turning it over in her fingers. The detective's direct line was printed in bold black letters, impossible to miss.

"Of course, Detective. I'll let you know if anything comes to mind."

Marlowe's gaze drifted back to Rebecca's wall of notes. "Your previous books—they were well-researched."

It wasn't a question, and Rebecca felt a chill. The detective had done her homework.

"I pride myself on accuracy."

"Good. Then you understand the importance of timely information in an investigation." Marlowe's voice remained even, but the implication hung in the air. "Evidence has a way of becoming less valuable the longer it sits unused."

Rebecca nodded, tucking the card into her pocket. "I understand completely."

"Do you?" Marlowe's eyes narrowed fractionally. "Because withholding evidence in a homicide investigation is obstruction of justice. Your professional curiosity doesn't supersede that."

The air between them tightened with unspoken tension. Rebecca maintained her composure despite the warning shot.

"I want to see justice done as much as you do, Detective."

"But perhaps not as quickly." Marlowe moved toward the door. "Thank you for your time, Ms. Sanders."

CHAPTER THIRTEEN

Office Whispers

The Horizon Financial office hummed with whispers and hushed conversations. Ethan stepped off the elevator to find clusters of employees huddled together, their voices dropping as he passed.

"Did you hear about Erika?" Melissa from accounting clutched her coffee mug with white knuckles. "Police found her yesterday. They're saying it was a robbery gone wrong."

"I heard she was strangled," whispered Tom, eyes wide. "Security is pulling all the badge access records."

Ethan's stomach clenched. He kept his face carefully neutral as he navigated toward his desk, catching fragments of conversations.

"...always flirting with the clients..."

"...wonder if it was someone she knew..."

"...police were asking about her work relationships..."

The office manager's voice cut through the speculation. "Everyone, please gather in the conference room in five minutes. Mr. Langford has an announcement."

Richard stood at the head of the conference table, his expression appropriately somber. No sign of the violent rage Ethan had witnessed. No indication he'd crushed the life from Erika just hours ago.

"As many of you have heard, we lost one of our own last night." Richard's voice carried the perfect note of professional grief. "Erika Jensen was found in her apartment. Police are investigating."

He paused, twirling his wedding ring once before continuing.

"In light of these tragic circumstances, the board has decided to accelerate our scheduled financial audit. Auditors will arrive tomorrow instead of next month."

A ripple of tension moved through the room. Several department heads exchanged glances.

"This is standard procedure when an employee with access to financial data dies unexpectedly," Richard continued smoothly. "I expect everyone's full cooperation."

Ethan's mind flashed back to a company holiday party two years earlier. He'd stayed late, working on a presentation when shouting erupted from Richard's office. Through the partially open door, Ethan had seen Richard grab a business associate by the throat, slamming him against the wall.

"You think you can threaten me?" Richard had snarled, his face contorted with the same rage Ethan had witnessed at Erika's apartment.

The next day, the associate was sporting a neck brace and a black eye. The official story: a car accident. The police report disappeared. The lawsuit vanished. Richard's wife, Judge Sophia Langford, had made calls to the right people.

Now, watching Richard calmly discuss security protocols and grief counseling resources, Ethan felt sweat beading along his spine. The man was capable of murder and returning to work as if nothing had happened.

* * *

The homicide department had commandeered the small conference room on the third floor. One by one, employees were called in to speak with the detectives. Ethan watched the door from his cubicle, his leg bouncing uncontrollably under his desk.

Detective Zoe Marlowe emerged, escorting a visibly shaken accountant back to her desk before consulting her notepad.

"Ethan Miller?" Her voice cut through the office noise.

Ethan's throat constricted. He stood on legs that felt disconnected from his body and followed her into the conference room.

"Have a seat, Mr. Miller." Detective Marlowe gestured to a chair while her partner, a younger detective with a tablet, positioned himself in the corner.

Ethan lowered himself carefully, hyper aware of his every movement. Don't fidget. Don't sweat. Don't look guilty.

"You worked with Erika Jensen." Not a question. Marlowe's eyes never left his face.

"Yes. Marketing department. Different teams, but same floor."

"How would you characterize your relationship?"

"Professional." Ethan focused on keeping his breathing even. "We didn't socialize outside work."

"According to several colleagues, Ms. Jensen was quite... social... with certain coworkers and clients."

Ethan's mind flashed to Erika's apartment, her naked body writhing against Richard's. He blinked hard, pushing the image away.

"I wouldn't know about that."

Marlowe tilted her head slightly. "Where were you Tuesday evening between eight and eleven PM?"

"Home. With my wife and daughter." The lie slipped out smoothly. "We had dinner, watched a movie."

"Your wife can confirm this?"

A flash of panic. Claire had been waiting up, angry about his absence.

"I stepped out for a walk after my daughter went to bed. I do that sometimes. Clear my head."

"A walk." Marlowe made a note. "Where exactly?"

"Just around our neighborhood." Ethan's collar felt suddenly tight. "Nothing specific. Just walking."

"Notice anything unusual that night? Anyone who seemed out of place?"

Ethan shook his head, afraid to speak.

Marlowe remained silent, studying her notepad. The silence stretched between them, thick and uncomfortable. Ethan fought the urge to fill it with nervous chatter, gripping the edge of his chair instead.

Finally, she looked up. "Is there anything else you can tell us about Ms. Jensen? From what we've learned she was very...amb itious and how should I phrase this...willing to go the extra mile to advance her career or to close a deal."

Ethan's mouth went dry. He knew exactly what Marlowe meant—he'd witnessed those "extra miles" firsthand through Erika's window.

"From my observations, that sounds fairly accurate. People talk, office gossip, you know. And that has pretty much been the scuttlebut on Erika."

"Have you engaged in any of these encounters with Ms. Jensen?"

"No, I have not." At least that wasn't a lie.

Marlowe leaned forward slightly. "It seems she has had quite a few of these inter-office encounters. Why do suppose you weren't included?"

The question caught Ethan off guard. His mind raced with images of Erika's naked body, her knowing smirk when she'd caught him watching. He cleared his throat.

"I really couldn't tell you. Maybe I wasn't her cup of tea, or more likely I couldn't help her career."

"I see, well thank you Mr. Miller." Marlowe reached into her jacket pocket and extracted a business card. "If you think of anything that might help in this matter please give me a call. This is my card. You can reach me at that number."

Ethan took the card, careful not to let his fingers tremble. He nodded and stood, desperate to escape the room.

Once the door closed behind him, Marlowe turned to the young detective. "He's hiding something. I don't know what yet, but he was nervous."

"He seemed normal to me."

"No, I could see it. I could sense it. A slight sweat on his upper lip. His leg fidgeting. I don't think he's the killer, but he's hiding something." She tapped her pen against the notepad. "Get me everything you can on this Ethan Miller."

* * *

Ethan returned to his desk, Detective Marlowe's card burning a hole in his pocket. He buried himself in spreadsheets, desperate to lose himself in the familiar patterns of data.

"Excuse me, is this desk seven-B?"

The voice startled him. He looked up and froze. For one heart-stopping moment, he thought Erika stood before him—blonde hair, similar height and build—but something was off. The woman's hair was pulled back in a practical ponytail instead of Erika's deliberate cascade. Her clothes were tailored but modest, nothing like Erika's calculated provocation.

"I—yes, that's the empty desk." Ethan struggled to find his voice. "Right across from mine."

"Perfect. I'm Vanessa Carter, new marketing associate." She extended her hand. "Starting today."

Ethan shook it automatically. Her grip was firm, professional—nothing like Erika's lingering touch that always promised more.

"Ethan Miller."

Vanessa nodded and began unpacking her things at the adjacent desk. Ethan couldn't stop staring. The resemblance was uncanny yet disturbingly wrong. Same facial structure, but her expressions were measured, thoughtful. Same lips, but they moved differently when she spoke—precise rather than seductive.

"I understand the circumstances of my hiring are unfortunate," Vanessa said quietly, arranging reference books on her desk. "I hope my presence isn't making things more difficult."

"No, it's fine." Ethan swallowed hard. "It's just—"

"The resemblance. I gathered that from everyone's reactions this morning." She met his gaze directly, her eyes analytical where Erika's had been calculating. "I assure you, it's purely coincidental."

Throughout the day, Ethan found himself repeatedly startled by Vanessa's presence in his peripheral vision. Each time he caught a glimpse of blonde hair, his heart raced before the cognitive dissonance hit—same physical package, completely different content. During the department meeting, she spoke articulately about financial trend analysis, her gestures economical and precise.

When she returned to her desk with a cup of tea—not Erika's preferred sugar-laden coffee—Ethan realized he was sweating. Seeing Vanessa was like watching someone wearing Erika's skin but moving all wrong inside it. The sensation left him profoundly unsettled.

* * *

Rebecca adjusted her unremarkable gray blazer and checked her reflection in her phone. She'd deliberately chosen clothing that would fade into the background—professional enough to belong in a corporate setting but forgettable enough that no one would remember her face afterward.

"I'm here to speak with someone about Erika Jensen," she told the receptionist. "I'm writing a memorial piece for the community newsletter."

The receptionist's expression softened. "How thoughtful. Let me call someone from her department."

Rebecca clutched her notebook—an actual physical notebook, not a digital device. People tended to be less guarded around old-fashioned notepads than laptops or phones. Her fingers traced the edge of the voice recorder hidden in her pocket.

"Ms. Sanders?" A middle-aged woman approached. "I'm Diane from HR. We can talk in the break room."

Rebecca followed, scanning faces as they walked. Which one was him? The man she'd seen watching from below Erika's window. She'd studied the company website, memorizing names and departments, but photographs couldn't capture the furtive body language she'd witnessed that night.

In the break room, several employees had gathered. Rebecca recognized Richard immediately from her research—the CFO looked haggard, with dark circles under his eyes.

"Thank you all for meeting with me." Rebecca smiled warmly. "I'm hoping to capture Erika's essence for those who didn't know her well."

She asked standard questions about Erika's work ethic and personality, watching reactions carefully. Richard contributed minimal responses, his wedding ring spinning continuously between his fingers.

"Did Erika have any close friends here?" Rebecca asked. "Anyone she confided in?"

A woman mentioned occasional happy hours. Rebecca nodded, writing notes while her eyes continued scanning the room. Her gaze stopped on a man sitting slightly apart from the others. Dark hair, average build, but something about his stillness caught her attention. Unlike the others who fidgeted with grief or discomfort, this man was too controlled, too deliberate in his movements.

When their eyes briefly met, Rebecca recognized the haunted look of someone carrying a terrible secret. She'd seen that expression in her research interviews with witnesses to violent crimes.

"And you are?" she asked him directly.

"Ethan Miller. Marketing department." His voice was steady, but his knuckles whitened around his coffee mug.

Rebecca made a show of writing his name while mentally confirming it against her research. This was him—the watcher in the shadows.

CHAPTER FOURTEEN

Claire's Journey

The next morning, Ethan's hands trembled as he fumbled with his tie. Three nights without his walks, and his body was betraying him. Sweat beaded along his hairline despite the cool air conditioning. He splashed cold water on his face, but it did nothing to calm the electric current humming beneath his skin.

"Ethan?" Claire called from the bedroom. "Emma's waiting for breakfast."

"I'll be right there." His voice came out sharper than intended.

In the kitchen, Emma chattered about her school project while Claire flipped pancakes. The normalcy of it all felt suffocating. Ethan's leg bounced uncontrollably under the table, his fingers drumming against his coffee mug.

"Dad, you're not listening," Emma complained.

"What? Sorry, sweetheart." He forced himself to focus, but his daughter's words seemed to blur together, drowned out by the pounding in his head.

Claire set a plate in front of him. "Are you feeling alright? You look flushed."

"I'm fine." He stabbed at his pancakes without eating. The sweet smell turned his stomach. "Just work stress."

"Maybe you should take a sick day."

"I said I'm fine." The words came out as a snarl.

Claire and Emma exchanged glances. The hurt in his daughter's eyes sent a flash of shame through him, but it wasn't enough to override the crawling sensation under his skin.

At work, Ethan locked himself in a bathroom stall, pressing his forehead against the cool metal partition. His heart raced like he'd sprinted up ten flights of stairs. Every nerve ending screamed for release—for the thrill of watching, of seeing what wasn't meant for his eyes.

He'd gone three nights without his fix. Three nights of lying beside Claire, staring at the ceiling, his body craving the rush. The compulsion clawed at him from the inside, worse than any physical addiction he could imagine.

Back at his desk, Vanessa stopped by with questions about a client presentation. Her resemblance to Erika sent a jolt through him.

"Are you even listening?" she asked, frowning.

"What? Yes, of course." He hadn't heard a word.

"You seem distracted."

Ethan gripped his pen so hard it snapped, ink spilling across his fingers. "I'm fine," he hissed, grabbing tissues to clean the mess.

Vanessa stepped back. "I'll come back later."

* * *

That night, Claire waited until Emma was asleep before confronting Ethan in their bedroom. He sat on the edge of the bed, staring at nothing, his body tense like a coiled spring.

"Ethan, we need to talk." She closed the door softly behind her. "You've been having nightmares. I hear you gasping for air in your sleep."

"It's just work stress." He didn't meet her eyes.

Claire sat beside him, careful to leave space between them. "I found a receipt in your car. From a restaurant near that woman's apartment. The one who was murdered."

Ethan's head snapped up. "You went through my things?"

"I'm worried about you." Her voice remained steady despite his accusatory tone. "You've changed. The nightmares, the mood swings, canceling your walks suddenly... Did you know her? The woman who died?"

"She was a colleague." His voice cracked. "It's been hard on everyone at work."

Claire took a deep breath. "I need to tell you something. My therapy—it's been more than just dealing with anxiety."

Ethan finally looked at her, confusion momentarily replacing the panic in his eyes.

"Three years ago, I started seeing Dr. Chen specifically for sexual trauma therapy." She twisted her wedding ring. "I've never told you the details of what happened in college because I couldn't bear to see your face when you heard it. But I've been working through it, and last month, Dr. Chen suggested I'm ready to start rebuilding our physical intimacy."

"That's why you've been... initiating?" His voice softened.

Claire nodded. "I want to want you again, Ethan. I'm trying. When you couldn't the other night, I thought maybe you'd given up on me."

"No," he whispered, guilt washing over his features. "Claire, I—"

"I know we've been distant. But I'm fighting to find my way back to you." She reached for his hand, her fingers trembling. "Whatever's happening with you now—please don't shut me out."

That night, after the intensity of their conversation, Claire sought to bridge the chasm between them with the physical connection Dr. Chen had encouraged her to pursue. The air in the bedroom was thick with tension and unspoken truths as she approached Ethan, her eyes steady and filled with determination.

"I want to try again," she said softly, her hands reaching for the hem of her blouse.

Ethan watched her, his face a mask of conflicting emotions. He opened his mouth to speak, but Claire silenced him with a gentle shake of her head. Her fingers worked deftly, undressing with a deliberate slowness that betrayed her underlying nervousness. Her clothing fell away, revealing the soft curves of her body bathed in the dim glow of the bedside lamp.

She moved towards him, her movements deliberate and measured. Ethan's breath hitched as she knelt between his legs, her fingers tracing the outline of his manhood through the fabric of his trousers. Claire's touch was tentative at first, exploring, seeking a response from his body that was reluctant to come.

With a deep breath, she unbuttoned his pants and eased down his zipper. Her hand slipped inside, freeing him from the confines of his clothing. Ethan's cock lay slack against his thigh, a tangible symbol of his internal turmoil.

Claire's heart pounded in her chest as she lowered her mouth to him, her lips brushing against the sensitive skin of his member. She caressed him gently, her tongue flicking out to taste him, her hand cupping and fondling his balls in an attempt to coax life into his flaccid flesh.

Ethan's body remained unresponsive, his mind trapped in a relentless cycle of anxiety and fear. The image of Erika's lifeless body, Richard's hands tightening around her neck, and the sound of his own company pin snagging on the branch as he fled, all played on an endless loop in his mind's eye.

Claire sucked furiously, desperate to make him hard, to feel some semblance of the connection they once shared. She bobbed her head, taking him deeper, her hand stroking in time with her mouth, willing him to respond.

But Ethan's body betrayed him. Despite the warmth of Claire's mouth, the wetness of her tongue, the tender touch of her hands, he remained soft, his arousal stifled by the weight of his guilt and the terror of being caught.

After a few minutes that felt like an eternity, Claire sat back on her heels, her breath coming in short, ragged gasps, the taste of defeat mingling with the saltiness of Ethan's skin on her tongue. She looked up at him, her eyes searching his face for some explanation, some reassurance that this was not the end of them.

Ethan reached out, brushing a strand of hair away from her face. "It's not you," he said, his voice barely above a whisper. "It's not your fault, Claire."

But as Claire dressed in silence, the realization dawned on her that the distance between them had grown even wider. And though she had bared her body and her soul to him, Ethan remained a fortress of secrets and lies, his walls impenetrable, his truths buried deep within.

Claire pulled her nightgown back on, her movements slow and deliberate. The silence between them felt heavier than ever before. She sat on the edge of the bed, her back to Ethan, shoulders slumped in defeat.

"I feel like I'm losing you," she whispered, her voice cracking. "And I don't even know why."

Ethan moved beside her, the mattress dipping under his weight. He stared at his hands, trembling slightly in his lap.

"Sometimes..." he began, then stopped, swallowing hard. "Sometimes I don't recognize myself anymore, Claire."

She turned to face him, surprised by the raw honesty in his voice.

"There are things I've done—" His voice broke. "Things I can't take back."

Claire reached for his hand, her touch gentle. "We all have regrets, Ethan."

"Not like this." He finally met her gaze, his eyes red-rimmed and glistening with unshed tears. "I've been so focused on what I want, what I need, that I stopped seeing you. Really seeing you."

Claire's breath caught in her throat. This wasn't the polished, controlled Ethan she'd grown accustomed to. This was the man she'd fallen in love with years ago—vulnerable, real.

"I didn't know about your therapy," he continued. "Three years, and I never noticed. What kind of husband does that make me?"

"The kind who's human," she whispered. "I hid it well."

Ethan's shoulders shook as a sob escaped him. "I don't deserve your kindness."

Without thinking, Claire wrapped her arms around him. For once, he didn't stiffen at her touch. Instead, he melted into her embrace, his tears dampening her nightgown.

"I'm scared, Claire," he confessed against her shoulder. "I'm so scared of losing everything."

She held him tighter, her own tears falling silently. "Then let me in, Ethan. Whatever it is, we can face it together."

For a brief moment, the walls between them crumbled. No secrets, no pretense—just two broken people clinging to each other in the darkness, neither knowing if they could find their way back to the light.

* * *

Detective Zoe Marlowe hunched over her desk, rubbing her eyes as she flipped through the stack of case files. The precinct hummed with the usual background noise—phones ringing, keyboards clicking, the occasional burst of laughter from the break room. She reached for her coffee, grimacing at the cold, bitter liquid before taking a sip anyway.

"Detective, this just came in from Records." Officer Perez dropped a thin folder on her desk.

Marlowe flipped it open, scanning the contents. A stalking report filed by Erika Jensen two weeks before her murder. Her posture straightened immediately, fatigue vanishing as her eyes narrowed on the details.

"Subject reports observing male figure outside her apartment on multiple occasions," she read aloud, her voice low. "Approximately six feet tall, athletic build, wearing dark clothing. Subject states perpetrator watches from position in landscaping across from east-facing windows, primarily between 9 PM and 11 PM."

She flipped the page, her finger tracing the timeline Erika had provided—Monday, Wednesday, Friday patterns. Regular as clockwork. The report noted that Erika couldn't identify the stalker's face due to distance and poor lighting, but had become aware of his presence after noticing movement in the bushes while closing her curtains.

"Victim states she deliberately left curtains partially open on three occasions to confirm suspicions," Marlowe continued reading. "Subject believes perpetrator may be connected to her workplace but cannot confirm identity."

The most telling detail came on the final page: "Complainant mentioned occasionally performing for her suspected audience, describing it as 'a strange power' to know someone was watching without their knowledge that she knew."

Marlowe pulled out her notepad, jotting down the times and locations. The positioning matched perfectly with the trampled vegetation they'd found at the crime scene. The schedule aligned with witness reports of a figure seen in the neighborhood on those specific evenings.

"This isn't random," she muttered. "Our perp had a routine, knew her schedule."

She reached for the employee roster from Horizon Financial, comparing it against the timeline in the stalking report. Several employees had the flexibility to be in that location during those hours, but something about the methodical nature of the stalking—the specific days, the consistent timing—struck her as significant.

CHAPTER FIFTEEN

A Calculated Comment

The conference room fell silent as Richard Langford entered, his custom Italian suit immaculate despite the visible strain around his eyes. The leadership team gathered for the emergency meeting looked up expectantly as he took his position at the head of the table.

"Thank you all for coming on such short notice," Richard said. "As you know, the police investigation into Erika's murder continues, and they've requested our full cooperation."

Ethan shifted in his seat, focusing on keeping his breathing steady. His fingers twitched toward his empty lapel where his company pin should have been.

"The detectives shared something disturbing with me yesterday," Richard continued, his voice dropping. "Based on evidence at the scene, they believe her killer had been watching her for some time. Stalking her, learning her patterns."

A murmur rippled through the room. Vanessa Carter, the new marketing associate, made a small sound of distress.

"Someone familiar with her schedule," Richard's eyes swept the room, "possibly even someone from this company."

His gaze landed on Ethan and locked. A moment of electric understanding passed between them—a silent acknowledgment that stretched for three heartbeats too long.

Ethan's mouth went dry. The knowledge hung between them like a tangible thing. Richard's eyes held no question, only cold certainty.

"We're implementing additional security measures," Richard continued, finally breaking eye contact. "And I'd ask everyone to be vigilant about reporting unusual behavior."

The meeting concluded with hushed, somber tones. As people filed out, Richard called across the room, "Ethan, a moment please."

Ethan froze, then turned back. The conference room emptied until only the two men remained.

"I noticed something was missing," Richard said, reaching into his pocket. He withdrew a company pin—identical to the one Ethan had lost. "Your department pin. I requested a replacement from HR."

He held it out, a seemingly innocent gesture that carried unmistakable menace.

"Found yours?" Richard asked.

"No," Ethan managed. "I've been looking everywhere."

"Interesting where things turn up sometimes." Richard pressed the pin into Ethan's palm, his fingers closing Ethan's hand around it with deliberate pressure. "I'd be more careful with this one."

* * *

Detective Zoe Marlowe sat across from Richard Langford in the small interview room at the precinct. Unlike most people called in for questioning about a murder, Richard appeared completely at ease—suit unwrinkled, posture relaxed, hands resting calmly on the table.

"Thank you for coming in, Mr. Langford." Marlowe placed a folder on the table without opening it. "I understand you were close with Erika Jensen."

"We worked together. She was a valuable member of my team." Richard's expression conveyed appropriate concern without excessive emotion.

"Just professional?" Marlowe watched his wedding ring—he wasn't twirling it.

"Of course." Not a flicker of change in his breathing pattern.

"Several colleagues mentioned seeing you two together outside of work hours."

Richard nodded once. "Business dinners. Client meetings sometimes run late."

Marlowe pulled out phone records. "Thirty-seven calls between your personal cell phones in the two weeks before her death. Most after 10 PM."

"We were finalizing the Anderson account. High-pressure situation." He smiled thinly. "I'm sure you understand demanding work environments, Detective."

"When did you last see Ms. Jensen alive?"

"Three days before her death, at the office." The answer came too quickly, too rehearsed.

Marlowe leaned forward. "Interesting. Because we have a witness who places you at her apartment building the night she died."

For a fraction of a second, something flickered behind Richard's eyes—not guilt or fear, but calculation.

"Your witness is mistaken." Richard straightened his already perfect cuffs. "I was having dinner with my wife, Judge Langford. You can verify with her."

Richard's face betrayed nothing, but Marlowe caught the almost imperceptible relaxation of his shoulders.

"Tell me about the company audit," she said, changing direction abruptly.

"Standard procedure. Nothing unusual."

"Ms. Jensen was involved?"

"Tangentially. She prepared some marketing reports." Richard's right index finger tapped once against his thumb—the first unconscious movement he'd made.

Marlowe nodded as if accepting his answer. "You know what I find interesting, Mr. Langford? Most people I interview about a murdered colleague show some emotion—shock, grief, anger. You're remarkably composed."

"I process tragedy differently than most." His smile never reached his eyes. "Is there anything else, Detective? I do have a company to run."

    * * *

Ethan locked the bathroom stall door and pressed his forehead against the cool metal partition. The fluorescent lights hummed overhead, the same sound that had formed the backdrop to Erika's breathless moans three weeks earlier. He closed his eyes and the memories flooded back.

The bathroom smelled of industrial cleaner, but underneath it, he caught a phantom trace of her perfume—jasmine with something darker beneath it. His hands trembled as he gripped the edges of the sink.

"God, yes, right there," Erika had whispered to the unknown man in the stall with her. The sound of her voice echoed in his mind, bouncing off the tile walls.

The memory shifted, distorted. Suddenly it wasn't the man's hands on her body but Richard's—not caressing but tightening around her throat. The pleasured gasps transformed into desperate, choking sounds.

Ethan splashed cold water on his face. In the mirror, his reflection looked hollow-eyed, haunted. Water dripped from his chin like tears.

He remembered how Erika had arched her back against the bathroom wall, her blonde hair cascading down her shoulders. The image morphed—her back arching not in pleasure but in the final spasm of death, her hair splayed across her living room floor.

The scent of jasmine gave way to something metallic. Blood. Had he actually smelled her blood that night, or was his mind inventing details?

"Even that pathetic Ethan could probably satisfy me better than you."

Her final taunt to Richard played on loop in his head. She had known he was watching. Had always known.

In his mind, Erika turned from Richard and looked directly at Ethan through the window, her eyes locking with his in the moment before Richard's hands closed around her throat. That hadn't happened—she never saw him that night—but in his fractured memory, she smiled at him as she died.

Ethan vomited into the sink, bile burning his throat. He rinsed his mouth and stared at his reflection again. Behind him, in the mirror, he thought he saw a flash of blonde hair in the stall he'd been watching from that day.

When he spun around, the bathroom was empty.

CHAPTER SIXTEEN

Night Terrors

Ethan jolted awake on the living room couch, a strangled "Erika!" escaping his lips before he could stop it. Sweat soaked through his t-shirt, heart hammering against his ribs. The Saturday afternoon sun streamed through the windows, casting long shadows across the floor.

In his dream, Erika's hands had been around his throat instead of Richard's around hers. "You watched me die," she'd whispered, her breath hot against his ear. "You just stood there."

"Daddy?" Emma stood in the doorway, clutching her stuffed rabbit. Her eyes were wide with fear. "Who's Erika?"

Ethan's mouth went dry. "Nobody, sweetheart. Just a bad dream."

"You were making scary noises." Emma's lower lip trembled. "Like the monster under my bed."

Claire appeared behind their daughter, her hand resting protectively on Emma's shoulder. Her expression was carefully neutral, but her eyes held questions.

"It's okay, Em. Daddy just had a nightmare." Claire squeezed Emma's shoulder. "Why don't you go finish your drawing? I'll be there in a minute."

After Emma left, Claire sat on the edge of the couch. "This is the third time this week."

"I'm fine."

"You're not fine. You haven't been fine for weeks." She reached for his hand. "Emma's scared. She asked me last night if you were sick like her friend's dad who went to the hospital."

Guilt twisted in Ethan's stomach. "I'm sorry."

"Don't apologize. Just... talk to me." Claire's fingers tightened around his. "Or if not me, someone. A doctor, maybe."

That evening, after Claire and Emma had fallen asleep watching a movie, Ethan stood in the entryway, keys in hand. His skin crawled with need. The walls of the house seemed to close in on him.

He couldn't stay here another night, pacing the floors, jumping at shadows.

The cool night air hit his face as he stepped outside. He deliberately turned away from his usual route toward Erika's apartment, instead heading toward Jenny's street. His feet remembered the way, muscle memory guiding him through the familiar shortcuts.

Jenny's kitchen light was on, her silhouette visible through the thin curtains. Ethan slipped into the shadows of the maple tree across from her window, feeling his breathing slow for the first time in weeks.

Jenny stood at her kitchen sink, tipping back a glass of water, her throat moving as she swallowed. The thin fabric of her negligee revealed the silhouette of her body against the kitchen light, curves softly outlined in the warm glow. Her long black hair cascaded down her back, catching hints of amber from the lamp above the counter. She looked peaceful, unaware of the eyes that tracked her movements through the darkness outside. She set the empty glass down with a soft clink against the countertop and padded back to her bedroom, her bare feet silent on the cool tile. The mattress dipped slightly as she slipped beneath the covers next to her husband, who stirred but didn't wake. His rhythmic breathing continued uninterrupted as she settled against her pillow. The light clicked off, plunging the room into darkness, leaving only the faint silver glow of moonlight filtering through the thin curtains.

Darkness. Nothing to see.

Ethan waited, but the house remained still and dark. Disappointment settled in his chest like a stone. Jenny's mundane nighttime routine felt hollow after what he'd witnessed with Erika. The memory of violence flashed behind his eyes—Erika's final moments, her wide eyes, Richard's hands around her throat.

His feet carried him away from Jenny's house, following familiar streets without conscious direction. The rhythm of walking calmed his racing thoughts. He turned left at the corner, then right at the next intersection. Only when he recognized the ornamental cherry trees lining the street did he realize where he was heading.

Erika's apartment building loomed ahead.

Ethan froze, his heart hammering against his ribs. Police tape still marked the side entrance to her building. He stepped back into the shadows of a nearby tree, breathing hard.

Three blocks away, Rebecca lowered her binoculars. The figure's silhouette matched her notes perfectly—average height, lean build, distinctive gait with a slight forward hunch. Same man who'd fled the night of the murder. Same man who'd been watching Erika's apartment for weeks before.

She slipped her notebook into her jacket pocket and eased out of her car, keeping to the shadows. Her years researching criminal behavior had taught her how to move unnoticed. She maintained distance as she followed him, documenting his movements with her phone camera.

The hairs on the back of Ethan's neck stood up. Something felt wrong. Different. He glanced over his shoulder, seeing nothing but empty sidewalk. Yet the sensation persisted—eyes on him, watching, cataloging his movements.

A strange thrill ran through him, mingling with the fear. This was how they felt—all the people he'd observed over the years. This vulnerability, this exposure. He'd never considered it before.

Ethan quickened his pace, heart racing. The watcher remained hidden, but he felt their presence like a physical touch. The hunter becoming the hunted.

Chapter Seventeen

Missing Pin

The company atrium transformed into a memorial space overnight. A large portrait of Erika—professionally taken at last year's company gala—stood on an easel, surrounded by white lilies. The image captured her radiant smile, golden hair cascading over bare shoulders, eyes bright with ambition.

Ethan tore through his dresser drawers, scattering socks and underwear across the bedroom floor. The replacement pin Richard had given him lay on the nightstand, gleaming accusingly in the morning light. He'd already checked every pocket of every jacket, emptied his desk drawers at work, and searched his car three times.

"Ethan? We're going to be late." Claire appeared in the doorway, dressed in a somber black dress. "What are you looking for?"

"Nothing. Just..." He gestured vaguely at the mess. "Thought I had a different tie."

He slipped the replacement pin into his pocket, unable to bring himself to attach it to his lapel. Not yet.

The atrium buzzed with hushed conversations when they arrived. Richard stood near Erika's portrait, accepting condolences with the appropriate gravity of a department head who'd lost a valued team member. His eyes found Ethan immediately.

"Please, everyone take your seats." Richard's voice carried across the room. "Before we begin, I'd like to acknowledge our collective grief with a small gesture."

An assistant distributed memorial pins—small silver E's with Erika's birth year and death year—to each employee.

"These will replace our standard company pins for the next month, in remembrance."

Ethan's fingers closed around the replacement pin in his pocket, panic rising in his throat.

Richard moved through the crowd, personally pinning each employee, murmuring quiet words of shared grief. He approached Ethan, eyes cold despite his sympathetic smile.

"Your pin, Ethan?"

Ethan's hand trembled as he withdrew the replacement company pin from his pocket.

Richard took it, examining it closely. "Interesting. This is your new replacement pin?" He glanced around at the other employees watching. "I thought for sure you would've found your original pin by now." He held the pin up to the light. "I wonder where the old one might have ended up."

Sweat beaded on Ethan's forehead as Richard leaned in to attach the memorial pin to his lapel.

"We should be careful with our possessions," Richard whispered, his breath hot against Ethan's ear. "You never know where they might turn up."

Richard's mind reflected back to the night of the murder sitting alone in his home office after discovering the company pin, methodically piecing together the puzzle. The company logo etched into the metal gleamed under his desk lamp as he rotated it between his fingers. Finding Ethan's name on the back. He pulled up the employee database on his laptop, Ethan Miller, marketing division.

"Ethan Miller," he whispered, pulling up the personnel file.

Richard's mind replayed the murder scene—the rustling in the bushes, the fleeting shadow. He clicked through the company's security footage archives, studying Ethan's gait and build, comparing it to his memory of the figure fleeing Erika's apartment. The timestamps from the parking garage showed Ethan leaving work unusually late on multiple evenings, including the night of the murder.

He opened his personal calendar, noting when he'd visited Erika over the past months, then cross-referenced with Ethan's work schedule and building access logs. The pattern emerged with chilling clarity—Ethan had been there, watching, many times before.

"You've been quite the voyeur, haven't you, Ethan?" Richard murmured, a cold smile forming.

At the memorial, Detective Marlowe stood near the back, her sharp eyes cataloging every interaction. She noted Richard's deliberate movements through the crowd, the lingering handshakes, the practiced grief. When he approached Ethan, she observed the younger man's posture stiffen, his face drain of color during their exchange.

After the ceremony, she collected the guest book, studying the signatures.

"Interesting turnout," her partner commented.

"Mmm." Marlowe flipped through the pages. "Notice how our financial director handled that exchange with the marketing analyst?"

"Miller? Yeah, looked like he was about to pass out."

"I want all security footage from their floor for the past month," she said. "And get me everything we have on their relationship."

Rebecca positioned herself near the refreshment table, notebook disguised as a small planner open beside her coffee cup. She documented the exchange between Richard and Ethan, noting the power dynamic, the visible tension.

Subject E visibly trembling during pin exchange. R maintaining dominance through physical proximity and prolonged eye contact. Clear intimidation tactics disguised as professional courtesy.

She watched Ethan's eyes dart nervously around the room after Richard moved away, his hand repeatedly touching the memorial pin as if it burned through his shirt.

Vanessa approached the podium last, her resemblance to Erika creating an unsettling ripple through the audience. Several executives shifted uncomfortably in their seats, eyes darting between her and Richard.

"Though I never had the privilege of meeting Erika Jensen," she began, her voice steady and clear, "I've come to know her through her work. The legacy she left behind speaks volumes about her professional dedication."

She detailed Erika's client acquisition strategies, her sales techniques, even personal touches like how she remembered client birthdays and preferences. Vanessa's analytical approach was markedly different from Erika's charismatic style, yet somehow more devastating in its precision.

"She maintained detailed records of every interaction," Vanessa continued, her fingers lightly tracing the edge of the podium. "Her notes on the Decker account particularly showed her meticulous attention to financial details. She tracked every transfer, every anomaly, with remarkable thoroughness."

Richard's wedding ring spun faster around his finger, a blur of gold catching the light as beads of sweat formed at his hairline.

CHAPTER EIGHTEEN

Necessary Sins

Richard sat alone in his home office that night, bourbon in hand, staring at Ethan's company pin on his desk. The house was silent—Sophia was working late at the courthouse again. Perfect. He needed the solitude to think.

"She gave me no choice," he whispered to the empty room.

Erika had backed him into a corner with her blackmail. The offshore accounts, the shell companies, the falsified contracts—she'd documented everything. Years of careful work dismantled by her prying eyes. What had started as passion had evolved into a calculated trap. He'd been a fool to trust her.

Richard took a long swallow of bourbon, feeling the burn down his throat. "She would have destroyed everything."

The moment replayed in his mind: her mocking smile as she demanded more money, her casual threat to expose him, the way she'd laughed when he'd pleaded. The feel of her throat beneath his hands—how quickly the life had drained from her eyes.

It wasn't murder. It was self-preservation.

And now there was Ethan. The voyeur. The witness.

Richard twirled the pin between his fingers. The marketing analyst was weak, frightened—a man with his own secrets. Richard had seen how he looked at Erika, how he skulked around after hours. Pathetic.

"He won't go to the police," Richard reasoned. "He can't explain why he was there."

Still, loose ends were dangerous. The pin gave him leverage, but was it enough? Perhaps Ethan could be useful. The man's observational skills were exceptional—his marketing presentations proved that. If properly motivated, he might even help with the ongoing audit.

Richard poured another drink. "Keep your friends close..."

He'd watched Ethan unraveling at work—the dark circles under his eyes, the trembling hands, the startled jumps at sudden noises. The man was terrified, guilt-ridden.

"Let him suffer a while longer," Richard decided. The pressure would make Ethan malleable, desperate for a way out.

If Ethan proved troublesome, well—Richard had connections through Sophia. One more problem could disappear, just like the assault charges last year.

* * *

The office stood empty except for Ethan and Richard, their faces illuminated by the harsh glow of computer screens. The clock read 10:37 PM. Ethan's eyes burned from staring at spreadsheets, but Richard had insisted they finish reviewing the quarterly reports before tomorrow's audit committee meeting.

"Almost done with those vendor payment reconciliations?" Richard leaned against Ethan's cubicle wall, coffee in hand.

"Just about." Ethan scrolled through the document, his attention caught by a recurring pattern. A consulting firm called Meridian Solutions appeared repeatedly—substantial payments for vaguely described services. He'd seen this name before in other reports.

Richard's phone rang. He stepped away to answer it, giving Ethan a moment alone with the files.

Taking advantage of Richard's absence, Ethan quickly opened another folder and cross-referenced the payments. Meridian Solutions led to another company, which connected to a third. Each transfer obscured the money's path a little more.

Then he saw it. A document Richard had mistakenly included in the shared folder—transfer instructions to an offshore account labeled "Decker." The amounts matched exactly what had been siphoned through the shell companies.

Footsteps approached from the hallway. Ethan's pulse spiked. He closed the document with a swift keystroke, pulling up the vendor payment spreadsheet just as Richard rounded the corner.

"Sorry about that. Wife checking in." Richard settled into the chair beside Ethan's desk, his cologne—expensive and overpowering—filling the small space. "Find anything interesting?"

"Just the standard reconciliations." Ethan kept his voice steady despite the thundering in his chest. "Everything seems to balance."

Richard nodded, eyes lingering on Ethan's screen. "You know what makes you so valuable to this company, Miller?"

"My marketing insights?"

"Your attention to detail." Richard swiveled Ethan's chair to face him directly. "You notice things others don't. It's a rare quality."

Ethan's mouth went dry. "Just doing my job."

"I've been observing your habits, you know." Richard's voice dropped lower. "The way you watch people."

The air in the cubicle seemed to vanish. Ethan's fingers tightened on his armrest.

"In meetings, at lunch—you're always observing." Richard leaned closer. "It's how you understand consumer behavior so well, isn't it? Watching people when they don't realize they're being watched."

"I—I suppose that's part of it."

"I'm the same way." Richard's smile didn't reach his eyes. "I've found that people reveal their true selves when they think no one's looking. Their desires. Their fears." He tapped the desk with his wedding ring. "Their secrets."

Ethan's collar felt too tight. Was Richard speaking in generalities, or did he know about Ethan's nighttime activities?

"Take Erika, for instance." Richard's voice was casual, but his eyes remained fixed on Ethan's face. "She never realized how transparent her ambitions were. Always putting on a show, thinking no one saw through it."

* * *

Back home, Claire sat cross-legged on the bed, her fingers hovering over Ethan's laptop keyboard. She hadn't planned to snoop, but when his computer chimed with an email notification while he showered, curiosity won.

The browser history tab revealed a digital trail of obsession. Dozens of searches about Erika Jensen—news articles about her murder, social media profiles, company directory information. Claire's stomach clenched as she clicked through page after page.

"Erika Jensen autopsy details"

"Erika Jensen personal life"

"Erika Jensen dating history"

Claire's hands trembled. One search particularly stood out: "Erika Jensen lingerie preferences." What kind of research was that?

She opened his email, finding a folder labeled "EJ" containing saved photos from Erika's social media—Erika at the beach, at company events, always stunning. In one, she wore a form-fitting dress at the holiday party, Ethan barely visible in the background, staring at her.

The shower water stopped. Claire quickly closed the tabs but couldn't unsee what she'd discovered.

When Ethan emerged from the bathroom, towel wrapped around his waist, she'd composed her face into neutrality.

"Your phone kept buzzing," she said, voice impressively steady.

"Thanks." He grabbed it, checking messages with his back to her.

Claire studied him—the husband she thought she knew. The late-night walks. The distracted behavior. The nightmares where he called out Erika's name. The pieces clicked into terrible place.

"Emma wants you to read her a story before bed," Claire said, watching him dress.

"I'll be there in a minute."

After he left the room, Claire returned to the laptop, staring at the search history. Not a stalker, then—a lover. The sexual dysfunction, the emotional distance—it all made sense now. He'd been having an affair with the murdered woman.

Claire closed the laptop, pressing her palm against its surface as if sealing away the truth she wasn't ready to confront.

* * *

Rebecca Sanders approached the police station with deliberate steps, clutching her leather portfolio against her chest like armor. Her heart hammered against her ribs as she checked her watch—exactly 3:15 PM, Detective Marlowe's shift according to the schedule she'd obtained through careful questioning of the front desk officer yesterday.

The fluorescent lights buzzed overhead as she approached the desk sergeant.

"I need to speak with Detective Marlowe about the Erika Jensen case."

The sergeant glanced up. "Your name?"

"Rebecca Sanders. I'm a neighbor. We spoke briefly during the canvassing."

Five minutes later, Marlowe appeared, sharp eyes assessing Rebecca before she motioned toward a small interview room.

"Ms. Sanders. You have information?"

Rebecca placed her portfolio on the table but kept her hand on it. "I've been thinking about that night. There are things about Richard Langford that don't add up."

Marlowe's expression remained neutral. "What things specifically?"

"I saw him at Erika's apartment multiple times before her death. I had no idea who he was until I saw him at their workplace. Their relationship was... volatile." Rebecca pulled out a small notebook. "I keep track of neighborhood patterns for my writing. Richard visited at least eight times in the two weeks before her murder."

"Your writing?"

"I'm a true crime author." Rebecca pushed her business card across the table. "Research habits die hard."

Marlowe examined the card. "That's right, I'd nearly forgotten. And you're just coming forward now because?"

"I needed to be certain. The last time they were together, two days before her death, they had a screaming match. I couldn't hear anything, but she raised her hand and rubbed her fingers together. I think she was threatening him about money." Rebecca leaned forward. "Detective, he lunged for her her throat during that argument—he stopped himself, but the intent was there."

Marlowe's eyes narrowed slightly. "You witnessed this?"

"From my apartment. I have a direct view."

"Did you photograph any of these encounters?"

Rebecca hesitated. "No. That would be crossing a line."

Marlowe's lips thinned. "Yet watching wasn't?"

"I observe patterns, Detective. It's what I do." Rebecca tapped her notebook. "Richard Langford has a pattern of violence when cornered."

"Anything else you've been observing that might be relevant?"

Rebecca's mind flashed to Ethan's figure fleeing the scene. She'd come prepared to share only part of what she knew.

"Just Richard. I thought you should know."

CHAPTER NINETEEN

Tension Rises

E than sat at his desk, methodically arranging documents for the upcoming presentation when Richard's heavy hand landed on his shoulder, startling him out of his concentration.

"Miller. Just the man I needed." Richard's smile didn't reach his eyes, remaining cold and calculating. "Let's chat in my office."

Inside Richard's sleek corner office, with its imposing mahogany desk and city view, Ethan perched on the edge of a leather chair, fighting to keep his expression neutral while his stomach knotted with unease.

Richard leaned back in his executive chair, the leather creaking beneath his weight. "Emma's soccer game went well Saturday, didn't it? She's quite the little athlete. That goal in the second half was impressive."

Ethan's mouth went dry, a chill crawling up his spine. "How did you—"

"Claire looked lovely in that blue sundress. Matches her eyes." Richard twirled his wedding ring between his thumb and forefinger, a nervous habit that belied his confident tone. "The one with the little white buttons down the front."

"Your hydrangeas are coming in nicely this year. Front yard looks immaculate." Richard's voice dropped lower, taking on a menacing quality. "Though your back fence could use some repair. Anyone could slip through that loose section by the maple tree. The one right outside Emma's bedroom window."

Ethan's pulse pounded in his ears, a roaring that nearly drowned out Richard's words. His hands gripped the armrests until his knuckles whitened. "What do you want?"

"Just checking in on a valued team member." Richard smiled, shark-like and predatory. "I know everything about you, Ethan. Your habits. Your schedule. Your family." He leaned forward, invading Ethan's space with deliberate intimidation. "Remember that."

That night, Ethan paced his living room, peering through blinds at every passing car. The sensation of being watched prickled across his skin like invisible needles. When headlights swept across the front window, he dropped to the floor with a muffled thud, crawling on hands and knees to adjust the blinds for a better view without exposing himself.

"Ethan, what are you doing?" Claire stood in the doorway, confusion etched on her face. Her arms were crossed protectively over her chest, a habit she'd developed years ago.

"Nothing. Thought I saw something." He rose, brushing off his knees with trembling hands. "Just checking the street. Neighborhood watch mentioned some suspicious activity."

Later, he double-checked every lock, testing windows and doors with obsessive thoroughness. He jiggled each handle three times, a ritual that had never seemed necessary before today. In Emma's room, he froze at the sight of her curtains partially open. As he reached to close them, movement across the street caught his eye—a shadow shifting behind a parked car, there and gone in an instant.

In bed, every creak of the house made him flinch. The familiar settling sounds that he'd ignored for years now seemed coded messages from an unseen threat. His phone buzzed with a text from an unknown number: "Nice pajamas." The three syllables hammered into his consciousness.

Ethan bolted upright, rushing to the window. The street appeared empty, but somewhere in the darkness, he knew eyes were watching. The familiar sensation of observing others had inverted itself with terrifying symmetry. The watcher had become the watched.

* * *

Detective Marlowe's office smelled of coffee and stale cigarettes, though Ethan had never seen her smoke. She sat across from him, a manila folder open between them. Her sharp eyes never left his face as she slid a series of grainy photographs across the desk.

"Recognize this vehicle, Mr. Miller?"

Ethan's throat constricted as he stared at his own sedan, clearly visible in the security footage. The timestamp showed 9:47 PM, three nights before Erika's murder.

"That's... my car."

"Indeed." Marlowe tapped another photo. "And here it is again. And again. Five separate nights in the two weeks leading up to Ms. Jensen's death, parked within viewing distance of her apartment building."

Ethan's palms dampened with sweat. "I sometimes drive through that neighborhood on my way home from work."

"At nearly ten at night? Several times a week?" Marlowe's voice remained even, clinical. "Hmmph, That's very interesting."

She shuffled through more papers, pulling out a printed call log. "You told me in our first interview that you had minimal interaction with Erika Jensen. That your departments rarely crossed paths."

"That's correct."

"Then perhaps you can explain why Ms. Jensen called your direct extension at 3:42 PM the day before her murder." Marlowe pushed the call log toward him.

Ethan stared at the evidence, his mind racing for an explanation that wouldn't incriminate him.

Ethan's collar felt suddenly tight. "I... I don't recall receiving that call."

"The log does show that the call was not answered, but I'm just curious, any idea why Erika would call you? You work in separate departments," she asked, her head tilting slightly as she studied his reaction.

"I assure you detective, I have no idea why she called me." Ethan leaned forward, fighting to keep his voice steady. "We rarely spoke. Clearly I wasn't there to answer the call." He spread his hands in a gesture of helplessness. "I wish I had been. Maybe I'd have more answers for you if I was."

Marlowe's expression remained unchanged as she made a note in her file. Her silence stretched uncomfortably, a tactic Ethan recognized—she was waiting for him to fill the void with nervous chatter.

He swallowed hard. "I can also assure you, I did not kill Erika Jensen, if that's what you're thinking."

"Interesting that your mind went there, Mr. Miller." Marlowe closed the folder with deliberate slowness. "I haven't accused you of anything."

She stood and walked to the window, her back to him. "We found traces of Erika's blood in places inconsistent with the primary crime scene. Places that had been cleaned." She turned back to face him. "Someone took considerable effort to stage this as a robbery gone wrong."

Ethan's heart hammered against his ribs. "I wouldn't know anything about that."

"No?" Marlowe returned to her seat. "You see, what puzzles me is why a marketing analyst with no connection to the victim would be so interested in her apartment building. Why her death would affect you so visibly that your colleagues have commented on your behavior."

She leaned forward. "People are watching you, Mr. Miller. They're noticing things."

The words hit Ethan like a physical blow. The hunter becoming the hunted.

"Is there something you'd like to tell me? Something that might explain why you've been visiting Ms. Jensen's neighborhood? Why she might have tried to contact you before her death?"

Marlowe leaned forward, her voice dropping. "Mr. Miller, I find it concerning that you've been less than forthcoming about your relationship with the victim. These discrepancies suggest a pattern of deception that raises some serious questions."

Ethan's chair scraped against the floor as he stood abruptly. His heart pounded in his ears, fight-or-flight instinct fully engaged.

"Am I under arrest, Detective? If not, then I'd like to go."

Marlowe's expression didn't change, but something flickered in her eyes—amusement, perhaps, or satisfaction at having provoked a reaction. She leaned back in her chair, studying him with the practiced patience of a predator.

"No, you're not under arrest, Mr. Miller." Her voice remained level, almost conversational. "Honestly, I don't think you killed her. You're not the type."

She closed the folder containing the evidence against him and tapped her fingers on its surface.

"But I do know your type, Mr. Miller. I know it very well."

The statement hung in the air between them. Ethan felt naked, exposed in a way that made his voyeuristic experiences pale in comparison. Marlowe's gaze seemed to pierce through his carefully constructed facade, seeing the shadow-self he kept hidden from everyone—even Claire.

"You're free to go," she continued, standing to signal the end of their interview. "But as they say in the movies, don't leave town."

Ethan grabbed his jacket from the back of the chair, desperate to escape her scrutinizing gaze. His fingers trembled as he fumbled with the material.

"I have no plans to travel, Detective."

Marlowe nodded, her eyes never leaving his face. "We'll be in touch, Mr. Miller. I'm sure we'll have more to discuss."

* * *

Back home, Ethan pulled a chair to the center of the living room and climbed up, examining the ceiling light fixture with methodical precision.

"What exactly are you doing?" Claire stood in the doorway, arms crossed over her chest.

"Just checking the wiring." Ethan's fingers probed the edges of the fixture, searching for anything that didn't belong. "Thought I heard a buzzing earlier."

Claire watched as he dismantled the light cover, his movements growing increasingly frantic. "Since when do you care about electrical wiring?"

Ethan didn't answer. He moved to the bookshelf, pulling volumes out and checking behind them, running his fingers along the edge of each shelf.

"Ethan, you're scaring me." Claire's voice trembled slightly. "First the nightmares, now this. What's going on?"

He paused, a book dangling from his hand. The rational part of his brain recognized how this must look to her—manic, paranoid, unhinged. But the fear coursing through his veins overrode everything else.

"Nothing's going on." He replaced the book and moved to the entertainment center, checking behind the television. "Just being thorough."

Claire stepped closer. "This isn't about wiring, is it?"

Ethan's hands froze on the cable box. For a moment, he considered telling her everything—about his voyeurism, about witnessing Erika's murder, about Richard's threats. The weight of his secrets pressed down on him, making it hard to breathe.

Instead, he moved to the window, checking the frame, the curtain rod, running his fingers along the sill.

"Do you think someone's watching us?" Claire's question cut through the room like a knife.

Ethan turned to face her, seeing the genuine concern in her eyes. For years, he'd been the watcher, invading others' private moments. Now the tables had turned, and the sensation of being observed made his skin crawl.

"Just being cautious," he muttered, moving to the next window.

Claire followed him, placing a gentle hand on his arm. "Ethan, please. Talk to me."

He pulled away, dropping to his knees to check under the coffee table. "There's nothing to talk about."

"You've been different since..." She hesitated. "Since that woman at your office died."

* * *

Ethan paced outside the conference room, his tie suddenly too tight around his neck. Detective Marlowe's questions lingered in his mind like cigarette smoke—acrid and impossible to ignore. Her pointed inquiries about his car near Erika's apartment and that mysterious phone call had left him shaking.

"Rough interview?"

He flinched at Vanessa's voice. She stood a few feet away, leaning against the wall with a manila folder pressed against her chest. Despite only being at the company for weeks, she'd already adopted an air of quiet competence that made her presence impossible to ignore.

"Standard procedure." Ethan tugged at his collar. "They're talking to everyone."

Vanessa's eyes—sharp and assessing—tracked the movement of his hand. "Interesting that they brought you back for a second round, though."

His stomach clenched. "What do you mean?"

"Just an observation." She stepped closer, lowering her voice. "I've been reviewing Erika's marketing research files. Trying to get up to speed."

"And?"

"She had notes about you." Vanessa tilted her head slightly. "Apparently, she found your consumer behavior analyses fascinating. She referenced your work in several proposals."

Ethan's mouth went dry. "We never worked together."

"That's what makes it interesting." Vanessa smiled, but it didn't reach her eyes. "She seemed to know a lot about your methods for someone in a different department."

The hallway suddenly felt too narrow, the walls closing in. Richard watching him from one side, Marlowe investigating from the other, and now Vanessa with her unsettling observations.

"We should grab coffee sometime." She pulled a business card from her folder and held it out. "I'd love to pick your brain about your approach to consumer psychology."

Ethan took the card automatically, his fingers numb.

"I have a feeling we could help each other out." Vanessa's eyes held his for a beat too long. "There's a lot happening beneath the surface here, isn't there?"

Before he could respond, she glanced over his shoulder. "Looks like Mr. Langford needs you."

Ethan turned to see Richard beckoning from his office doorway, his replacement company pin gleaming on his lapel like a tiny, mocking eye.

"Don't forget about that coffee," Vanessa called as she walked away. "I think we have a lot to discuss."

CHAPTER TWENTY

Reversal of Fortune

The company-wide email arrived at 9:03 AM. Ethan read it twice, his coffee growing cold beside his keyboard.

"Following preliminary findings of the internal audit, financial irregularities have been identified in several offshore transactions. Pending a full investigation, Financial Director Richard Langford has been placed on administrative leave..."

The office erupted in hushed conversations. Ethan sat frozen, watching as two security guards appeared at Richard's office door. The CFO stood beside them, face grim as stone.

"They're escorting him out," someone whispered.

Richard emerged, jacket folded over his arm, expression unnervingly calm. His eyes swept the floor until they locked with Ethan's. A slight smile curved his lips before he turned away.

By noon, Richard's name had been removed from the company directory. His assistant was reassigned. The CFO announced an emergency leadership meeting for department heads, including Ethan.

"The audit uncovered a complex network of shell companies," the CFO explained, sliding documents across the conference table. "Transactions disguised as consulting fees to entities that don't exist. At least four million diverted through an off-shore account codenamed 'Decker.'"

Ethan recognized the transaction records—the same ones he'd glimpsed on Richard's computer. The same ones Erika had threatened him with.

"The police have been notified," the CFO continued. "We'll need everyone's cooperation."

Back at his desk, Ethan's phone buzzed with a text from an unknown number:

I know what you saw that night. And I know what you were doing every night before that. We should talk about your options. Soon.

His fingers went numb. The phone slipped, clattering against his keyboard. He snatched it back, glancing around to see if anyone had noticed his reaction.

The message glowed on his screen, each word a small explosion in his mind. Someone else knew. Someone who wasn't Richard.

Ethan's thumbs hovered over the keyboard. *Who is this?* he typed, then deleted it. Responding would confirm receipt. Confirm guilt.

Another text arrived: *Your window-watching hobby makes for interesting material. Especially when it escalates to murder.*

His heart hammered against his ribs. He fumbled with the phone settings, checking if the number was blocked or restricted. It wasn't—just a number he didn't recognize with a local area code.

A third message appeared: *Check your email. Personal account, not work.*

Sweat beaded on his forehead as he opened his personal email on his phone. A new message waited, sender listed only as "Observer." The subject line: "Night Vision."

The email contained a single attachment. His finger trembled as he tapped it.

The image loaded—a dark, grainy photo taken at night. A figure stood in shadow, looking up at an apartment window. Though the quality was poor, the silhouette was unmistakably his own, captured outside Erika's building.

His phone buzzed again.

Coffee tomorrow, 2PM. Riverside Café. Come alone or these go to Detective Marlowe.

Richard sat in his home office, phone pressed to his ear.

"It's accelerated. They found Decker." He twirled his wedding ring furiously. "Yes, the same problem as before. Someone who's seen too much."

He listened, eyes fixed on Ethan's company pin resting on his desk.

"No, not like last time. This one's smarter. More careful." Richard shifted in his seat and lowered his voice. "I need it handled permanently."

The voice on the other end asked a question.

"Of course Sophia will help with the aftermath. She always does." Richard's jaw tightened. "But first, I need our friend from the Hartford situation. The one who helped with that nosy accountant."

He scribbled a phone number on a notepad.

* * *

Ethan approached the Riverside Café and checked his watch. 1:45. He'd arrived early to scope the location, a habit born from years of surveillance. The café sat on a corner with large windows overlooking the river—too exposed for his comfort. He walked in and sat at a table in the back, positioning himself to see both entrances while keeping his back to the wall, mentally mapping escape routes as he settled in.

His hands wouldn't stop shaking. He ordered black coffee he didn't want, just to have something to do with them. Every person who entered sent a jolt of adrenaline through his system. A businessman with a briefcase. A young couple holding hands. Each silhouette in the doorway made his stomach clench with dread.

At precisely 2:00, she walked in. Average height, unremarkable clothes, but with observant eyes that scanned the room methodically before landing on him. Recognition flickered across her face. She approached his table with deliberate steps, moving with the confidence of someone who knew exactly who she was looking for.

"Ethan Miller." Not a question. Her voice was calm, matter-of-fact.

"Who are you?" He fought to keep his voice steady, fingers tightening around his coffee cup.

"Rebecca Sanders." She sat down without invitation. "I've been watching you watch others for weeks now. Interesting hobby you have."

His throat went dry. "I don't know what you're—"

"Save it." She placed her phone on the table, screen down. "I saw you the night Erika died. Standing in the bushes outside her window. I saw you run. The police might be interested in knowing you were there."

Ethan's pulse hammered in his ears. He glanced toward the exit, calculating the distance, wondering if he could make it before she could stop him.

"Don't," Rebecca said quietly. "Running now only confirms everything. Besides, I'm not your biggest problem right now."

"Are you working with the police?" His voice had dropped to a whisper.

"No. I'm a writer. True crime, specifically." She leaned forward. "I live in the building across from Erika's. Perfect view of her apartment—and anyone who might be lurking outside it. I've been documenting patterns for weeks."

Ethan's coffee cup trembled in his grip. "What do you want?"

"Information. I'm putting together a book about what happened to Erika." Her eyes narrowed. "But I'm also interested in justice. Richard killed her, didn't he? You witnessed it. That's why you've been so jumpy at work."

The directness of her question stunned him. "Why would you think—"

"Because I've been piecing it together. The company audit. His suspension. The way he looked at you at the memorial." She tapped her finger on the table. "I could be your ally, Ethan. You need one right now. We both know Richard is guilty as hell and he is dangerous."

"An ally who's blackmailing me?" He tried to inject indignation into his voice, but it came out as desperate.

"I prefer to call it mutually beneficial cooperation. You help me understand exactly what happened, I help keep your... nocturnal habits... private." She held his gaze. "And together, we make sure Richard pays for what he did to Erika. Before he realizes you were there that night."

Ethan's facade crumbled. His shoulders slumped forward as he leaned across the table, voice dropping to a desperate whisper.

"I think he already knows I was there that night."

Rebecca's expression shifted, her professional detachment giving way to genuine concern. "Why do you think that?"

"My pin. My company fucking pin." His words tumbled out in a frantic rush. "It's missing and I think he found it in the bushes outside her window. He gave me a new one while subtly letting me know mine was missing." Ethan's hands trembled violently, sloshing coffee onto the table. "He's been watching me, toying with me. My God, I'm going out of my mind."

His voice cracked on the last word. The weeks of terror, guilt, and isolation finally broke through. Tears welled in his eyes, then spilled over, tracking down his cheeks. He didn't bother wiping them away, past caring about appearances.

Rebecca glanced around the café, then slid her chair closer. Her voice softened, losing its clinical edge.

"It's going to be okay Ethan. I'm here to help you." She reached across the table,

placing her hand gently on his arm. The unexpected contact startled him, and he flinched before looking up to meet her eyes.

"I have evidence too," Rebecca said. "Photos from that night. I caught the silhouette of someone—you—fleeing the scene. I've been documenting Richard's comings and goings as well."

Ethan stared at her hand on his arm. The simple human contact felt alien after weeks of isolation. He couldn't remember the last time someone had touched him with genuine concern rather than obligation.

"Why would you help me?" His voice was barely audible. "You don't know me."

Rebecca withdrew her hand and considered him for a moment. "Because I've been watching this neighborhood for months. I've seen you on your... walks. I've seen Richard visiting

Erika. I've pieced together enough to know you're not the villain in this story, despite your questionable hobbies."

She opened her bag and pulled out a small notebook. "I'm a writer, Ethan. I observe people, just like you do. Different methods, same result." She flipped through pages of handwritten notes. "I know Richard killed her. I know you saw it happen. And I know he's dangerous."

Ethan wiped his face with a napkin. "If he found my pin, he knows I was there. He could frame me. Or worse."

"That's why we need each other." Rebecca leaned forward. "I need your testimony for my book, and you need protection. Together, we can build a case against Richard that even his judge wife can't make disappear."

Ethan looked down at his trembling hands. "What about the other things I've done? The watching?"

"One battle at a time." Rebecca's expression hardened. "First, we deal with a murderer. Then we can discuss your... issues."

CHAPTER TWENTY-ONE

The First Warning

The conversation with Rebecca left Ethan simultaneously relieved and terrified. Someone else knew his secret—not just his voyeurism, but his presence at Erika's murder. The knowledge should have crushed him with anxiety, yet sharing the burden had loosened the vice grip on his chest. For the first time in days, he could almost breathe normally.

He arrived home late, mentally rehearsing excuses for Claire. The house was quiet, unnervingly so. A note on the kitchen counter informed him that she'd taken Emma to her mother's for the weekend—something about giving him space to work through whatever was bothering him. The thoughtfulness of the gesture only intensified his guilt.

The emptiness of the house pressed against him like a physical weight. He grabbed a beer from the fridge and headed upstairs to shower, desperate to wash away the day's accumulated tension. The bathroom light flickered as he entered—the bulb needed changing. He'd add it to his list of neglected household tasks, growing longer by the day.

Steam filled the room as he undressed, tossing his clothes into the hamper. He paused, noticing his jacket pocket bulging slightly. Had he forgotten something? He reached in and pulled out a folded piece of paper he didn't recognize, the crispness of it unfamiliar against his fingertips.

His heart rate accelerated as he unfolded it, the paper crackling in the humid air. The message was typed in a plain font, clinical and impersonal:

"You were there. I know. Voyeurs like us understand each other."

The paper slipped from his fingers, landing on the tile floor with a soft pat. The shower continued to run, forgotten, water streaming down the glass door. Someone had slipped this into his pocket. When? How? His mind raced through the day—the tense meeting, the rushed lunch, coffee with Rebecca at that crowded café.

Richard? It had to be. But the wording... "Voyeurs like us." Richard wasn't a voyeur. He was a killer, an embezzler, but not a watcher. He was the type who demanded attention, not one who lurked in shadows.

Unless there was something else Ethan didn't know about the man who signed his paychecks.

He picked up the note again, examining it more carefully, turning it over in his trembling hands. No fingerprints would remain on the glossy paper. No handwriting to analyze. Just eleven words that shattered any hope that his secret remained contained between him and Rebecca.

Whoever had written this knew both about his presence at Erika's murder and his nightly habit of watching. They had gotten close enough to slip it into his pocket without him noticing, invading his personal space with surgical precision.

The thought of being watched, of being the observed rather than the observer, made him physically ill. His stomach clenched as the roles reversed—predator becoming prey.

The house creaked with ordinary night sounds, but each pop of settling wood sent electric jolts through Ethan's nervous system. He paced the living room, scanning the street through gaps in the blinds. Every passing car became a potential surveillance vehicle. Every shadow morphed into a watcher.

He double-checked the locks on the front door, then the back. Then the front again. The windows came next—he moved methodically through the house, testing each latch, drawing curtains tight. No gaps. No cracks. No way for anyone to see in.

The irony wasn't lost on him. The voyeur now terrified of being viewed.

Upstairs, he stood in the darkness of Emma's bedroom, peering through her unicorn curtains at the neighbor's house. Was that movement in their upstairs window? He squinted, heart hammering. Just the wind stirring a houseplant. Maybe.

In the master bedroom, he crawled beneath the window rather than walk past it, convinced someone might be tracking his silhouette. He flattened himself against the wall, edging toward the glass, then carefully lifted one slat of the blinds with his index finger.

The streetlight illuminated an empty sidewalk, but the shadows between houses seemed darker, deeper than usual. Perfect hiding spots for someone watching his windows.

"Get it together," he whispered, but immediately regretted making noise. What if someone had directional microphones pointed at the house? What if Richard had hired professionals to monitor him?

His phone buzzed on the nightstand. Claire checking in. He couldn't bring himself to answer—what if his voice betrayed his panic?

The bathroom offered no refuge. The small frosted window above the shower suddenly seemed like a vulnerability. He showered in darkness, unable to shake the sensation of eyes on his naked body.

Back in the bedroom, he pulled the desk chair to the window and sat in shadow, watching the street below. Two hours passed. His neck stiffened. His eyes burned. But he couldn't stop scanning for threats, couldn't silence the whispers of paranoia.

When headlights swept across the front of the house at 2 AM, he dropped to the floor, heart nearly bursting from his chest. Just a car turning around in the cul-de-sac.

* * *

Richard drummed his fingers against the polished mahogany of his home office desk, the rhythmic tapping a counterpoint to the thundering panic in his chest. The suspension letter from Horizon Financial lay open before him, corporate letterhead gleaming under his desk lamp. The words "pending investigation" and "financial irregularities" seemed to pulse on the page.

His phone lit up with another email from the audit team requesting additional documentation for vendor payments to Atlantic Consulting Group—one of his shell companies. They were getting closer. Each day brought new questions, new threads being pulled from his carefully constructed web of fraud.

"They're finding everything," Richard muttered, swirling amber liquid in a crystal tumbler. The whiskey burned his throat but did nothing to calm his nerves. "Three years of work, all those careful transfers through Decker, gone."

He glanced at the small wall safe hidden behind his diploma—inside lay Ethan's company pin, the only physical evidence connecting anyone else to Erika's murder. His insurance policy. His leverage.

The doorbell rang precisely at nine. Richard checked the security camera feed on his tablet before disabling the alarm system.

Jackson Mercer stood on the doorstep, ramrod straight in a black tactical jacket despite the warm evening. His close-cropped hair and vigilant eyes spoke of military discipline. No small talk, no pleasantries as Richard led him to the office and closed the door.

"The situation has accelerated," Richard said, handing Jackson a folder. "This is everything on Ethan Miller. Home address, work schedule, family details. I need eyes on him 24/7."

Jackson flipped through the documents, pausing on Ethan's employee photo. "What exactly am I looking for?"

"Patterns. Vulnerabilities. Points of access." Richard twisted his wedding ring—a tell he couldn't control. "I don't just need information. I need leverage."

"Leverage for what?"

Richard's jaw tightened. "He was there the night of the incident with Ms. Jensen. He saw everything."

Jackson's expression remained neutral, professional. "And what do you want done with him?"

"Nothing. Yet." Richard refilled his glass. "First, I need him scared. Paranoid. Off-balance. Let him know he's being watched. Leave... evidence of your presence. Nothing traceable."

Jackson nodded once. "And his family?"

"His wife and daughter could possibly be used for leverage, for motivation. I don't really care one way or the other about them. They might prove useful, or they might be collateral damage."

* * *

Jackson settled into the driver's seat of his nondescript gray sedan, parked with perfect sightlines to Ethan Miller's suburban home. The vehicle—clean, untraceable, and forgettable—blended seamlessly with the neighborhood's weekend traffic. He adjusted his baseball cap lower over his eyes and raised his camera with telephoto lens.

The front door opened. Jackson's finger pressed the shutter button in rapid succession as Ethan emerged, looking haggard and jumpy. Every few steps, Ethan glanced over his shoulder, his movements jerky and uncoordinated.

"Amateur," Jackson muttered, documenting Ethan's transparent paranoia. The man was practically announcing his guilt with every furtive glance.

Ethan got into his car and pulled away. Jackson waited thirty seconds before following at a careful distance. He maintained three cars between them at all times, a technique honed during private security contracts in places where being spotted meant death.

At the grocery store, Jackson abandoned his vehicle and continued surveillance on foot, camera concealed against his side. He captured Ethan examining produce with unseeing eyes, checking his phone obsessively, startling when a store clerk asked if he needed assistance.

Rebecca Sanders adjusted her position in her car seat, training her own camera lens on Ethan's house. She'd been monitoring the residence since dawn, documenting his nervous departure in her notebook.

"Subject exhibits classic hypervigilance," she murmured into her digital recorder. "Constant checking of surroundings, inability to maintain normal gait pattern."

Her apartment walls were now covered with timeline charts, character profiles, and surveillance photos. Her laptop displayed the growing manuscript—"Watched: The Erika Jensen Murder"—with a new chapter titled "The Watchers and The Watched."

Rebecca's phone buzzed with a text from her literary agent: "Any progress on the new pages?"

She smiled, typing back: "You won't believe what's developing. This story has layers."

When a gray sedan pulled away from the curb shortly after Ethan left, Rebecca's instincts flared. She captured several frames of the vehicle and its driver.

"New player entered surveillance field," she noted, zooming in on the driver's face. "Military bearing, professional technique."

Rebecca added a note to her chapter outline: "Surveillance hierarchy—the watcher becomes the watched."

Rebecca locked her apartment door behind her and dropped her camera bag onto the couch. The day's surveillance had yielded more than she'd anticipated—not just Ethan's nervous movements but the emergence of a professional tail. Her wall of evidence had grown into an intricate web of connections, photos, and timelines.

She settled at her desk, fingers hovering over the keyboard. The manuscript file opened with a satisfying click.

"WATCHED: The Erika Jensen Murder" stared back at her in bold type, followed by "FIRST DRAFT - SECTION ONE: THE VICTIM."

Rebecca scrolled through the completed chapters, making minor adjustments. The section began with Erika's discovery, the sanitized police report contrasted against Rebecca's own observations from her window. She'd crafted Erika not as the office seductress that gossip painted her to be, but as a strategic player in a male-dominated industry.

"She used what she had," Rebecca had written, "in a world that valued her body over her mind. But behind closed doors, she was meticulously documenting everything."

The chapters detailed Erika's calculated relationship with Richard, drawing from Rebecca's observations and subsequent research. She'd included a psychological profile that examined how Erika's childhood with her con artist father had shaped her approach to survival.

Rebecca added a final paragraph to the section:

"The night Erika Jensen died, three people occupied three different vantage points around her apartment. Inside, Richard Langford stood over her body, his hands still warm from the pressure against her throat. Outside, Ethan Miller watched from the shadows, a voyeur unexpectedly witness to murder rather than intimacy. And across the street, I documented it all, unaware that what I was capturing would become the framework for understanding not just a murder, but the intricate web of watching and being watched that defined all their lives—and increasingly, mine."

She saved the file and printed a complete copy of the first section. Seventy-three pages. The foundation was laid.

* * *

The upscale bistro bustled with lunch crowds when Ethan arrived five minutes late. Vanessa Carter sat at a corner table, her back to the wall, surveying the room with quiet intensity. She'd chosen the most private spot in the restaurant—a detail that heightened Ethan's unease.

"Sorry I'm late," Ethan mumbled, sliding into the seat across from her.

"Not at all. I ordered sparkling water for both of us." Vanessa's smile didn't reach her eyes. Though she resembled Erika physically, the similarities ended there. Where Erika had projected calculated warmth, Vanessa radiated cool assessment.

The waiter appeared, took their orders, and vanished. Ethan fidgeted with his napkin.

"I appreciate you agreeing to meet." Vanessa leaned forward slightly. "I've been trying to understand the office dynamics since I started. It's... complicated when you're replacing someone who died so tragically."

"We're all still processing it," Ethan replied, the rehearsed line sounding hollow even to his own ears.

"I've been reviewing some of Erika's client files. She had quite an approach to relationship management."

"She was good at what she did."

Vanessa tilted her head. "Interesting choice of words. What exactly was she good at, Ethan?"

The question hung between them. Ethan reached for his water glass to hide the tremor in his hand.

"Sales, obviously."

"Obviously." Vanessa nodded. "Though her methods seem unconventional. I noticed you two had several meetings scheduled that were canceled last minute."

Ethan's throat tightened. "We worked in different departments."

"Yet she called you the day before she died."

The room seemed to compress around him. "How would you know that?"

"It was in her calendar. 'Call E.M. re: documentation.' " Vanessa's expression remained neutral. "I assumed E.M. was you. What documentation was she referring to?"

"I don't—I never spoke to her."

"But you watched her, didn't you?"

Ethan knocked over his water glass. Ice cubes scattered across the table as he fumbled to right it.

"Professionally, I mean," Vanessa clarified, dabbing at the spill with her napkin. "You observed her sales techniques. That's what good analysts do, isn't it? Watch people?"

"Yeah, I guess so. I try to keep up on people's motivations. What makes a person buy one product over another." Ethan dabbed at the remaining water with his napkin, avoiding her gaze. His fingers trembled slightly as he meticulously arranged the soaked napkin into a neat square.

"Yeah, but I'm talking more than that, Ethan." Vanessa leaned closer, lowering her voice to just above a whisper. "Surely you saw how Erika closed many of her deals. I mean, I've only just started here and going through her files, it's pretty obvious that she used, oh hell I'll just say it. She used her body to close deals, Ethan. You know it and I know it." Her eyes never left his face, studying his reaction with an analyst's precision.

The waiter arrived with their food, the plates landing between them like a temporary reprieve. Ethan waited until he departed before responding, using the interruption to compose himself.

"That would not surprise me. There has been office gossip of that nature." He kept his voice deliberately neutral, professional distance his only shield.

"Thank you for being honest with me." Vanessa's expression softened, the hard edges of her inquiry melting away. "I'll be honest with you as well. I'm finding disturbing things in her files, Ethan."

His fork paused halfway to his mouth, a piece of chicken suspended in midair. "What kind of things?" The question came out more strained than he intended.

"I'm not quite sure yet, but my suspicions are that she had dirt on people...several people as a matter of fact." Vanessa pushed her salad around her plate, arranging the greens into a careful pattern. "With what's going on with Richard, it makes me wonder if he was one of them, and if he was, that's one hell of a motive for murder."

"That's quite an accusation, Vanessa." Ethan's heart hammered in his chest, each beat a thunderclap he was certain she could hear across the table.

"I'm not accusing anyone. I'm just speculating." She took a small bite of her food, chewing thoughtfully before continuing. "From what I've read in her files, I just thought you might be the right person to connect with. Erika seemed to think you had your finger on the pulse of this place. She seemed to really think quite a lot of you."

"I'm utterly shocked at that. She barely ever spoke to me." His collar felt suddenly tight, the restaurant too warm.

Vanessa placed her hand on Ethan's thigh, the touch light but deliberate. "Well from what I've read and what I've seen, you're quite a guy. I hope that we can get to know each other much better."

Ethan shifted nervously in his seat, acutely aware of her hand, the proximity, the echo of Erika in her features. "Yes, I think that would be nice." His mind confused, suspicious but thoroughly aroused.

CHAPTER TWENTY-TWO

Erika's Voice

Rebecca approached the building superintendent's office with practiced confidence, a sympathetic smile already in place. The nameplate on the door read "Frank Mendoza." She knocked twice, adjusting her posture to appear appropriately somber yet professional.

"Mr. Mendoza? I'm Rebecca Sanders, I live across the street." She extended her hand when he opened the door, maintaining just the right amount of eye contact. "I'm working on a memorial piece for Erika Jensen."

Frank's weathered face softened, crow's feet deepening around his eyes. "Terrible thing, what happened to her. Such a pretty young lady."

"Absolutely heartbreaking. I've been speaking with her colleagues, but I wanted to include something more personal, something that captures her essence." Rebecca pulled out a business card from her previous book, the one that had briefly put her on the literary map. "I'm a writer. This piece will help people remember her as more than just a victim—as the vibrant woman she was."

Frank studied the card, running his thumb over the embossed lettering. "What do you need from me exactly?"

"Just fifteen minutes in her apartment. The police have released the scene, and I'd like to get a sense of who she really was." Rebecca leaned in slightly, lowering her voice to a confidential tone. "Her family mentioned they'd appreciate a thoughtful tribute. Something dignified to counter all the sensationalism."

Frank hesitated, keys jingling in his hand. "I don't know... management has rules about these things..."

"I understand your concern." Rebecca pulled out two fifties, folding them discreetly between her fingers. "For your time and trouble. I promise I'll be quick and respectful—in and out with no disturbance."

Twenty minutes later, Rebecca stood in Erika's living room, breathing in the lingering scent of expensive perfume. Frank had agreed to give her thirty minutes, no more, waiting down the hall. She worked methodically, examining bookshelves, drawers, closets—anywhere Erika might have hidden something important, something that would give Rebecca insight into the woman's true nature.

In the bedroom, Rebecca noticed a loose baseboard behind the nightstand, slightly discolored compared to the others. Prying it open with her fingernail revealed a small cavity containing a flash drive labeled "Insurance" in neat, precise handwriting.

Rebecca pocketed it without hesitation and continued her search, making notes about Erika's expensive tastes—designer clothes still bearing tags, high-end cosmetics arranged with military precision—and the conspicuous absence of personal photos or mementos. When Frank knocked to signal her time was up, she thanked him warmly and left, slipping him another fifty as a final gesture of goodwill.

Back in her apartment, Rebecca kicked off her shoes and immediately plugged in the flash drive, her heart racing with anticipation. It contained a single folder labeled "Journal" with dozens of dated entries stretching back nearly two years. She opened the earliest one, settling into her desk chair with the focused intensity of a surgeon beginning a delicate operation.

Rebecca clicked through the journal entries, her heart racing. These weren't organized chronologically—they jumped between dates and topics, revealing glimpses of Erika's calculated life.

April 17 - Richard's latest "consulting" payment went to Decker Holdings. $175,000. Traced it to a Cayman account. He thinks I don't understand financial structures. What a fucking idiot.

March 3 - Drinks with the VP of Sales. Laughably easy to get him talking about Q1 projections. Men love feeling smart around a beautiful woman. Especially when their cock is in your mouth. Information is currency and I sucked him dry. Will leverage this during bonus discussions next month.

Rebecca scrolled to another entry, fingers trembling slightly with the thrill of discovery.

May 12 - Someone's been watching my apartment. Not Richard—he's too arrogant to be discreet. The quiet one from marketing—Ethan—likes to watch from the oak tree. Not as discreet as he thinks. Could be useful leverage someday. Noticed him three times this week, always after 10pm.

Rebecca's breath caught. This confirmed her suspicions about Ethan. She leaned closer to the screen, hungry for more.

February 9 - Dad called from prison. Wanted money again. Said no. He taught me everything about manipulating people, then got caught in his own con. I learned the most important lesson: never leave evidence. Always maintain plausible deniability. His mistake was getting sloppy when he thought he was untouchable.

A more recent entry appeared:

June 1 - Richard threatened me today. Laughable. Everything Is documented in the safe deposit box at First National, box #773. Key taped under bathroom sink at mom's old place on Sycamore. If anything happens to me, Richard goes down. He doesn't realize I've been ten steps ahead since the beginning. His embezzlement scheme is child's play compared to what dad taught me.

Must remember to pay property taxes on Mom's place due August 1st. Cannot lose that property—too valuable as a secure location.

Rebecca continued reading, surprised by an entry that revealed unexpected vulnerability:

March 28 - Dream about mom again. Wonder if she ever thinks about me. Twenty years since she left. Sometimes I hate how much I still care. Found myself looking at her old photos last night. Dad always said sentiment was weakness, but I can't seem to let her go completely.

May 22 - Richard's wife called his office while we were together. Watched him lie effortlessly. I recorded the entire conversation. Added it to the file. He twirled his wedding ring the entire time—his tell when he's nervous. The great Richard Langford, so predictable beneath his expensive suits.

April 30 - Someone's definitely watching. Ethan. I feel his eyes on me constantly, even at work. Started performing for him a little. Might as well give him a show while gathering leverage. I'm sure he wouldn't want his wife to find out about him watching me fuck my clients. Left the curtains open last night deliberately. His silhouette was visible against the streetlight. What a fucking amateur.

Rebecca leaned back, processing what she'd discovered. Erika had been several steps ahead of everyone—documenting Richard's crimes while noticing Ethan's voyeurism. And somewhere in an abandoned house on Sycamore Street was a key to evidence that could solve everything.

CHAPTER TWENTY-THREE

Home Invasion

Ethan returned home Saturday afternoon, exhausted from wandering the city to escape his thoughts. With Claire and Emma at her mother's until tomorrow, the empty house should have felt like a sanctuary. Instead, it felt like a trap, walls closing in with each passing second.

He locked the door behind him, tossed his keys onto the entryway table—and froze. The ceramic bowl where they kept spare change sat two inches left of its usual position. He'd developed a photographer's eye for spatial relationships; this wasn't a mistake. Someone had been here.

Heart hammering against his ribs, he moved through the living room with cautious steps. The cushions on the couch were perfectly aligned, but the throw blanket was folded with the tassels on the right side instead of the left. Claire always folded it the same way, a habit born from years of routine.

"Hello?" His voice echoed through the empty house, bouncing off walls that suddenly seemed foreign.

In the kitchen, a coffee mug stood in the dish rack he'd emptied before leaving. The refrigerator magnets had been rearranged—subtle, but unmistakable to someone who noticed details for a living. His fingers traced the edge of the counter, searching for more evidence.

Upstairs, the bedroom door stood slightly ajar. He always closed it completely. Inside, the dresser drawers were perfectly shut, but the handles weren't aligned horizontally as he kept them. Someone had opened them, searched through his things, then tried to return everything to its place—but not perfectly enough to fool his meticulous eye.

In the bathroom, his toiletries had been shifted slightly, toothbrush angled differently, razor moved an inch to the left. The medicine cabinet mirror reflected his pale face as a terrible realization washed over him, cold and sickening.

This was how they felt. Jenny, Erika, all the others—this violation of privacy, this feeling of being exposed, vulnerable. Of having someone touch your things, invade your space, observe without consent. The invisible boundary between public and private, shattered.

He sank onto the edge of the bathtub, hands trembling uncontrollably. For years, he'd justified his voyeurism as harmless—they never knew, so how could it hurt them? But someone had been in his home, touching his possessions, learning his habits, and the knowledge made his skin crawl with revulsion.

The intruder had been methodical, careful not to break anything or leave obvious signs. Just like him watching through windows. They wanted him to know they'd been here, watching, violating. A message, not a robbery. A deliberate psychological assault.

He'd done this to others for years. Now someone was doing it to him, and the symmetry of it was unbearable.

* * *

In the bedroom, Ethan found it. A cigarette butt left on his nightstand—Richard's brand, the distinctive gold band unmistakable. His stomach lurched. Richard was sending a clear message: I can get to you anytime.

His phone buzzed with a text:

"It's Rebecca. Need to talk. Have new information. Riverside Cafe 1 hour. Come alone."

He stared at the message, paranoia flaring. What "new information" could she possibly have? Was this a trap?

His thumb hovered over the buttons as he hesitated. Rebecca had seen him the night of the murder. She knew things—had been watching him just as he'd watched others. But unlike Richard, she hadn't threatened him. Yet.

He typed back: "See you there, 1 hour."

The walls of his sanctuary had been breached from all sides. Richard watching, Rebecca watching, perhaps others he didn't even know about. The hunter had become the hunted, observed from every angle.

He pulled the blinds shut throughout the house, checking locks twice, three times. Sleep would be impossible tonight. The irony wasn't lost on him—how many nights had he robbed others of their peace, their security, their privacy?

* * *

Vanessa Carter stayed late at the office again, her third night this week. The emptiness of the building provided perfect cover. With Richard suspended, his files were technically off-limits, but the temporary reassignment of his projects gave her just enough legitimate access to continue her digging.

She pulled up another spreadsheet of vendor payments, her trained eye immediately spotting the pattern. The shell company names varied, but the payment amounts followed a mathematical sequence—each transfer precisely 17.3% larger than the previous one.

"Amateur," she whispered, fingers flying across her keyboard as she documented the trail.

Before Horizon Financial, she'd spent three years specializing in fraud detection. The skills that had made her excellent at catching financial criminals were the same ones that made her dangerous to them.

Vanessa opened her personal encrypted drive and added the latest findings to her growing documentation. The transactions all eventually linked to an offshore account labeled "Decker"—Richard's poorly disguised embezzlement funnel. She'd already traced over two million dollars moving through it.

Her resemblance to Erika had been coincidental but useful. People projected their feelings about the dead woman onto her, revealing themselves in small ways. Richard couldn't look her in the eye. Ethan stared too long, as if seeing a ghost.

Vanessa closed the file and shut down her computer. She'd gathered enough evidence to approach the authorities, but something held her back. The office politics surrounding Erika's death suggested something more sinister than financial crimes.

She slipped her notebook back into her purse. Patience had always been her strength. The right moment to act would present itself.

* * *

The Riverside Cafe hummed with activity. Ethan arrived fifteen minutes early, choosing a corner table with his back to the wall. His eyes darted to each new customer, his fingers drumming an anxious rhythm on the ceramic mug.

Rebecca slid into the seat across from him, her movements deliberate and controlled. She placed her laptop bag on the empty chair beside her.

"You look terrible," she said.

"Someone was in my house today." Ethan's voice cracked. "They moved things, left cigarette butts. The same brand Richard smokes."

Rebecca nodded, unsurprised. "I know. I've been watching your place." She pulled out her camera and turned the display toward him. "This is the man who's been following you."

The screen showed a broad-shouldered figure in a dark jacket moving toward Ethan's front door. The next photo captured his face in profile—hard features, military-short hair.

"I don't recognize him," Ethan whispered.

"He's professional. Ex-military maybe." Rebecca put the camera away and leaned forward. "I found something in Erika's apartment. Her journal."

Ethan's eyes widened. "How did you—"

"That's not important. What matters is what she wrote about you." Rebecca pulled out her phone and showed him a photo of a journal page. "She knew you were watching her. Mentioned the oak tree specifically."

Ethan's face drained of color. "What else?"

"She documented everything about Richard's embezzlement scheme. Called it her 'insurance policy.' There's a reference to a safe deposit box where she kept evidence." Rebecca swiped to another entry. "*Everything Is documented in the safe deposit box at First National, box #773. Key taped under bathroom sink at mom's old place on Sycamore.*

"I want to be clear about something," Rebecca said, closing her phone case with a decisive snap. "I've got enough evidence to go to Detective Marlowe right now. Photos of you watching Erika's apartment, timestamps that place you at the scene during the murder, and now her journal entries mentioning you specifically."

Ethan's throat tightened. "So why haven't you?"

"Because I want something more valuable than just seeing you arrested." Rebecca's eyes locked with his. "I want exclusive rights to this story. Your full testimony about what you saw that night, everything you know about Richard's embezzlement, and your... unique perspective as a witness."

"You want to profit from Erika's murder?"

"I want to expose the truth. And yes, write a book that will resurrect my career." She shrugged, unapologetic. "You need me, Ethan. Richard hired that man to silence you. Without protection, you won't survive the week."

Ethan stared into his coffee. "What exactly are you proposing?"

"An alliance. My evidence combined with your testimony is enough to put Richard away. I'll help you find what Erika hid in that safe deposit box. In exchange, I get exclusive rights to your story—the voyeur who witnessed murder."

"And if I refuse?"

Rebecca gathered her things. "Then I'll go to Marlowe with what I have. You'll still go down, just not as a witness." She stood. "Think about it. I'll need your answer before morning."

The drive home stretched Ethan's nerves to breaking. Every red light became an opportunity for someone to pull alongside him. Each car maintaining the same distance behind felt like surveillance.

He checked his rearview mirror for the twelfth time. The blue sedan three cars back had been there since the cafe. Or was it a different blue car? He couldn't tell anymore.

At a four-way stop, Ethan caught a pedestrian staring directly at him. The man's gaze lingered too long before he continued crossing.

Passing shop windows, Ethan felt eyes following from within. A woman on her phone seemed to track his movement as he drove past. Was she reporting his location to someone?

Even the traffic cameras at intersections seemed to swivel toward his car. The sensation of being watched—so familiar when he was the observer—now crawled across his skin like insects.

The irony wasn't lost on him. The watcher was now the watched, jumping at shadows, seeing threats in every glance.

CHAPTER TWENTY-FOUR

The Power Shifts

E than's alarm vibrated silently at 4:30 AM Sunday. He hadn't slept more than twenty minutes at a stretch, jerking awake at every house creak and passing car. The empty bed beside him—Claire and Emma still at her mother's—felt like both blessing and curse.

He dressed in layers: dark jeans, black thermal shirt, and a navy windbreaker. The telephoto lens and camera body went into a nondescript messenger bag along with binoculars, water bottle, and protein bars. His movements were mechanical, practiced from years of predawn preparations for his voyeuristic excursions.

Richard's Tudor-style home sat on a half-acre lot in Oakwood Heights, the neighborhood where judges, surgeons, and executives clustered behind manicured hedges. Ethan parked three blocks away, walking the rest with his head down, just another early morning jogger stretching his legs.

The public park across from Richard's house offered perfect cover—a dense cluster of rhododendrons with sight lines to both the front entrance and backyard patio. Ethan settled into position while the sky remained charcoal gray, his breath fogging in the morning chill.

5:47 AM: Lights came on in what Ethan assumed was the master bedroom.

6:15 AM: Richard emerged in a bathrobe to retrieve the Sunday paper. Ethan's camera clicked rapidly, capturing the financial director's haggard appearance—unshaven face, hair uncombed, dark circles beneath bloodshot eyes.

6:30 AM: Richard appeared on his back patio with coffee and the business section. Ethan zoomed in on the man's hands—they trembled slightly when turning pages. The wedding ring twirled constantly between thumb and forefinger.

7:12 AM: Richard's phone rang. He answered immediately, standing to pace the flagstone patio. His gestures grew increasingly agitated—jabbing the air, running fingers through his hair, checking his watch repeatedly. Ethan captured it all, frame by frame.

The conversation lasted nine minutes. When it ended, Richard slammed his fist against the patio table, sending the newspaper fluttering and coffee spilling across stone. He stared at the mess for a long moment before retrieving his phone again, dialing with deliberate precision.

This call was shorter. Richard nodded several times, spoke briefly, then ended the call. His posture changed—shoulders squaring, chin lifting. He gathered the scattered newspaper and returned inside.

* * *

Ethan arrived home an hour before Claire and Emma were due back. He swept the kitchen floor, emptied the dishwasher, and changed the sheets on all beds. His movements were purposeful, almost frantic—a man desperate for normalcy. He wiped down countertops that were already clean, straightened picture frames that didn't need adjusting, and checked his phone repeatedly for the time.

The spaghetti sauce simmered on the stove—Emma's favorite—filling the house with garlic and basil. He'd stopped at the farmer's market for fresh ingredients, choosing plump tomatoes and fragrant herbs with unusual care. He'd spent nearly five minutes selecting the perfect bunch of basil, inhaling its scent as if seeking some kind of absolution in its freshness.

Headlights swept across the living room wall. Ethan wiped his hands and headed outside, reaching the car just as Claire turned off the engine. The cool evening air felt clarifying against his skin, a brief respite from the steam of his anxious preparations indoors.

"Daddy!" Emma scrambled from her booster seat, launching herself into his arms with the unrestrained joy only an eight-year-old could muster.

He caught her, burying his face in her hair. "Hey, monkey. Missed you." The familiar weight of her small body against his chest anchored him momentarily to something real and uncomplicated.

"We got Grandma a new bird feeder and the cardinals came right away! They were so red, like flying fire!" Emma's words tumbled out in excited bursts.

"That's amazing." He squeezed her tighter than usual, eyes closed for a moment too long, breathing in the scent of her strawberry shampoo and the faint trace of her grandmother's cinnamon cookies.

Claire watched from beside the car, her expression guarded, one hand absently touching the pendant at her throat. "You're in a good mood."

"Just glad to have my girls back." He set Emma down and moved to the trunk, hefting out their overnight bags with exaggerated ease. "Made spaghetti. Thought we could eat together before bedtime. Table's already set."

Claire's eyebrows lifted slightly. "That sounds nice." Her eyes searched his face, looking for clues to this sudden domesticity.

At dinner, Ethan listened to Emma's weekend adventures, asking questions and laughing at her dramatic retelling of a squirrel stealing bird seed. His hand occasionally brushed Claire's when passing bread, lingering a second longer than necessary. He refilled her wine glass without being asked, remembered details about her mother's garden that Claire had mentioned weeks ago.

Claire passed Emma a napkin, studying Ethan when his attention was on their daughter. The tension lines around his eyes had softened. His smile reached his eyes when Emma spoke. But something flickered beneath the surface—a watchfulness, a deliberate quality to his attentiveness. Twice she caught him glancing toward the windows, his focus momentarily elsewhere before snapping back to their family tableau.

After tucking Emma in, Ethan joined Claire on the couch with two mugs of tea, the chamomile aroma rising between them like a peace offering. "How was your mom?" he asked, settling into the cushions with calculated casualness.

"Good. Asked about you." Claire accepted the mug, her fingers wrapping around its warmth. "She wants us to visit for Thanksgiving. Said she misses having us all there."

"I'd like that." He sat closer than he had in weeks, the fabric of his sleeve just brushing against her arm.

Claire sipped her tea, observing how his gaze periodically drifted to the windows, checking reflections, shadows. When he turned back to her, his expression shifted—vulnerability replacing vigilance, as though remembering to play a part. His shoulders would relax, then tense again, a rhythm she was beginning to recognize.

But the gentle touch on her hand felt genuine, as did the soft kiss he placed on her temple before standing to take their empty mugs to the kitchen. For a moment, she allowed herself to lean into his touch, wondering if this version of her husband—attentive, present, tender—was real or merely another reflection, distorted by whatever secret lay behind his watchful eyes.

* * *

Monday morning brought the familiar fluorescent hum of Horizon Financial's open office plan. Ethan buried himself in spreadsheets, grateful for the distraction of quarterly projections and market analysis. The weekend's domestic performance had drained him—maintaining the façade of normalcy required a vigilance that left him exhausted.

"Excuse me, Ethan? Got a minute?"

He looked up to find Vanessa standing beside his desk, a folder tucked against her chest. Her blonde hair was pulled back in a sleek ponytail, emphasizing the clean lines of her face. Unlike Erika's deliberately provocative attire, Vanessa's charcoal pencil skirt and cream blouse were understated, yet somehow more magnetic for their restraint.

"Sure. What's up?" He straightened, closing the document he'd been staring at for twenty minutes without absorbing a single number.

"I'm preparing for the Westridge presentation Thursday." She settled into the chair beside his desk. "Marketing projections need to align with financial forecasts, and I'm seeing some inconsistencies."

As she leaned forward, a subtle scent drifted toward him—not Erika's overwhelming floral perfume that announced her presence before she entered a room, but something more

complex. Sandalwood and amber with hints of vanilla. Sophisticated rather than seductive, yet equally intoxicating.

"Let me see." He swiveled his monitor so they could both
view it.

Vanessa moved her chair closer, her shoulder nearly touching
his as she placed the folder between them. "Here's what I've
prepared. But when I cross-reference with last quarter's actual
s..." She opened a spreadsheet on his screen, her fingers moving
efficiently across the keyboard.

Her proximity was disarming. Where Erika had wielded her
sexuality like a weapon, Vanessa's effect was more subtle—a
quiet intensity that commanded attention without demanding
it.

"The variance is in these segments." She leaned closer, her
arm brushing his as she pointed to specific cells. Then, with
deliberate pressure, her hand rested on his forearm while she
traced figures with her other hand. "Do you see the pattern?"

The contact sent an unexpected current through him. Her
fingers were cool against his skin, the pressure light but unmistakably intentional.

Ethan looked up from the spreadsheet to find her eyes already
on his face, studying his reaction with the same analytical precision she'd applied to the numbers. Something passed between
them—recognition, attraction, possibility—hanging in the air
like static before a storm.

Vanessa held his gaze for three heartbeats before withdrawing her hand and leaning back with a professional smile that didn't quite reach her eyes.

"I'll need your input on reconciling these figures before Thursday," she said, her voice resuming its business-like tone.

* * *

"I'm seeing patterns that concern me," Claire said, her fingers twisting in her lap as she sat across from Dr. Chen. The therapist's office felt smaller today, the walls pressing in with each revelation.

Dr. Chen adjusted her glasses. "What kind of patterns, Claire?"

"The nights he's gone. The distance. I thought it was me—my inability to..." Claire's voice trailed off. "But last week, I checked his laptop history."

"And what did you find?"

Claire's eyes fixed on the potted fern in the corner, its leaves perfectly still in the climate-controlled air. "Searches about Erika Jensen's murder, doctor. So many searches. It's like an obsession." Her voice cracked. "News articles, police updates, forum discussions about theories. Pages and pages."

Dr. Chen made a note on her pad. "Have you confronted Ethan about this?"

"How could I?" Claire's laugh held no humor. "Admit I violated his privacy? Besides, I'm afraid of what he'll say." She swallowed hard. "There are so many searches."

"What are you thinking Claire?"

"I don't know what to think. I can only conclude he was sleeping with her. Did he kill her?" The words hung in the air, solid and terrible. Claire's hands trembled. "The timing of his 'walks' matches when she was killed. The restaurant receipt near her apartment. His nightmares where he calls her name."

Dr. Chen leaned forward. "Claire, these are serious concerns. But correlation isn't causation."

"I've spent three years here trying to fix myself. Trying to be whole again for him." Claire's eyes filled with tears. "What if the problem was never me? What if I've been trying to heal myself for a man who's been unfaithful all along? Or worse did I drive him to infidelity? Can I blame him for seeking intimacy?"

"Have you considered other explanations?"

"Like what? That my husband is obsessed with a murdered woman he worked with? How is that better?" Claire wiped her eyes. "Either way, I don't know who I'm married to anymore."

* * *

Judge Sophia Langford entered the police station with the measured steps of someone accustomed to being watched. Her charcoal Armani suit—crisp and severe—projected authority even as her eyes darted nervously around the bustling precinct. Officers glanced up, recognizing her instantly. Sophia had sentenced many of the criminals they'd arrested.

Detective Marlowe emerged from her office. "Judge Langford. Thank you for coming."

Sophia's hand tightened around her leather handbag. "Is there somewhere private we can speak?"

Marlowe led her to an interview room with institutional green walls and a table scarred by years of nervous fingers. The fluorescent lights cast harsh shadows across Sophia's carefully composed face.

"You mentioned on the phone you had something to show me?" Marlowe kept her voice neutral, professional.

Sophia placed her handbag on the table, opened the clasp with manicured fingers that trembled slightly. She withdrew a small evidence bag—store-bought, not police-issue—containing a company lapel pin.

"I found this in Richard's safe." Her voice remained steady, betraying nothing of the turmoil that had led to this moment. "He doesn't know I have the combination."

Marlowe studied the pin through the plastic. The company logo gleamed under the harsh lighting.

"This isn't Richard's department." Sophia smoothed an invisible wrinkle from her sleeve. "I checked. It belongs to marketing. You can see the name on the back."

Marlowe reached for the bag. Sophia's fingers lingered, reluctant to release it.

"You understand what you're doing, Judge Langford?"

Sophia finally let go of the bag. "I understand exactly what I'm doing, Detective." Her perfectly lined lips pressed together. "Twenty-three years of marriage, and I've looked the other way more times than I care to admit. But murder..." She shook her head. "I won't be an accessory to murder."

"Even if it means your husband goes to prison?"

"Even if it means I go with him." Sophia's eyes hardened. "I helped him once before, when he assaulted that business partner. Used my influence. Called in favors." Her voice dropped. "I've spent my career upholding the law while compromising it for him. No more."

Marlowe slid the evidence bag into her pocket. "We'll need a formal statement."

"Of course." Sophia straightened her already-straight jacket. "I've prepared what I need to say."

* * *

Rebecca hunched over her laptop, fingers flying across the keyboard. The manuscript was taking shape—not just a murder story, but an exposé of corporate power dynamics with Richard Langford as its centerpiece. The clock read 2:17 AM. She hadn't moved in hours.

She scrolled through her latest chapter draft:

Richard Langford wielded power like a scalpel—precise, cutting, and ultimately destructive. During the quarterly review meeting, he systematically dismantled the marketing team's proposal not through logical argument but through calculated intimidation. "Interesting approach, Melissa," he'd said to the team lead, his voice dripping with condescension. "Perhaps if you'd consulted with someone who understands our market position..." He left the sentence hanging, the unspoken criticism more devastating than any direct attack.

The pattern repeated across departments. In finance, he created artificial competition between team members by "accidentally" sharing salary information. In operations, he pitted project managers against each other for limited resources. The result: departments that should have collaborated instead fought for scraps of his approval.

Rebecca paused, reviewing her notes from interviews with Horizon Financial employees. She added:

His most insidious tactic was the strategic assignment of credit. When junior analyst Daniel Chase developed the cost-cutting protocol that saved the company millions, Richard presented it to the board as a collaborative effort "developed under my guidance." Yet when the implementation hit early snags, Richard made sure everyone knew it was "Chase's model" that had failed. Chase resigned three months later.

For women in the company, Richard's manipulation took on additional dimensions. He promoted attractive women just enough to keep them engaged but never to positions that threatened his authority. Erika Jensen was the exception—her ambition matched his own, and she'd gathered enough leverage to force his hand.

Rebecca reached for her coffee, grimacing at the cold bitterness. Her notes contained dozens more examples—Richard creating impossible deadlines then "generously" stepping in to help, Richard withholding critical information until the last moment to appear indispensable, Richard's strategic use of praise in public and criticism in private.

The pattern was clear. Richard Langford didn't just commit financial crimes—he created a culture of fear and dependency that allowed those crimes to flourish unchecked.

CHAPTER TWENTY-FIVE

Collateral Damage

Morning light filtered through the kitchen blinds, casting golden stripes across the breakfast table. Claire poured milk over Emma's cereal while Ethan hunched over his coffee, dark circles shadowing his eyes.

"Did you sleep at all?" Claire asked, her voice low enough that Emma wouldn't hear.

Ethan shrugged. "Enough."

Emma spooned Cheerios into her mouth, milk dribbling down her chin. The television murmured in the background—morning news Claire kept at minimal volume during breakfast.

"Mommy, what's a stalker?" Emma asked, her eight-year-old pronunciation making the word sound almost innocent.

Claire's hand froze mid-air. "Where did you hear that word, sweetie?"

Emma pointed toward the television. "The lady on TV said police are looking for a stalker who hurt someone."

Ethan's head snapped up. The news anchor's voice suddenly seemed deafening: "...continued investigation into Erika Jensen's murder. Police are exploring connections to reported stalking incidents in the weeks before her death..."

"Turn that off," Ethan barked.

Claire reached for the remote, but Emma wasn't finished.

"Was she the lady from your work? The one in the picture at the remembering party?" Emma's eyes widened. "Did a bad man hurt her like in the scary movies I'm not supposed to watch?"

"I said turn it OFF!" Ethan slammed his palm against the table. Coffee sloshed over the rim of his mug, spreading across the tablecloth.

Emma flinched, her spoon clattering into her bowl. Her lower lip trembled.

"Ethan!" Claire stood abruptly. "That's enough."

"Daddy's mad at me," Emma whispered, tears welling.

"I'm not—" Ethan began, but Emma had already slid from her chair, fleeing toward her bedroom. The door slammed shut behind her.

Claire turned to Ethan, fury etched across her face. "What is wrong with you? She asked a question—a perfectly innocent question—and you exploded at her."

"She shouldn't be listening to that stuff."

"She's eight, Ethan. She hears things. What she shouldn't be experiencing is her father screaming at her over breakfast."

"I didn't scream—"

"You terrified her!" Claire's voice rose. "And this isn't the first time. You've been a powder keg for weeks. Emma's walking on eggshells around you. We both are."

* * *

Ethan's phone buzzed on his desk. Vanessa Carter's name appeared on the screen with a message: "Need your expertise on Westfield account. Conference Room B, 2pm, just us."

He glanced across the office where Vanessa sat reviewing documents, her long hair falling forward as she made notes. Despite her physical resemblance to Erika, everything else about her was different—methodical, reserved, intellectually focused. Yet there was something unsettling about her interest in him, a persistent attention he couldn't quite decode.

At 2:05, Ethan pushed open the door to Conference Room B. Vanessa stood at the far end of the table, arranging folders in neat stacks, her movements precise and economical.

"Sorry I'm late," he said, hovering at the threshold.

"Perfect timing." Vanessa moved to the windows and pulled the blinds shut with a deliberate motion. "For privacy. These numbers are sensitive."

The room dimmed, creating an intimate atmosphere that made Ethan's pulse quicken. He took a seat as Vanessa spread documents across the table, aligning them with meticulous care.

"I've been reviewing Erika's client files." Vanessa slid into the chair beside him—not across the table, but right next to him, close enough that he could feel the warmth radiating from her body. "There's something off about the Westfield account."

She leaned toward the documents, her shoulder pressing against his. The contact sent an electric current through him, triggering his hyperawareness. Her perfume was subtle, nothing like Erika's bold scent—more like clean paper and something faintly floral.

"Look at these invoices." Her voice dropped to an intimate whisper that seemed to travel directly to his ear. "The consulting fees increased quarterly with no additional services rendered."

Ethan tried to focus on the numbers, but Vanessa's proximity made concentration impossible. His voyeuristic tendencies had never prepared him for being the object of such focused attention. She flipped to another page, leaning even closer, her breath warm against his cheek.

"The same pattern appears in transactions to Meridian Solutions and Decker Holdings."

Ethan froze. Decker—Richard's offshore account. The name that had appeared in Erika's journal multiple times.

"How did you find these?" he asked, his mouth suddenly dry, heart hammering against his ribs.

"I have experience with financial fraud detection." Her eyes met his, intelligent and unflinching. "My previous company specialized in it."

She reached across him for another document, her hand brushing his thigh under the table. The touch lingered longer than necessary. Her fingers pressed slightly into his leg as she retrieved the paper, a gesture too deliberate to be accidental.

"These patterns are distinctive," she continued, her voice husky. "Someone was siphoning money through shell companies. The trail is sophisticated but unmistakable."

Ethan's phone vibrated in his pocket. He shifted away from Vanessa to check it, grateful for the momentary reprieve from her intensity.

A text from Rebecca: "TARGET FOLLOWING YOU. BLACK SUV. BE CAREFUL."

* * *

Ethan's drive home felt like moving through quicksand. Every traffic light stretched into minutes, each car behind him a potential threat. The black SUV Rebecca mentioned had disappeared three turns back, but the weight of being watched pressed down on his shoulders.

He pulled into his driveway at dusk, killing the engine and sitting in silence. The house looked normal—lights on in the kitchen where Claire was likely preparing dinner, Emma's bike propped against the garage door. The ordinariness of it all made what came next even more jarring.

As he approached the front porch, his steps slowed. Five cigarette butts lay on the steps, arranged in a perfect pentagon. Not scattered as if someone had carelessly smoked while waiting, but positioned with mathematical precision—equidistant from each other, filter ends pointing inward to form a star pattern.

The brand matched the ones he'd found inside his house—Richard's preferred luxury import. Marlboro would have been coincidence. These were Dunhill International, impossible to dismiss.

Ethan crouched, studying the arrangement without touching it. The butts weren't fresh; they'd been placed deliberately after being smoked elsewhere. No ash residue surrounded them. This wasn't someone smoking on his steps—this was a message.

The intimacy of the intrusion hit him like a physical blow. Someone had stood here while Claire and Emma were inside, taking their time to create this macabre artwork. The voyeur was now the viewed, the watcher now the watched.

His phone buzzed with another text from Rebecca: "Did you make it home safe?"

Before he could respond, the front door swung open. Claire stood in the doorway, silhouetted against the warm light from inside.

"Ethan? What are you doing?"

He rose quickly, positioning himself to block her view of the cigarettes butts. "Just checking something. Thought I dropped my keys."

Her eyes narrowed slightly, not believing him but too tired to press. "Dinner's almost ready. Emma's been asking for you."

"I'll be right in."

CHAPTER TWENTY-SIX

Shared Shadows

Ethan stayed late Tuesday evening, the office emptying around him as he combed through marketing reports. The distraction of work felt safer than home, where Claire's suspicion hung thick in the air and cigarette butts appeared with unsettling regularity.

The marketing floor fell silent except for the hum of the air conditioning. He gathered his belongings, his footsteps echoing as he made his way to the elevator. The parking garage beneath the building was nearly empty, most spaces vacant under the sickly yellow lighting that flickered intermittently.

Ethan fumbled for his keys, the sound of his own breathing suddenly loud in his ears. A car engine started somewhere in the distance, then fell silent. The sensation of being watched prickled along his spine.

"Working late again, Miller?"

Richard's voice came from behind a concrete pillar. He stepped into view, his expensive shoes clicking against the concrete. Despite his suspension, he wore a tailored suit, the only sign of his unraveling the loosened tie at his throat.

Ethan froze, keys dangling from his fingers. "What are you doing here? You're suspended."

"Forgot some personal items." Richard's smile never reached his eyes. He moved closer, backing Ethan against his car. "Funny thing about personal items. They turn up in the strangest places."

The garage lighting cast harsh shadows across Richard's face, deepening the hollows of his eyes.

"Like that old oak tree across from Erika's apartment," Richard continued, his voice dropping to a near whisper. "The one with the split trunk about twenty feet up. Perfect little nook there, isn't it? Good sightline to her bedroom window, especially when she left the curtains open just enough."

Ethan's mouth went dry. That exact spot—his preferred vantage point—described with intimate precision.

"The branches are just thick enough to support a man's weight," Richard continued. "Though they creak if you shift position too quickly. Must have been uncomfortable standing there night after night."

Richard leaned closer, close enough that Ethan could smell the whiskey on his breath. "Tell me, what did you see from that tree the night Erika died?"

Ethan's back pressed against the cold metal of his car door. His mind raced through possible escapes, but Richard's larger frame blocked his path.

"I don't know what you're talking about," Ethan managed, his voice barely audible.

Richard's laugh was hollow. "Every Monday, Wednesday, Friday. Always wearing that navy jacket." He reached out and flicked the lapel of Ethan's coat. "This one, actually. The one with the missing pin."

Ethan's stomach dropped. The precision of Richard's knowledge was paralyzing.

"Always gone by 11:15," Richard continued, checking his watch with theatrical emphasis. "Just enough time to get home before Claire starts wondering where you are. Though lately she's been wondering anyway, hasn't she?"

The fluorescent lights buzzed overhead, casting Richard's face in sickly yellow. His eyes never left Ethan's.

"The first couple weeks, you'd park three blocks away. Then you got bolder—started parking just around the corner from Erika's building." Richard's fingers drummed against the roof of Ethan's car. "Always the same routine. You'd circle the block once, checking for witnesses. Then you'd slip between those two hedges and take up your position."

Ethan's throat constricted. Every detail was correct—the exact pattern he'd followed for months.

"You weren't the only one watching, Ethan." Richard's voice dropped to a whisper. "I've been watching you watch her."

The garage seemed to shrink around them, the air growing thinner with each passing second.

"So," Richard's wedding ring glinted as he twirled it anxiously, "let's talk about what happens next. Because we both have secrets worth keeping, don't we?"

Ethan's heart hammered against his ribs. His entire body tensed, fight-or-flight instincts screaming while his feet remained frozen to the concrete.

Richard's expression shifted, a strange intimacy replacing the threat. He stepped back slightly, creating breathing room between them.

"We're not so different, you and I." Richard's voice softened, almost conspiratorial. "We both appreciate... observation. The power of seeing without being seen."

The words landed like a blow. Ethan stared, unable to formulate a response.

"You think I didn't notice how you catalog everything?" Richard continued. "The way you watch people in meetings, noting their tells, their weaknesses?" He chuckled. "I've had my eye on you for quite a while Ethan."

Richard leaned against the adjacent car, his posture relaxing as if they were having a casual conversation between colleagues.

"There's something... intoxicating about it, isn't there? Knowing things others don't know you know." Richard's eyes gleamed in the harsh garage lighting. "Seeing them when they think they're alone, when all the masks come off."

The familiarity with which Richard described Ethan's addiction sent chills down his spine. This wasn't just manipulation—Richard understood the compulsion.

"I used to follow my wife's lovers," Richard admitted, his voice dropping lower. "Before Erika. I'd watch them meet Sophia in hotel rooms, restaurants with private booths. Never confronted her—that wasn't the point. The point was knowing."

Ethan swallowed hard, recognizing the twisted reflection of his own compulsion.

"The difference between us," Richard said, straightening his tie, "is that I've learned to channel it. To use what I see." He smiled thinly. "You've been wasting your talent, Ethan."

"I have to go," Ethan said abruptly, fumbling behind him for the door handle.

Richard's expression hardened. "We're not finished."

"My wife is expecting me." The lie tumbled out as Ethan yanked the door open, creating a barrier between them.

Richard's hand shot out, gripping the door frame. "This conversation isn't over, Miller."

Ethan slammed the door shut, jamming the key into the ignition with trembling fingers. The engine roared to life, and he reversed so quickly the tires squealed against the concrete. In his rearview mirror, Richard stood motionless, watching him flee.

Ethan circled up the garage ramp, heart thundering against his ribs. His breath came in short, desperate gasps. He had to get out, had to put distance between himself and Richard.

As he rounded the final turn toward the exit, headlights from an approaching car momentarily blinded him. He swerved, narrowly avoiding a collision, and skidded to a stop.

Vanessa Carter stood frozen in the headlight beams, clutching a stack of files to her chest, her eyes wide with surprise.

Ethan lowered his window, struggling to control his breathing. "Jesus, I'm sorry. I didn't see you."

She approached cautiously. "Are you okay? You look like you've seen a ghost."

The garage suddenly felt too exposed. Richard could appear at any moment. Ethan glanced nervously toward the lower levels.

"Working late?" he asked, voice still unsteady.

"Just finishing some quarterly projections." Vanessa tilted her head, studying him with that unnervingly perceptive gaze. "You're shaking."

"I'm fine," Ethan insisted, though his white-knuckled grip on the steering wheel betrayed him. "Just... in a hurry to get home."

Vanessa glanced toward the lower levels of the garage, then back to Ethan. "Did something happen down there?"

The question hung between them. Ethan considered telling her about Richard, about the threat, but the words died in his throat.

"Nothing," he managed. "Nothing happened."

Vanessa's eyes narrowed as she studied his face. "You're in no shape to drive." She gestured to his trembling hands. "Your adrenaline's through the roof."

"I'm fine," Ethan insisted, though his voice betrayed him.

"You nearly hit me just now," she pointed out. "Let me drive you home."

Ethan hesitated, glancing again toward the lower levels of the garage. The thought of Richard potentially watching made his skin crawl.

"My car—"

"Will be perfectly safe here overnight," Vanessa finished. "The security cameras cover every angle." She stepped closer, lowering her voice. "Something happened with Richard, didn't it?"

The accuracy of her guess startled him. Ethan's silence was answer enough.

"Come on," she said, her tone softening. "My car's just over there. We can talk where it's safer."

The word "safer" decided it. Ethan killed the engine and stepped out, locking his car with shaking hands. Vanessa led him to her modest sedan, unlocking it with a chirp.

Once inside, Ethan exhaled deeply, the tension in his shoulders easing slightly as they pulled out of the garage.

"He was waiting for me," Ethan admitted as they merged onto the main road. "He knows... things. About me."

Vanessa nodded, keeping her eyes on the road. "I've been reviewing some files since taking over his projects. Richard has dirt on half the executive team."

She made a sudden turn, deviating from the route to Ethan's house.

"This isn't the way to my place," he said, tensing again.

"I know." Vanessa checked her mirrors. "I think we should stop at my apartment first. I have some files there that might help protect you from Richard."

"Files?"

"Financial records, emails." Her hands tightened on the steering wheel. "Things that suggest he was embezzling much more than anyone realizes. And that Erika knew."

* * *

Vanessa's apartment caught Ethan off guard. Located in an upscale high-rise downtown, it opened into a space of calculated minimalism—white walls, hardwood floors, and sparse furniture that looked both expensive and uncomfortable.

"Nice place," he managed, taking in the pristine environment.

"It serves its purpose," Vanessa replied, setting her keys in a small ceramic dish by the door—the only decorative item on an otherwise empty entryway table.

What the apartment lacked in warmth, it made up for in intellectual presence. Floor-to-ceiling bookshelves dominated one wall, filled not with novels but with oversized art books—monographs on Rothko, Koons, and artists Ethan didn't recognize. Several featured Japanese characters alongside English titles.

"Make yourself comfortable," she said, gesturing to a sleek gray sofa. "I'll get the files."

As she disappeared into another room, Ethan wandered toward a series of framed photographs arranged in a perfect grid on the wall. Each showed Vanessa in different locations around the world—standing before the Eiffel Tower, hiking on what appeared to be the Great Wall of China, silhouetted against a sunset in what might have been Morocco. In each, she wore the same expression—not quite smiling, but intensely present, as if cataloging every detail of her surroundings.

Unlike the chaotic warmth of his own home filled with Emma's toys and Claire's collection of throw pillows, Vanessa's space felt curated, deliberate. Nothing was accidental. Nothing was out of place.

"You travel a lot," Ethan observed when she returned carrying a sleek laptop and a manila folder.

"I did. Before settling here." She set the items on a glass coffee table. "My previous job involved financial fraud investigations for an international firm. I spent three years traveling to different branches."

The revelation shifted something in Ethan's understanding of her. This wasn't just a marketing associate who'd replaced Erika. This was someone with specific expertise in exactly what Richard had been doing.

Vanessa perched on the edge of the kitchen counter, crossing one leg over the other, her posture relaxed despite the tension that crackled in the air between them. Ethan stood before her, his hands braced against the polished stone on either side of her hips, trapping her in the cage of his arms.

"You seem on edge," Vanessa said, her voice low and soothing, a stark contrast to the heat that smoldered in her eyes. "Let me help you unwind."

Before he could respond, she reached out and began to unbutton his shirt, her fingers deft and sure. Ethan's breath caught in his throat as her nails grazed his skin, the sensation sending jolts of electricity straight to his core.

The pretense of comfort quickly transformed into something much more intense. With a sudden urgency, Vanessa pulled him closer, her mouth finding his in a kiss that was all teeth and tongues. It was wild, untamed, a stark departure from the carefully controlled environment of her apartment.

Ethan's hands moved of their own accord, exploring the curves of her body, slipping beneath the hem of her skirt. He found her already wet, her panties a mere whisper of fabric against his fingers. With a growl, he tore them away, letting the scrap of lace fall to the floor as he dropped to his knees before her.

Vanessa's head fell back, a moan escaping her lips as Ethan buried his face between her thighs. He lapped at her relentlessly, his tongue tracing circles around her clit before delving inside her, savoring the taste of her arousal.

The questions came between gasps and moans, her voice barely above a whisper, yet each word cut through the fog of lust enveloping them. "You wanted to do this to Erika, didn't you? Did she know?"

Ethan's body tensed, but he didn't stop. He couldn't. The need to possess Vanessa, to claim her in a way he never could with Claire or Erika, was overwhelming.

With a final, shuddering cry, Vanessa came apart, her fingers tangling in his hair as she ground herself against his mouth. But there was no respite for Ethan. As soon as she caught her breath, she pushed him back against the counter, her hands fumbling with his belt.

She freed his erection, her fingers cool against his heated flesh. Ethan groaned as she stroked him, her grip firm and unyielding. And then she was on her knees before him, her lips parted, her eyes locked on his as she took him into her mouth.

The visual of Vanessa, so put-together and in control, now on her knees in a moment of vulnerability and raw need, was nearly his undoing. Ethan's hips jerked forward instinctively, driving himself deeper into her eager mouth.

Vanessa's questions continued, between each deep stoke, each one driving the stakes higher, blurring the lines between intimacy and interrogation. "Did she tease you? Did she ever let you have a taste of her? Are you imagining her sucking your cock right now?"

Ethan's control snapped. With a guttural roar, he pulled away from her, spun her around, and bent her over the kitchen counter. He entered her in one hard thrust, her gasp of surprise music to his ears.

Vanessa gasped at the sudden intrusion. "Fuck me Ethan, fuck me."

He pounded into her mercilessly, each stroke a savage affirmation of his need for her, for this, for the chance to forget—if only for a moment—the guilt and fear that had been his constant companions since Erika's murder.

And when he finally reached his climax, Vanessa was there to swallow his release, her moans of pleasure mingling with his own as they both tumbled over the edge into sweet oblivion.

As their breathing slowed and the tremors of their shared climax subsided, Ethan braced himself against the counter, his forehead resting on the cool glass of the coffee table. Vanessa stood, adjusted her skirt, and returned to the kitchen counter with a grace that belied the intensity of what had just transpired.

She opened the manila folder and began to lay out financial documents with a precision that felt almost surgical. "Erika's client files were a mess," she said, her voice steady, as if they hadn't just been entwined in a frenzy of passion and secrets. "But I've started to find patterns, anomalies in the vendor payments. It's almost like she was trying to tell someone what Richard was doing."

Ethan watched her, his mind racing. Vanessa's abrupt shift from lover to investigator was disorienting. He pulled his shirt back on, his fingers fumbling with the buttons. "You've been looking into Erika's files?"

"Of course," Vanessa said, glancing up at him with an expression that suggested the answer should have been obvious. "It's part of my job. And after what you've told me, I think it's more important than ever to understand what happened."

She pointed to a series of numbers on a printout. "See here? These are payments to a shell company called 'Decker.' Richard was using it to siphon funds out of Horizon Financial."

Ethan moved closer, his eyes scanning the documents. The lines of text and numbers blurred together, but Vanessa's finger traced a clear path through the financial labyrinth.

"I think Erika knew," Vanessa continued. "She was documenting everything. Maybe she planned to expose him, or perhaps she was gathering leverage to secure her own position. Either way, it's clear she was playing a dangerous game."

Ethan's heart pounded in his chest. Vanessa's discoveries were a double-edged sword. They could help him clear his name, but they also implicated him deeper in the sordid affair. "What are you going to do with this information?" he asked, his voice barely above a whisper.

"I haven't decided yet," Vanessa replied, her gaze fixed on the papers before her. "But I assure you, I will use it. Richard has to be stopped, and the truth about Erika's death needs to come out."

She looked up at him then, her eyes piercing. "You want to be a part of this, don't you, Ethan? To make things right."

Ethan felt the weight of her words settle on his shoulders. The opportunity to right his wrongs was within reach. All he had to do was grasp it. But could he trust Vanessa? Could he trust anyone in this web of deceit and betrayal?

For now, he had no other choice. He needed her, needed her skills and her insight, if he was going to survive the fallout from Erika's murder.

"Yes," he said finally, the decision solidifying within him. "I'm in. Let's bring Richard down."

* * *

Ethan slipped his key into the lock, his mind still reeling from his encounter with Vanessa. The house was dark except for a single lamp in the living room casting long shadows across the hardwood floor. He closed the door quietly behind him, hanging his keys on the hook.

"You're home late." Claire's voice floated from the darkness.

Ethan's heart slammed against his ribs. He hadn't seen her sitting in the armchair, still as a statue, hands folded in her lap.

"Jesus, Claire. You scared me." He flipped on another light, blinking as his eyes adjusted.

Claire didn't move. Her face remained impassive, but her eyes—those eyes that once looked at him with such tenderness—were hard as flint. On the coffee table between them sat their wedding photo, removed from its usual place on the mantel. The glass caught the lamplight, reflecting it back in fractured beams.

"I called your office at six. Janine said you'd left hours ago." Claire's voice was unnervingly calm. "I texted. Called. Nothing."

Ethan's throat constricted. The scent of Vanessa's perfume seemed to cling to him like a second skin. He ran a hand through his hair, buying time.

"I was following up on some leads about Richard. Lost track of time." The lie came easily, practiced.

Claire picked up the wedding photo, studying it. "Remember this day? How you promised there would never be secrets between us?" She set it down with deliberate care. "What happened to that man, Ethan?"

The question hung in the air between them, weighted with years of unspoken truths. Ethan stood frozen, unable to cross the invisible line that separated them.

* * *

The morning air held a chill as Rebecca settled into the driver's seat of her sedan, parked strategically across from the downtown parking garage. She'd been there since 6:30 AM, thermos of coffee in the cupholder, camera bag open on the passenger seat. Her research had paid off—Richard's schedule was predictable, at least on Tuesdays.

She adjusted her position, stretching her stiff neck. The telephoto lens felt heavy in her hands, but she kept it trained on the garage exit. Her notebook lay open beside her, filled with times, dates, and observations in her tight, economical handwriting.

Movement caught her eye. Richard's car emerged from the garage, pulling into a secluded corner of the lot. Rebecca lifted the camera to her eye, focusing the lens with practiced precision.

"Come on, give me something good," she murmured, finger hovering over the shutter button.

Richard stepped out, checking his surroundings with quick, nervous glances. He didn't notice her vehicle among the dozens parked along the street. A moment later, a nondescript gray sedan pulled up beside him. Jackson emerged, military posture unmistakable even from this distance.

Rebecca's heart rate quickened. She steadied her breathing as she'd learned to do during stakeouts, keeping the camera stable. The shutter clicked rapidly as she captured the sequence: Richard reaching into his jacket, extracting a manila envelope, Jackson's hand extending to take it.

The envelope passed between them. Click. Richard's mouth moving, giving instructions. Click. Jackson nodding, tucking the envelope inside his coat. Click. The two men separating without a handshake. Click.

"Gotcha," Rebecca whispered, reviewing the images on her camera's display. Crystal clear—Richard's face in profile, the envelope clearly visible, the exchange undeniable. She quickly switched to her longest lens, capturing Jackson's license plate as he drove away.

She lowered the camera, heart pounding with the thrill of evidence gathered. This wasn't just material for her book any-more. This was proof—concrete, undeniable proof connecting Richard to the intimidation campaign against Ethan.

Rebecca slipped the camera into its bag and started her car. The weight of what she'd witnessed settled over her. These photos changed everything.

CHAPTER TWENTY-SEVEN

Closing In

Ethan's focus on the quarterly marketing report shattered when he glanced up to see Detective Marlowe standing in his office doorway. Her sharp eyes surveyed his workspace, lingering on the family photo beside his monitor.

"Mr. Miller. Got a minute?" Her tone made it clear this wasn't a request.

Ethan's mouth went dry. "Of course, Detective." He gestured to the chair across from his desk, noticing his hand trembled slightly.

Marlowe sat, placing a manila folder on his desk. She didn't open it immediately, instead studying his face with clinical detachment.

"Your car is quite distinctive, Mr. Miller. That custom blue Honda Accord with the dent in the rear bumper."

Ethan's stomach clenched. "Is it?"

"Indeed. We've been reviewing security footage from the area surrounding Ms. Jensen's apartment." She opened the folder, sliding across three grainy but unmistakable photos. "Your vehicle appears on traffic cameras near her building on seven different evenings last month. Including the night of her murder."

The room seemed to tilt. Ethan stared at the photos, each showing his car at different intersections within blocks of Erika's apartment.

"We've been through this before detective. As I told you before, I drive through that area sometimes," he managed.

"Seven times in one month? Always after dark?" Marlowe's voice remained level. "Ms. Jensen filed a stalking report two weeks before her death. Described someone watching her apartment from outside. Couldn't identify them."

Ethan's collar felt too tight. "That's unfortunate, but it has nothing to do with me."

"Our theory is shifting, Mr. Miller." Marlowe leaned forward. "Perhaps you weren't having an affair with Ms. Jensen. Perhaps you were watching her. A peeping tom she eventually confronted. Things escalated. Accidents happen."

"That's absurd." Ethan's voice cracked.

"Is it? We have your car repeatedly in the area. We have her stalking report. We have your evasive answers." Her eyes narrowed. "People who watch others often think they're invisible. They're not."

Ethan's palms were slick with sweat. "You can't prove that because it simply didn't happen."

Marlowe's eyes never left Ethan's, filling the room with tension before finally breaking her long silence. "I can't prove anything yet, Mr. Miller, but I'll be honest with you, it's not looking good for you."

Ethan visibly shaken, his voice cracking. "Detective, you can't prove something that never happened."

"Maybe not, Mr. Miller, but I think you know more than you're sharing." Marlowe leaned forward, her voice dropping to just above a whisper. "I think you're a peeper and you saw something and now you're scared. Tell me what you know, Ethan. We can protect you."

The accusation hit like a physical blow. She knew. Not everything, but enough. The walls seemed to close in around him as sweat beaded along his hairline. His carefully constructed façade was crumbling under her penetrating gaze.

Ethan swallowed hard, gripping the edge of his desk. "Are we done, detective?"

Marlowe studied him for a long moment, noting his white knuckles, the pulse throbbing at his temple. She gathered the photos, sliding them back into the folder with deliberate slowness.

"Okay, we're done... for now. But do yourself a favor, think about what I've said."

She stood, straightening her jacket. Her expression remained impassive, professional, but her eyes promised return visits. More questions. More evidence.

Marlowe walked out of the office, her footsteps fading down the hallway, leaving Ethan sweating and more on edge than ever before.

* * *

Ethan stumbled into the emergency stairwell, the heavy metal door slamming behind him with a hollow clang. His legs gave out as he slid down the concrete wall, gasping for air that wouldn't come. The fluorescent lights overhead pulsed and swam in his vision.

She knows. She knows what I am.

His tie felt like a noose. He clawed at it, fingers fumbling with the knot until it came loose. Still not enough air. The stairwell spun around him, gray walls closing in. His heartbeat thundered in his ears, drowning out everything else.

I'm going to prison. For voyeurism. For a murder I didn't commit.

Dark spots danced at the edges of his vision. Ethan's hands trembled violently as he tried to brace himself against the cold floor. His breaths came in shallow, rapid bursts that only intensified the lightheadedness.

Claire and Emma. The images of their faces swirled together, accusing, disappointed, afraid.

The stairwell door opened with a metallic creak. Ethan couldn't even lift his head to see who had found him in this pathetic state.

"Ethan?"

Vanessa's voice. Great. The new hire seeing him fall apart.

Cool fingers touched his wrist, checking his pulse. "You're having a panic attack. Try to focus on my voice."

Something cold pressed against his hand. "Water. Small sips."

Ethan forced his eyes to focus. Vanessa knelt beside him, her expression concerned but not pitying. He took the water bottle with shaking hands, managed a small sip.

"I saw Detective Marlowe leaving your office," Vanessa said quietly. "Then you rushed out looking like you'd seen a ghost."

Ethan's breathing began to slow, the tunnel vision gradually receding. "I'm fine."

"No, you're not." Her voice was matter-of-fact.

In the stark isolation of the stairwell, the air was thick with tension and the scent of stale cigarette butts from the floor above. Ethan's panic began to ebb, replaced by a different kind of turmoil as he became acutely aware of Vanessa's presence. She was close, too close, yet he found himself unable—unwilling—to pull away.

Vanessa's hand moved from his wrist, her fingers lightly brushing the side of his face before tangling in his hair. The gesture was tender, almost maternal, yet it sent a jolt of electricity through him, igniting dormant fires.

Their eyes locked, and something unspoken passed between them—a desperate acknowledgment of their shared secrets and the precariousness of their situation. In that moment, they were two lost souls seeking refuge in the shadowed corners of their fractured world.

Ethan's hand found its way to Vanessa's waist, pulling her closer as their lips met in a frenzy of passion and fear. It was reckless, wrong, yet it felt like the only right thing in a world turned upside down.

Their bodies moved against each other with a frantic urgency, the cold concrete wall at her back contrasting with the heat radiating between them. Clothes were a nuisance, pushed aside just enough to allow the barest contact of skin on skin. Vanessa's leg hitched around his hip, granting him deeper access as they moved in a rhythm as old as time.

Ethan's mind was a whirlwind of sensation, his control slipping as he lost himself in the act. And then he saw it—the subtle tilt of Vanessa's head, a calculated move that mirrored Erika's practiced allure with her clients. It was a fleeting moment, but it pierced through the haze of desire, a stark reminder of the manipulation and games that seemed to permeate every aspect of his life.

His breath caught in his throat, a gasp that could have been pleasure or pain, as his phone vibrated insistently in his pocket. He ignored it, trying to hold onto the fleeting escape he had found in Vanessa's arms.

But the phone wouldn't be silenced. With a growl of frustration, Ethan pulled away to retrieve it. The display flashed Claire's name, and a sense of dread filled him as he answered.

"Emma's school called, she's sick," Claire's voice was tense, laced with concern. "I'm on my way to get her now."

The world came crashing down around him. The raw reality of his family's needs struck him like a physical blow, amplifying the guilt that gnawed at his conscience. The intimate moment with Vanessa, already tainted by echoes of Erika, now seemed sordid and wrong.

Ethan's eyes met Vanessa's, the gravity of the interruption etched on both their faces. "I have to go," he said, his voice barely above a whisper.

Vanessa nodded, straightening her clothes with swift, efficient movements. There was no recrimination in her eyes, only a shared understanding of the complexities they both faced.

As Ethan descended the stairs, the echo of his footsteps seemed to mock him, a stark reminder of the dangerous path he had veered onto. He had sought solace in the arms of another woman, only to find himself more lost than ever before.

The cool air of the parking garage hit him like a slap in the face as he made his way to his car. The taste of Vanessa's lipstick was still on his lips, a bitter reminder of the betrayal that now stained his soul.

He had no right to seek comfort when his actions had only added to the chaos of his life. Claire and Emma needed him, and he had failed them once again.

Ethan's hands gripped the steering wheel tightly as he pulled out of the parking lot. His thoughts were a tumultuous sea, crashing against the walls of his carefully constructed facade.

In the rearview mirror, the office building faded into the distance, but the consequences of his actions were now etched indelibly into the fabric of his existence. The road ahead was shrouded in shadows, and the journey back to his family was fraught with the weight of his betrayal.

* * *

Rebecca sealed the large manila envelope with deliberate pressure from her palm, making sure the adhesive caught every millimeter of the flap. Inside lay a carefully curated selection of evidence—photos of Richard meeting with Jackson, time-stamps meticulously noted in her precise handwriting, and a timeline connecting Richard's financial irregularities with Erika's death.

She'd spent the night organizing it all, cross-referencing dates against her notes and the fragments of Erika's journal. The work felt familiar—the same methodical process she'd used for her previous books—but this time the stakes were real, immediate. Not some cold case she was reconstructing, but a murder whose aftershocks still rippled through the present.

Rebecca checked the address one final time. No return information, nothing to connect the package to her. Detective Marlowe would receive it tomorrow morning.

Her fingers lingered on the envelope. Once she dropped this in the mail, there was no taking it back. The information would move beyond her control, becoming part of Marlowe's investigation rather than material for her book.

"Evidence first, book later," she whispered to herself, echoing the mantra she'd repeated throughout the night as her professional ambition warred with her conscience.

She glanced at her laptop, where her manuscript sat open—eighteen chapters now, with detailed character studies of Ethan, Richard, and Erika. The narrative was taking shape, becoming something powerful, something that could resurrect her stalled career.

But some truths couldn't wait for publication schedules and editorial reviews.

Rebecca stood, tucking the envelope into her messenger bag. Through her window, she could see Erika's apartment across the way, its darkness a constant reminder of what had happened there. Her gaze drifted down to the spot where she'd first seen Ethan watching.

She'd been a silent observer long enough. The weight of the envelope in her bag felt like a step toward something resembling justice—or at least accountability.

Detective Zoe Marlowe spread the photographs across her desk, methodically arranging them in chronological order. The manila envelope had arrived that morning—no return address, no note, just a series of high-resolution images showing a man with military bearing meeting with Richard Langford. The timestamp metadata remained intact, establishing a clear timeline of their interactions.

"Jackson Mercer," she murmured, comparing the surveillance photos to the DMV record she'd pulled. Former military, then private security. The kind of man you hired when you needed something handled quietly.

Marlowe didn't waste time wondering about her anonymous source. The evidence was what mattered, not who provided it. She assembled a small surveillance team within the hour.

"Three teams, rotating shifts. I want eyes on Mercer around the clock," she instructed her junior detective. "Document every interaction, especially with Langford."

They established their first position by 2PM, a nondescript sedan parked with clear sightlines to Mercer's apartment building. Marlowe took the first shift herself, camera with telephoto lens resting on her lap.

At 4:17PM, Mercer emerged, moving with practiced awareness of his surroundings. Marlowe captured a series of shots as he met Richard in a coffee shop two blocks from the financial district. The men spoke for exactly eleven minutes. No physical items exchanged hands, but Richard's agitation was evident in his body language—leaning forward, fingers drumming on the table, wedding ring twirling.

At 11:43PM, the night team documented their second meeting—a brief encounter in the parking garage beneath an office building. This time, an envelope changed hands. The photographer captured the transaction with perfect clarity.

The final meeting occurred at 7:22AM the following morning. Richard jogged along his regular route through the park,

Mercer falling into step beside him for precisely three minutes before peeling off in another direction.

Marlowe reviewed the surveillance logs, noting the pattern. Three meetings in less than 24 hours suggested urgency. Whatever Richard had hired Mercer to do was accelerating.

"Get me phone records for both of them," she told her team. "And put a tail on Langford too. Whatever they're planning, I want to be three steps ahead."

Chapter Twenty-Eight

Watching the Watcher

The evening shadows stretched across the sidewalk as Ethan left his house, hands jammed into his jacket pockets. His first walk in weeks felt different—the familiar rush of anticipation replaced by a churning anxiety that settled like lead in his stomach.

He chose a route he'd never taken before, cutting through an unfamiliar neighborhood where the houses stood further apart. Every few steps, he glanced over his shoulder, scanning for followers.

A car slowed behind him. Ethan ducked between two parked vehicles, heart hammering against his ribs. The car passed without stopping, but the momentary panic left him shaking.

He continued walking, this time angling toward a commercial street where shop windows provided reflective surfaces. He pretended to examine a display of electronics, eyes focused on the glass to check the sidewalk behind him. A woman with a stroller. A teenager on a skateboard.

At the next intersection, Ethan abruptly crossed the street, then doubled back in the opposite direction. The defensive maneuver felt foreign—a prey's tactic, not a predator's.

"You're being paranoid," he whispered to himself, but couldn't shake the certainty of being watched.

He passed a bank with mirrored exterior panels and slowed his pace, studying the reflections. A shadow moved—someone matching his pace half a block behind. Ethan's pulse spiked. He turned suddenly into an alley, pressed himself against the brick wall, and waited.

No one followed. False alarm.

The realization brought no relief. He'd spent years moving through these neighborhoods with predatory confidence, invisible by choice, controlling what others saw. Now he jumped at shadows, constantly looking over his shoulder, hyper aware of every passing car and pedestrian.

When a couple emerged from a restaurant ahead, Ethan instinctively stepped back into a doorway. The woman laughed at something her companion said, the sound carrying in the quiet street. Ethan watched them walk away, remembering how he once derived pleasure from these stolen glimpses into others' lives.

Tonight, he felt only vulnerability, the unsettling awareness that someone else controlled the narrative now. Someone watched him watching others, transforming his secret dominance into exposed weakness.

Ethan's erratic path eventually led him to a section of town where the homes stood dark and silent, the residents either asleep or out for the night. His breath came in short, ragged bursts, fogging the crisp air. The adrenaline surge from his paranoia had given way to a numbing exhaustion, and the familiar itch beneath his skin demanded satisfaction.

He found himself in front of a narrow townhouse with a single illuminated window. The curtains fluttered gently in the breeze, revealing glimpses of movement inside. Ethan hesitated, his instinct for self-preservation warring with the voyeuristic compulsion that had dictated his actions for years.

The desire to watch won out. He slipped into the shadows of a nearby tree, its leaves providing sparse cover. The risk of exposure heightened his senses, each pulse of blood through his veins a drumbeat echoing his escalating heart rate.

Inside, the room was bathed in soft light, casting a warm glow on the two figures entwined on the bed. They were young, college-aged perhaps, their bodies lean and unmarked by time. One had her back to the window, her dark hair spilling over the pillow. The other was a tangle of limbs and curves, her fair skin almost luminous against the tangled sheets.

Ethan watched, transfixed, as the fair-haired girl trailed kisses down her partner's neck, her hand disappearing beneath the covers. The dark-haired girl arched her back, a soft moan escaping her lips as her lover's skilled fingers found their mark.

The heat of arousal surged through Ethan, obliterating his fear. His hand moved to the bulge in his pants, stroking himself through the fabric. The friction sent waves of pleasure coursing through him, a temporary balm for the chaos in his mind.

He freed himself from his clothing, his erection springing forth, hard and aching. Ethan's grip tightened around his shaft, his movements synchronized with the rhythmic undulations of the girls on the bed.

The fair-haired girl straddled her partner now, her hips rocking back and forth as she rode the dark-haired girl's fingers with abandon. Their breaths came faster, punctuated by gasps and sighs that Ethan imagined he could hear even from his hiding place.

He matched their pace, stroking himself with increasing urgency. His focus narrowed to the erotic tableau before him, the outside world fading into insignificance.

As the girls reached their climax, their cries of ecstasy mingling in the night air, Ethan found his own release. His body shuddered, a low groan caught in his throat as he spilled himself onto the ground.

Spent, he leaned against the tree trunk, his heartbeat gradually slowing to match the quiet cadence of the night. The window remained a square of light in the darkness, a silent testament to the stolen moment that had just passed.

Ethan tensed as a new sound reached his ears—the metallic click of a gate latch nearby. He quickly tucked himself away, every nerve on high alert. A figure emerged from the shadows, moving with purpose toward the townhouse.

It was a man, his features obscured by the dim lighting. He glanced around before slipping a key into the front door and disappearing inside.

The sudden intrusion of a third party sent a jolt of adrenaline through Ethan. He didn't wait to see what would happen next. With one last look at the window, he turned and fled into the night, leaving the echoes of passion and the threat of discovery behind.

* * *

Ethan's return home was a journey through a looking glass, from the shadowed realm of his compulsions to the sanctuary of his presented life. The house stood silent, the only illumination coming from the soft glow of candles flickering in the master bedroom.

Claire had transformed their room into a tableau from their early days together, when passion was as simple as a breath drawn in unison. Van Morrison's "Moondance" played softly in the background, the melodic strains weaving a tapestry of nostalgia that filled the air with a palpable longing.

She had chosen their song, a subtle invocation of the tenderness and desire that once flowed effortlessly between them. The bed was turned down, revealing satin sheets that whispered promises of warmth and reconnection.

Claire emerged from the bathroom, her form bathed in the candlelight, casting soft shadows across her skin. She wore a silk robe, the fabric draping lovingly over her curves, a sensual armor designed to shield and reveal in equal measure.

Her eyes met Ethan's, a silent entreaty passing between them. She approached him, the scent of jasmine trailing in her wake, a fragrant reminder of their honeymoon. Her hands reached for his, her touch a gentle plea, an invitation to step back into the dance they had once known by heart.

With deliberate grace, Claire led Ethan to their bed, the tension in her frame betraying the importance of this moment. She reached for the hem of his shirt, her fingers brushing against the bare skin of his abdomen, the contact a spark that should have ignited a fire.

Ethan's breath hitched, the ghost of arousal stirring within him. He willed his body to respond, to meet the unspoken need in Claire's eyes. But the echoes of his earlier release lingered, a spectral barrier between desire and physical capability.

Claire's hands moved with practiced ease, exploring the contours of his chest, her nails lightly raking over his nipples, sending jolts of sensation through him. She kissed him, her lips soft and searching, coaxing his mouth open, her tongue teasing his into a slow, sultry waltz.

Ethan's mind reeled, torn between the twin pulls of guilt and pleasure. He yearned to lose himself in Claire's tender ministrations, to bridge the chasm that had opened between them. His heart pounded in his chest, a drumbeat of yearning that his body failed to answer.

Claire's hand slipped lower, her fingers deftly unfastening his belt, tugging at the zipper of his trousers with a quiet determination that spoke volumes of her desire to reclaim what had been lost.

She freed him from his constraints, her palm cupping his flaccid member, her thumb stroking the sensitive underside in a rhythmic caress designed to stoke the embers of his arousal.

Ethan closed his eyes, concentrating on the feel of Claire's touch, the warmth of her breath against his skin, the soft whimper of need that escaped her lips as she sought to will his flesh to harden.

Minutes stretched into an eternity, each second a testament to Ethan's inability to bridge the gap between mind and body. His cock lay quiescent in Claire's hand, a silent confession of his betrayal.

Claire withdrew, the hurt evident in the tightening of her jaw, the slight tremble of her lips. She retreated to the edge of the bed, her gaze fixed on the flickering candlelight that danced across the walls, a silent witness to their shared pain.

Ethan reached for her, a whispered apology hanging in the air between them. But Claire was already pulling away, the delicate thread of connection severed by his failure to respond. The silence that enveloped the room was a shroud, smothering the embers of their attempted reunion.

The night that had promised a return to intimacy had instead delivered a stark reminder of the distance that lay between them—a chasm that Ethan feared they might never cross.

* * *

The break room hummed with the white noise of office life—the hiss of the coffee machine, the rustle of newspapers, the low murmur of conversations. Ethan stood by the window, his gaze fixed on the cityscape below, a distant reflection of his own fractured existence.

Vanessa approached him, her steps measured, her presence commanding an unspoken authority that seemed to hush the room. She stood close, her shoulder brushing against his, close enough that colleagues looked up, their eyes narrowing with curiosity.

Leaning in, her breath warm against his ear, Vanessa whispered, "My place, 8pm. It's important." Her voice was a low purr, the urgency in her tone cutting through the fog of Ethan's daily routine.

Ethan's breath caught in his throat, the unexpected invitation sending a jolt of adrenaline coursing through his veins. He nodded, a silent acknowledgment of the rendezvous, and watched as Vanessa walked away, the sway of her hips a hypnotic promise of the night to come.

The evening air was cool against Ethan's skin as he stood outside Vanessa's apartment. The door opened to reveal Vanessa, her form silhouetted against the soft light of her home. She ushered him inside, her hand lingering on the small of his back, a silent affirmation of their shared understanding.

Vanessa led him to a pristine gray sofa that seemed to dominate the room. She handed him a stack of financial documents, her eyes grave with the weight of the information they contained. Ethan scanned the pages, his mind racing as he pieced together the intricate web of Richard's financial misdeeds.

Their conversation was a dance of words and implications, each revelation drawing them closer until the tension between them snapped like a taut bowstring.

Vanessa's lips crashed against Ethan's, her kiss fierce and demanding. Ethan responded with a hunger that bordered on desperation, the taste of her mouth a potent drug that flooded his senses.

They tore at each other's clothes, the urgency of their need rendering finesse irrelevant. Vanessa straddled Ethan on the sofa, her nails raking down his back as she guided him inside her.

Their coupling was a frenzied tangle of limbs, a raw and animalistic expression of their mutual desire. Ethan thrust into her with an intensity that bordered on violence, each stroke eliciting a sharp gasp from Vanessa's lips.

As they moved together, Ethan caught Vanessa studying his face, her eyes sharp with observation, cataloging his expressions with the meticulous care of a scientist conducting a critical experiment.

The moment of climax was a white-hot explosion of sensation. Ethan's release was a torrent that left him spent and gasping for air. The evidence of their union seeped out, staining Vanessa's pristine couch with a visceral testament to their passion.

The fervor of their union subsided, leaving Ethan and Vanessa entangled on the now tainted sofa. Ethan's breath came in ragged gasps, his body slick with the sweat of their exertions. He rolled off Vanessa, his mind a whirlwind of conflicting emotions.

"I'm sorry," Ethan murmured, his voice barely above a whisper. He was apologizing for more than just the physical mess they had made—it was an apology for the chaos they had invited into their lives.

Vanessa propped herself up on her elbow, her eyes softening as she looked at him. "It's okay," she assured him, her hand reaching out to gently caress his now limp member. "We're both consenting adults. We're allowed to want this."

Ethan's gaze dropped to the stained fabric beneath them, the stark evidence of their betrayal. "But what are we doing?" he asked, the question hanging heavy in the air between them.

Vanessa sat up, pulling her knees to her chest, her expression thoughtful. "I've been attracted to you since the first day I walked into Horizon Financial," she admitted, her voice steady despite the vulnerability of her confession. "There's something about you, Ethan. It's more than just your looks. You're intelligent, perceptive, and there's a depth to you that I somehow find irresistible."

Ethan's eyes met hers, the weight of his own attraction mirrored in his gaze. "I feel the same way about you, Vanessa. But my marriage... Claire has been through so much. She struggles with intimacy because of her past, and I've felt so guilty for needing... this."

Vanessa reached out and took his hand, her fingers intertwining with his. "No one has to know," she said, her voice low and persuasive. "This can be our secret. We can have this—this connection—without tearing apart what you have with Claire."

Ethan nodded, the tension in his shoulders easing somewhat at her words. They lay back down on the couch, their bodies fitting together as if they were two pieces of a puzzle. With Vanessa's head resting on his chest, Ethan closed his eyes and allowed himself to bask in the warmth of her embrace.

As they lay there, the stark irony of his situation was not lost on him. Ethan, a man living a double life, had now added another layer to his deception. He was a husband who craved the intimacy his wife couldn't provide, a voyeur who had become the subject of someone else's watchful gaze, and now, a man caught in the throes of an illicit affair.

The room was silent save for the soft, rhythmic sound of their breathing. Ethan's thoughts drifted to Claire, and the guilt that gnawed at him was a familiar ache. He told himself that this—his tryst with Vanessa—was a necessary release, a pressure valve for the pent-up needs that threatened to suffocate him.

But as he held Vanessa close, Ethan couldn't shake the feeling that he was walking a dangerous tightrope, balancing precariously between the life he had and the one he might yet fall into. For now, though, he indulged in the illusion of simplicity, the comfort of skin on skin, and the fleeting sense of being understood and more importantly, desired.

Their secret, safely tucked away in the sanctuary of Vanessa's apartment, was a testament to the complex dance of human desire and the lengths people would go to in order to fulfill their deepest yearnings.

* * *

The streetlights cast rhythmic patterns across Ethan's dashboard as he drove home from Vanessa's apartment. His body still hummed with the afterglow of their encounter, but the satisfaction was rapidly giving way to a cold, creeping dread. He'd betrayed Claire in the most fundamental way possible.

Ethan adjusted his rearview mirror and frowned. A black SUV had been maintaining the same distance behind him for the past ten minutes. Three cars back, never closer, never farther. Too consistent to be coincidence.

At the next intersection, Ethan took an abrupt right turn without signaling. The SUV followed after a brief pause, matching his speed precisely. Ethan's heart rate accelerated as he made another unexpected turn, this time left.

Again, the SUV followed.

"Shit," Ethan muttered, gripping the steering wheel tighter.

He slowed as they passed under a particularly bright streetlight. In his mirror, he caught a clear glimpse of the driver—close-cropped military haircut, broad shoulders, expressionless face. Jackson. Richard's hired muscle.

Ethan's mouth went dry. The intimidation was escalating from subtle signs to open surveillance. Jackson wasn't even trying to hide anymore. This was a message: You're being watched. We know where you go. We know what you do.

The irony wasn't lost on Ethan. The voyeur was now the observed. He thought of all the women he'd watched through their windows, the private moments he'd stolen. Now he was experiencing that same violation—the knowledge that someone was tracking his movements, cataloging his secrets.

His affair with Vanessa was no longer just a betrayal of Claire; it was potentially dangerous ammunition for Richard. If Richard discovered this new relationship, he'd have even more leverage to use against Ethan.

Ethan took several random turns, but the SUV remained fixed behind him, a dark shadow that refused to be shaken. Jackson was sending a clear message—there was nowhere Ethan could go that he wouldn't be followed, nothing he could do that wouldn't be observed.

* * *

Ethan pulled into his driveway, the SUV slowing as it passed his house before disappearing around the corner. His hands trembled as he turned off the ignition. The weight of being watched—of having his own tactics used against him—left him nauseated.

Inside his darkened house, he moved from window to window, checking locks, drawing curtains. Claire and Emma were

asleep upstairs, unaware of the predator their husband and father had become—or the predators now hunting him.

Blocks away, Rebecca sat at her desk, the blue glow of her
laptop illuminating her concentrated expression. Her fingers
moved rapidly across the keyboard as she drafted a new section
for her manuscript:

The Psychology of Surveillance: Predator and Prey

*The observed inevitably change behavior when aware of obser-
vation - a quantum principle applied to human psychology. Just as
particles behave differently when measured, humans alter their
patterns when conscious of being watched.*

She paused, considering Ethan's recent behavior. Since re-
alizing he was under surveillance, his movements had become
erratic, paranoid. The confident voyeur had transformed into a
hunted animal.

*The voyeur derives power from invisibility—the asymmetry of
seeing without being seen. When this dynamic inverts, the psychological impact is profound. The watcher, now watched, experiences
the violation they've inflicted on others. This creates a recursive
loop of awareness: they know they're being observed, they know the
observer knows they know, and so on.*

Rebecca scrolled through her photos of Ethan from the past
week—his hunched shoulders, the constant glances over his
shoulder, the new routes he took to avoid predictability.

*Subject E has displayed classic counter-surveillance behav-
iors since becoming aware of observation. His previous methodical patterns have dissolved into unpredictability. The*

hunter-turned-hunted exhibits heightened stress responses, territorial marking behaviors (checking perimeters, securing entrances), and paradoxically, increased risk-taking—perhaps a psychological reaction to the loss of control.

She saved her work and leaned back, considering the ethical implications of her project. She was documenting a psychological unraveling in real-time—valuable material for her book, but at what cost to the human being she was observing?

CHAPTER TWENTY-NINE

Vanessa's Truth

E than hesitated outside Vanessa's apartment door, hand suspended before knocking. The financial documents she'd given him yesterday had confirmed his suspicions about Richard's embezzlement scheme—and offered potential leverage. But coming here felt dangerous, like stepping into another trap.

He knocked anyway.

Vanessa opened the door wearing a simple gray sweater and jeans, her resemblance to Erika still jarring despite her completely different demeanor. "You came," she said, stepping aside. "Come in."

Her apartment was nothing like Erika's. Where Erika's had been sleek, minimalist, designed to showcase herself, Vanessa's was warm with overflowing bookshelves and framed photographs covering nearly every wall. Academic texts on financial fraud and psychology lined one shelf—not the decorative books people displayed for show, but worn volumes with sticky notes protruding from pages.

"Let me get us something to drink," Vanessa said, disappearing into the kitchen. "Red okay?"

"Perfect," Ethan replied, drawn to the photographs. Family gatherings, graduation ceremonies, hiking trips. Vanessa smiling with friends against mountain backdrops. A life documented with genuine connections rather than carefully curated impressions.

His eyes fixed on a particular frame—a sun-drenched beach scene. A stunning woman in a bikini laughed while building a sandcastle with a young girl, perhaps five or six years old. The woman's hair caught golden in the sunlight, her smile radiant.

Vanessa returned with two glasses of wine.

"Wow, what a great picture," Ethan said, nodding toward the beach photograph.

"That's my mom and me," Vanessa replied, handing him a glass.

"She is stunning," Ethan said. "I can certainly see the family resemblance."

Vanessa gestured toward her couch. "Let's sit. I've been going through those transactions all week. There's more than what I showed you."

Ethan sank into the cushions, grateful for the wine's warmth spreading through his chest. "How did you spot it? Most people wouldn't recognize those patterns."

"Before Horizon, I worked for a firm that specialized in detecting financial fraud." She tucked one leg beneath her, turning to face him. "The shell companies, the consulting fees to 'Decker Associates'—it's textbook embezzlement, just executed well enough to fool most people."

"But not you." Ethan studied her over his glass.

"Not me." Her smile carried a hint of pride. "I recognized it immediately, but as the new hire, I needed to be careful who I told."

The wine disappeared quickly as they talked. Vanessa poured second glasses, sitting closer when she returned. Their conversation shifted from Richard's crimes to office politics, then to personal stories—her childhood in Seattle, his college years. The shared confidences created an unexpected intimacy.

"You know what's strange?" Vanessa set her empty glass on the coffee table. "I feel like I've known you longer than a few weeks."

Her hand brushed his arm, lingering. The touch sent electricity through him—not the predatory excitement of watching but something warmer, more genuine.

She stood suddenly, her movements deliberate as she pulled her sweater over her head, exposing her supple curves. Ethan froze, wine glass suspended halfway to his lips.

She approached, taking his glass and setting it aside before straddling him. Her fingers worked at his shirt buttons, methodically exposing his chest.

"Vanessa, you know I'm married—" The protest sounded hollow even to his ears.

Vanessa's fingers worked Ethan's belt with practiced efficiency. "I know, and as I told you, this is about us. No one needs to know." Her voice dropped to a whisper, lips brushing against his ear. "Ethan, I want to feel you inside me again. You want this too, why deny yourself?"

His body responded even as his mind raced with conflicting thoughts. Claire's face flashed before him—their broken intimacy, her struggle to heal, Emma waiting at home. Yet Vanessa's touch obliterated his resistance, igniting something primal he'd suppressed for too long.

She stood, her jeans sliding down slender legs. The resemblance to Erika was uncanny, yet fundamentally different. Where Erika had been calculated seduction, Vanessa's desire seemed authentic, her eyes reflecting genuine want rather than strategic manipulation.

"Come," she whispered, taking his hand and pulling him to his feet.

The bedroom door stood half-open at the end of a short hallway. Ethan followed, his steps unsteady. The room beyond was dimly lit by a bedside lamp, casting golden shadows across a queen-sized bed with rumpled sheets.

Vanessa guided Ethan to the bed, her touch both insistent and gentle. The back of his knees hit the mattress, and she pushed him down onto the soft comforter. Ethan's heart thundered in his chest, a mixture of arousal and the thrill of doing something so reckless, so unlike him. He watched as Vanessa's fingers curled around the waistband of his boxer briefs, tugging them down to join his discarded pants on the floor.

His erection sprang free, and Vanessa's eyes darkened with desire as she took in the sight of him. She didn't speak, but her burning gaze communicated volumes. With a swift, fluid motion, she straddled his hips, her knees sinking into the bed on either side of his thighs.

Ethan's breath caught in his throat as he felt the warmth of her body pressing against his own. Vanessa reached down, her fingers closing around his shaft, guiding him to her entrance. She was slick with arousal, the evidence of her desire making it easy for him to slide inside her.

As she lowered herself onto him, Ethan let out a low groan. The sensation of being enveloped by her heat was almost too much to bear. He fought the urge to thrust upward, allowing Vanessa to set the pace. She began to move, her hips rolling in a deliberate, unhurried rhythm that drove him wild with need.

The room filled with the sounds of their lovemaking—the soft, wet noises of their bodies joining together, Vanessa's breathy moans, the creak of the bedsprings beneath them. Ethan's hands found their way to Vanessa's hips, gripping her firmly as she rode him.

He could feel the pressure building within him, a storm of pleasure that threatened to sweep him away. But he held back, wanting to prolong this moment—this illicit connection that felt more real and more necessary than anything he'd experienced in a long time.

Vanessa leaned forward, her breasts brushing against Ethan's chest as she captured his lips in a searing kiss. Her tongue danced with his, exploring and tasting, as her movements above him grew more fervent.

Ethan's self-control began to crumble. He met Vanessa's thrusts with his own, driving deeper into her. Their bodies moved together as one, a symphony of desire and need.

"Ethan," Vanessa gasped, her voice ragged with pleasure. "Oh god, don't stop."

Her words spurred him on, and he felt himself teetering on the edge of release. Vanessa's muscles tightened around him, and she cried out as her orgasm crashed over her, her body shuddering with the force of it.

The sensation of her climax triggered Ethan's own. With a guttural moan, he surrendered to the waves of ecstasy that washed over him, his hips bucking involuntarily as he spilled himself into her.

For a few moments, there was nothing but the sound of their ragged breathing filling the room. Vanessa collapsed onto Ethan's chest, her body slick with sweat. He wrapped his arms around her, holding her close, feeling the rapid beat of her heart syncing with his own.

As their breathing returned to normal, Vanessa lifted her head, her eyes meeting Ethan's. There was a tenderness in her gaze that took him by surprise. She smiled at him—a small, private smile that seemed to contain a world of understanding.

Ethan knew he should feel guilty, that he should be thinking of Claire and Emma at home. But in that moment, lying there with Vanessa in his arms, he allowed himself to bask in the warmth of their connection. It was a connection that had nothing to do with his voyeuristic compulsions, nothing to do with manipulation or deceit. It was, he realized with a start, the first genuine moment of intimacy he'd experienced in years.

And as Vanessa's fingers traced lazy patterns on his chest, Ethan found himself wanting to hold onto that feeling for as long as he possibly could.

Her eyes, heavy-lidded with satisfaction, locked with his.

"Do you have any idea how much you turn me on?" she murmured, her voice husky.

"Really? Little ol' me?" Ethan replied with a hint of playfulness.

Vanessa's gaze traveled downward, her hand following the trail of hair on his stomach until her fingers found him. She stroked gently with her fingernails. "Yeah you and not so little by the way."

Ethan laughed, a warm sound that filled the intimate space between them. "Well thank you, is that what turns you on?"

"That's definitely a part of it but you turned me on even before I ever saw that." Her fingers continued their gentle exploration. "I can't explain it, you just make me want to do everything with you."

"Everything? What does everything entail?" His eyebrow arched with curiosity.

Vanessa continued to slowly coax Ethan's cock back to life. "Oh you know, everything."

"No I don't know. Tell me what things do you want to do?" He propped himself up on one elbow, genuinely intrigued.

"I want to explore your body completely, slowly. I want to play role playing games with you."

"Role playing? Like what?"

"Trust me, I'll think of some good ones." Her smile turned mischievous. "Maybe we're at a hotel and you're a travelling businessman from out of town and I'm a hotel maid."

Ethan laughed. "Oh, now that sounds interesting."

"Maybe I'm a bad employee that needs some special attention or a good spanking."

"You do have a wonderfully exciting imagination. I think I might enjoy this role playing of yours."

"And toys," she added.

"Toys? What kind of toys?"

"I love to play with my toys. Vibrators, dildos, butt plugs."

Ethan chuckled. "Are you serious, I never pictured you into things like that. Don't get me wrong, I love the idea. Claire would never..." his voice trailed off.

"I'm very serious Ethan. Open the drawer of that night stand next to you."

Ethan reached over and pulled open the drawer. Inside lay an assortment of sex toys—vibrators in various sizes, sleek butt plugs, dildos, and even a small whip. Laughing, he said, "You weren't kidding, you're some kind of nympho."

"Don't make fun of me. I just have...well I'll just call it an appetite."

"No, I'm not making fun of you. I think I'm going to have a lot of fun with you though."

As he rummaged through the drawer, Ethan's fingers brushed against something flat. He pulled out a small framed photograph. "What's this? That's your mom again."

"Here give it to me." Vanessa reached for the picture, her playfulness suddenly replaced with urgency.

Ethan pulled the picture further away, keeping it from Vanessa's grasp. His eyes widened as recognition dawned. "That's your mom with...Erika?"

"Give me the picture." Her voice turned sharp.

"That is Erika. She's younger but there's no mistaking her." Ethan stared at the photo, confusion etched across his face. "Vanessa, what's your mom doing with Erika?"

Vanessa snatched the photograph from Ethan's hand, her eyes suddenly glistening with tears.

"You weren't supposed to see that." She clutched the photo to her chest, all playfulness vanished.

"Vanessa, what's going on? How do you know Erika?" Ethan sat up, pulling the sheet around his waist.

She stared at the wall for several long moments, her breathing uneven. When she finally spoke, her voice was barely above a whisper.

"She's my half-sister."

Ethan's mouth fell open. "Half-sister? But—how is that possible? You never mentioned—"

"I didn't know about her until last year." Vanessa's shoulders slumped as she turned the photograph to look at it again. "My mother died of cancer eleven months ago. While I was going through her things, I found a box of letters and photos."

Her fingers traced the outline of her mother's face in the photograph.

"There were birthday cards my mother had written but never sent. School photos of a little girl growing up. And finally, recent pictures of Erika as an adult." Vanessa's voice cracked. "My mother had been keeping tabs on her all these years without ever reaching out."

Ethan remained silent, processing this revelation.

"I found out my mother had another daughter before me, with a different man. She left that man... and her daughter." Vanessa wiped away a tear. "According to her journals, she regretted it her entire life but was too ashamed to try to reconnect."

She looked up at Ethan, her eyes filled with pain.

"Can you imagine discovering you had a sister your entire life and never knew? I spent months trying to work up the courage to contact her. I researched everything about her. Found out where she worked."

"And then she was murdered before you could meet her," Ethan said softly.

Vanessa nodded, fresh tears spilling down her cheeks.

"I applied for the job at Horizon to be close to the people who knew her. To understand who my sister was." She let out a bitter laugh. "Everyone talked about her like she was this manipulative seductress, but I needed to know the real Erika."

Ethan's heart ached for Vanessa. Her revelation had transformed everything—what he'd assumed was a casual fling suddenly carried the weight of her tragic connection to Erika.

"I'm so sorry," he whispered, gently taking the photograph and placing it on the nightstand.

Vanessa looked up, her face streaked with tears, vulnerability replacing the confident woman who had seduced him minutes earlier. Her shoulders trembled with each sob.

"I was too late," she whispered. "All those years wasted, and then when I finally found out about her—" Her voice broke.

Ethan reached out and pulled her against him. Vanessa's head leaned on Ethan's chest and she cried, her tears warm against his skin. Her body shook with grief as he held her, one hand stroking her hair while the other wrapped protectively around her shoulders.

"I just wanted to know her," Vanessa mumbled against his chest. "To tell her she had family who cared. That she wasn't abandoned by everyone."

Ethan tightened his embrace, rocking her gently. The intimacy of this moment felt more significant than their physical connection earlier. He remained silent, letting her grief flow without interruption.

Her fingers curled against his chest as she clung to him. Ethan closed his eyes, overwhelmed by the twisted irony—he had watched Erika die while her sister, who never got to meet her, now wept in his arms.

"I should have contacted her sooner," Vanessa said between sobs. "I was just so scared she'd reject me."

"You couldn't have known," Ethan whispered, his throat tight with emotion.

CHAPTER THIRTY

Unexpected Alliance

They sat in silence for several minutes, her breathing gradually steadying against him. Ethan's mind raced, weighing what he knew against what he should share.

"Vanessa," he said finally, his voice low. "There's something I need to tell you."

She pulled back slightly, wiping her eyes. "What is it?"

Ethan took a deep breath. "Erika kept a journal. She documented everything—including evidence against Richard."

Vanessa's eyes widened. "You knew her that well?"

"No, I..." Ethan hesitated, choosing his words carefully. "Rebecca—she's a writer who lives across from Erika's building—she found entries from Erika's journal. There are references to a safe deposit box. Some kind of 'insurance policy' against Richard."

"Insurance policy?" Vanessa sat up straighter, her grief momentarily suspended by curiosity.

"Financial records, I think. Proof of his embezzlement." Ethan paused. "And I know where the key is."

Vanessa stared at him. "How could you possibly know that?"

"One of the journal entries mentioned her mother's old house on Sycamore Street. Rebecca and I think it's the key to the safe deposit box."

"Sycamore Street?" Vanessa's voice trembled. "Yeah, years ago that's where my mother lived. Our mother."

"Exactly." Ethan nodded. "Erika must have gone back there, maybe trying to connect with her past. The journal said she hid the key there."

Vanessa's face transformed, shock replacing grief. She rose up abruptly.

"You've known this for how long exactly?" Her voice had an edge he hadn't heard before. "While I've been pouring through financial statements trying to piece together Richard's scheme, you've been sitting on actual evidence?"

Ethan raised his hands. "It's complicated—"

"No, it's not. You knew where evidence was hidden that could bring down Richard—the man who I'm pretty sure murdered my sister—and you kept it to yourself." Her eyes narrowed. "Why? What aren't you telling me?"

"I couldn't be sure it was real," Ethan said. "And I didn't know you were her sister until just now."

"That's not good enough." Vanessa crossed her arms. "You're holding something back. I can see it in your face."

Ethan looked away. The moment stretched between them, taut with unspoken truths.

"I need to know I can trust you," Vanessa said finally. "All of it, Ethan."

"Rebecca and I were planning to go to the house," he admitted. "We've been working together to build a case against Richard."

Vanessa's expression hardened. "I'm coming with you."

"It could be dangerous. Richard has someone watching me—"

"She was my sister." The words fell like stones between them. "I've spent weeks pretending I barely knew her, watching everyone grieve while hiding my own pain. Whatever you're involved in, I'm in it now too."

Ethan studied her face—so like Erika's yet completely different. Where Erika had been calculating, Vanessa was direct. Where Erika manipulated, Vanessa confronted.

"Okay," he said finally. "We'll go together. Tomorrow after work."

Vanessa nodded, some of the tension leaving her shoulders. "I have a rental car. We'll take that instead of yours. Less chance of being followed."

"Smart."

"And Ethan?" She leaned forward, her voice dropping. "Whatever you're not telling me—and I know there's something—it better not put us in danger. Because if it does, and if it keeps us from nailing Richard for what he did to my sister, I'll make sure you regret it."

The threat wasn't delivered with malice, just absolute certainty. Ethan believed her completely.

"I understand," he said quietly.

CHAPTER THIRTY-ONE

Evidence

The abandoned house on Sycamore Street loomed against the twilight sky, its weathered Victorian facade a patchwork of peeling paint and rotting wood. Ethan parked Vanessa's rental car a block away, behind a stand of overgrown bushes.

"No one's lived here in years," Vanessa whispered as they approached through the tangled yard.

Ethan glanced over his shoulder. The street remained empty, but his skin prickled with the sensation of being watched.

"You're sure we weren't followed?" Vanessa asked, noticing his vigilance.

"No. That's why we need to hurry."

They reached the back porch, its steps sagging beneath their weight. Vanessa tried the door handle—locked.

"There used to be a spare key under—" She knelt and felt along the edge of a cracked flowerpot, coming up empty. "Gone."

Ethan moved to a window, testing its frame. "This one's loose."

He slipped his fingers beneath the warped wood and pushed upward. The window resisted, then gave with a groan that seemed deafening in the quiet neighborhood.

"Someone's going to hear us," Vanessa hissed.

"We don't have a choice." Ethan hoisted himself through the opening, landing on creaking floorboards. He reached back to help Vanessa through.

Inside, the house smelled of mildew and abandonment. Dust motes swirled in the beam of Ethan's flashlight. Vanessa pulled out her phone, activating its light.

"The journal said the key was taped under a bathroom sink." Ethan whispered, scanning the debris-strewn kitchen.

"There is one bathroom downstairs and one upstairs." Vanessa moved toward the hallway, then froze as headlights swept across the front windows. "Car."

They killed their lights and pressed against the wall. The vehicle slowed, then continued past.

"That could have been anyone," Ethan whispered, his heart hammering.

"Or it could have been Jackson," Vanessa countered. "We need to hurry."

They moved cautiously through the downstairs hallway, floorboards protesting beneath their weight. The bathroom door hung askew on rusted hinges.

"Wait here," Ethan whispered as he slipped inside.

The downstairs bathroom was small and decrepit. Cracked tiles lined the floor, and the porcelain sink had yellowed with age. Ethan crouched, his knees popping as he ran his fingers along the underside of the basin.

"Nothing," he muttered after a thorough search. "Just cobwebs and rust."

Vanessa glanced nervously toward the front of the house. "We need to check upstairs."

The staircase curved upward into darkness. Each step elicited a protest of ancient wood that seemed to echo through the empty house. Ethan winced with every sound, imagining Jackson materializing from the shadows.

At the top landing, they paused to listen. The house remained silent except for the occasional settling of its frame.

"This way," Vanessa whispered, directing her light down a narrow hallway.

The upstairs bathroom was larger than its downstairs counterpart, with a claw-foot tub dominating one wall. Moonlight filtered through a small, frosted window, casting everything in ghostly blue.

Ethan dropped to his knees in front of the pedestal sink. "Keep watch," he instructed Vanessa, who positioned herself at the doorway.

He ran his fingers along the underside of the basin, feeling nothing at first. Then his fingertips brushed against something that wasn't porcelain or plumbing—a small rectangular shape secured with duct tape.

"I think I found it," he whispered, his pulse quickening.

Carefully, he peeled back the aged tape. A small brass key dropped into his palm.

"Got it," he said, holding it up to catch the moonlight. "Exactly where her journal said it would be."

Vanessa exhaled in relief. "That's the safe deposit box key?"

Ethan nodded, closing his fingers around it. "This is what Richard couldn't find. This is what Erika was using to blackmail him."

They descended the stairs with painstaking care, each step calculated to minimize noise. Outside, a dog barked in the distance, causing them both to freeze midway down the staircase.

"Just a dog," Ethan whispered after a moment, pocketing the small brass key.

When they reached the first floor, Vanessa pointed toward the back of the house. "Same way we came in."

Ethan nodded, leading the way through the kitchen. The window frame creaked as he pushed it open wider. He climbed through first, then turned to help Vanessa, his hands steadying her waist as she navigated the opening.

The night air felt clean after the musty interior. They crept across the overgrown yard, every rustling leaf magnified in the darkness. At the edge of the property, Ethan scanned the street before motioning Vanessa forward.

They moved quickly between pools of streetlight, staying close to hedges and parked cars. When they finally reached Vanessa's rental, Ethan glanced over his shoulder one last time before sliding into the passenger seat.

Vanessa started the engine but kept the headlights off until they'd rolled several houses down. Only then did she switch them on and accelerate.

The tension that had gripped them inside the abandoned house suddenly broke. Vanessa pulled the car to the curb a few blocks away, put it in park, and turned toward Ethan. Without warning, she threw her arms around him, her body trembling with relief.

Ethan returned the embrace, feeling the warmth of her against his chest, the scent of her shampoo mingling with the dusty smell still clinging to their clothes.

"Unbelievable," he whispered, his chin resting on her shoulder.

Vanessa pulled back, her eyes bright in the dim glow of the dashboard lights. "We did it. We actually found it."

Her smile faded as she checked her mirrors and pulled back onto the road. The streetlights flashed rhythmically across their faces as they drove in silence for several blocks.

"First thing tomorrow we make a trip to First National Bank," Ethan said, rolling the small key between his fingers.

First National Bank stood imposingly on the corner of Main and Elm, its limestone facade gleaming in the morning sun. Ethan checked his watch—9:05 AM. The bank had just opened.

"Ready?" Vanessa asked, smoothing her blazer.

Ethan nodded, clutching the small brass key in his pocket. They'd agreed to arrive separately; Vanessa had been waiting in her car when he pulled into the parking lot.

Inside, the marble floors echoed with their footsteps as they approached the customer service desk. A middle-aged woman with immaculate hair greeted them with a practiced smile.

"We need access to a safe deposit box," Ethan said, keeping his voice low.

"Certainly. Do you have the key and your identification?"

Ethan produced the key and his driver's license. "The box belonged to Erika Jensen. I'm not the owner, but—"

"I'm afraid only the registered box holder can access it," the woman interrupted, her smile tightening.

Vanessa leaned forward. "Ms. Jensen is deceased. We're helping with her estate matters."

The woman's expression shifted to concern. "In that case, you'll need proper documentation—a death certificate, court order, or executor authorization."

Ethan's heart sank. They hadn't anticipated this obstacle.

"One moment," Vanessa said, opening her purse. She extracted an official-looking document and slid it across the counter. "I have power of attorney from Ms. Jensen's family."

Ethan stared at her, trying to mask his surprise. The document looked authentic, complete with notary stamps.

The woman examined the paperwork, comparing signatures. After what felt like an eternity, she nodded. "This appears to be in order. Please follow me."

They were led through a security door into a room lined with metal boxes of various sizes. The woman used her master key along with Ethan's brass key to unlock box #773, then discreetly withdrew.

Vanessa pulled out the long metal container and placed it on the private table. Ethan's hands trembled slightly as he lifted the lid.

Inside lay a thick manila envelope labeled "DECKER" in Erika's distinctive handwriting. Beneath it were USB drives, bank statements, and a handwritten ledger.

Ethan opened the envelope. It contained detailed financial records—wire transfers, shell company registrations, and offshore account numbers. Each document connected to Richard's embezzlement scheme.

"My God," Vanessa whispered, examining a spreadsheet. "He diverted over two million dollars."

Ethan flipped through the ledger. "Look at this—dates, amounts, account numbers. She documented everything."

"This is what got her killed," Vanessa said, her voice barely audible. "She had him completely exposed."

Vanessa carefully organized the documents into the manila envelope. "This is everything we need to take Richard down."

"Yeah, but I'm damn curious what's on these flash drives." Ethan held up two small USB sticks labeled with dates.

"Let's go to my car. I've got my laptop, we can check them out there."

"Sounds like a plan." Ethan gathered the evidence while Vanessa returned the empty box.

Outside, morning sunlight glinted off the bank's windows as they crossed the parking lot to Vanessa's car. Ethan glanced over his shoulder, the habit now second nature. The lot remained quiet except for an elderly couple slowly making their way toward the entrance.

Vanessa unlocked her car and slid into the driver's seat. Ethan joined her on the passenger side, closing the door with a solid thunk that sealed them in privacy. The interior smelled of vanilla air freshener and new leather.

She reached into the backseat and retrieved a slim silver laptop. "Let's see what Erika thought was worth hiding."

Ethan handed her the first flash drive. Their fingers brushed during the exchange, a brief moment of warmth that seemed to linger. Vanessa plugged the drive into her laptop and waited for it to register.

Finally a single folder appeared titled "Media". Vanessa double clicked on the icon.

The screen filled with thumbnail images—dozens of photographs. Vanessa clicked on the first one, and it expanded to fill the screen. Richard and Erika locked in an embrace, partially undressed in what appeared to be a hotel room.

"Jesus," Ethan whispered.

Vanessa scrolled through more images—Richard and Erika in various compromising positions, some clearly taken without Richard's knowledge. The dates in the file names spanned months.

"She was documenting everything," Vanessa said, her voice tight.

Beside the photo folder sat an audio folder. Vanessa clicked it open, revealing MP3 files labeled by date.

She selected one at random and pressed play. Erika's voice emerged from the laptop speakers, unnervingly clear:

"So you'll transfer the funds tomorrow?" Her tone was businesslike despite the intimate setting.

Richard's voice followed, relaxed and confident: "Yes, yes. Now come back to bed."

"And the promotion paperwork?"

A sigh. "I told you, it's complicated. HR is watching these things closely after that lawsuit last year."

"Not complicated for me to explain those fake invoices to the board, is it?"

Silence, then Richard's voice, suddenly cold: "Don't threaten me, Erika."

Vanessa stopped the recording. "She was blackmailing him with evidence of both the affair and the embezzlement."

"No wonder he snapped," Ethan murmured, staring at the screen filled with damning evidence.

Vanessa stared at the screen, her expression shifting from shock to something more complicated. She closed the laptop with a decisive click and leaned back against the headrest.

"Wow. My sister was..." She shook her head, struggling to find words. "I don't even know what to say. I guess the talk around the office I heard was right. She used her body to get what she wanted." Her voice cracked slightly. "I am a bit shocked."

Ethan shifted uncomfortably in his seat, unsure how to respond. The images on the screen had been explicit, undeniable evidence of Erika's methods.

"She was very smart and very... successful," he offered awkwardly. "She uhm—"

"There's no need to whitewash it, Ethan," Vanessa interrupted, her eyes suddenly sharp. "My sister was a tramp. She used her body and sexuality to climb the corporate ladder."

The bluntness of her statement hung in the air between them. Ethan noticed how Vanessa's hands trembled slightly as she pushed the laptop away, creating physical distance between herself and the evidence of her sister's life.

CHAPTER THIRTY-TWO

The Pursuit

"We can't just sit here in the parking lot," Vanessa said, sliding the laptop into her bag. "Let's go to my place—figure out our next move."

"Good call. I'll follow you."

"Actually, can you drive? I'm a bit shaken." She handed him her keys.

As they pulled out of the bank parking lot, Ethan checked the rearview mirror—a habit that had become second nature. A black SUV with tinted windows three cars back caught his attention. Something about its aggressive stance triggered his instincts.

"Don't look now, but I think we're being followed." He kept his voice level despite the adrenaline surging through him. "Black SUV, tinted windows."

Vanessa's eyes widened. "Are you sure?"

"Let's find out." Ethan made a sudden right turn at the next intersection. The SUV followed, maintaining the same distance.

"Coincidence maybe?" Vanessa whispered.

Ethan made another unexpected turn onto a residential street. The SUV appeared again, hanging back but definitely tracking them.

"That's no coincidence." His knuckles whitened on the steering wheel. "That's Jackson—Richard's guy."

Vanessa's breathing quickened. "What do we do?"

"We need to lose him." Ethan accelerated slightly, mind racing through options. "Any ideas?"

"Lakeside Mall is three blocks ahead," Vanessa said. "It has a multi-level parking structure with multiple exits."

"Perfect."

Ethan drove casually toward the mall, making no sudden moves that might alert their pursuer. The SUV maintained its distance, a predator patiently stalking its prey.

They entered the parking garage, climbing to the third level before pulling into a space near the elevator bank. The black SUV appeared at the ramp, moving slowly as the driver scanned for them.

They slipped out and walked briskly toward the mall entrance, Ethan's hand at the small of Vanessa's back. Inside, they merged with the afternoon shopping crowd.

"Don't look back," he murmured as they passed through the food court. "Head for the north exit."

They walked quickly through the mall, weaving between shoppers, occasionally changing direction to confuse any pursuit. After exiting on the opposite side, they jogged to a bus stop where a city bus was just pulling in.

"Get on," Ethan urged, following Vanessa up the steps. They dropped into seats near the back as the doors closed.

Through the window, Ethan spotted Jackson emerging from the mall, scanning the parking lot with frustrated intensity.

The bus pulled away, carrying them to safety—at least for now.

The bus dropped them off downtown. They ducked into an office building with public access to the first few floors, still vigilant for any sign of Jackson.

"In here," Vanessa whispered, pulling Ethan into a service stairwell. The heavy door clanged shut behind them, sealing them in concrete silence broken only by their ragged breathing.

"You think we lost him?" Her voice echoed slightly in the enclosed space.

Ethan leaned against the wall, heart hammering. "For now."

Their eyes locked, adrenaline still coursing through their systems. Vanessa moved toward him first, her lips crashing against his with desperate intensity. His hands found her waist, pulling her against him as the fear transmuted into something electric.

"We shouldn't—" he started, but she silenced him with another kiss.

"I know," she breathed against his mouth. "I don't care."

They collided against the wall, hands tearing at clothing, seeking skin. Ethan lifted her, her legs wrapping around his waist as he pressed her against the cold concrete. Their coupling was urgent, almost violent—each thrust an affirmation of life against the threat that stalked them.

Vanessa buried her face against his neck, muffling her cries as her body tensed around him. Ethan followed moments later, his world narrowing to this single point of connection, temporarily forgetting Richard, Jackson, even Claire.

Reality returned slowly as their breathing steadied. Ethan gently lowered Vanessa to her feet, both of them adjusting clothing in awkward silence.

"That was..." she started.

"Unexpected," he finished.

A small laugh escaped her. "That's one word for it."

They slid down to sit side by side on the stairs, shoulders touching.

"This thing between us," Vanessa said quietly. "It's not just about Erika or Richard anymore, is it?"

Ethan stared at his hands. "No. I don't think it is."

"We barely know each other."

"I feel like I've known you longer." He turned to face her. "Maybe because we've been through more in weeks than most people experience in years."

She nodded. "Shared trauma—the ultimate bonding experience."

"Is that all this is?" he asked.

Vanessa reached for his hand, interlacing their fingers. "No. There's something else here. Something real. And that scares me more than Jackson does."

CHAPTER THIRTY-THREE

Triggers

Moonlight sliced through the blinds as Jackson moved methodically through Ethan's home office. His gloved hands pulled open desk drawers, rifling through papers, searching for anything that could be used to leverage Ethan. The house stood silent around him, empty since Ethan had left an hour earlier. Jackson had watched him drive away, waited ten minutes to ensure he wouldn't return, then picked the lock on the back door to gain entrance.

He found nothing in the desk. Moving to the bookshelf, he ran his fingers behind rows of books, checking for hidden compartments or taped envelopes.

The sound of a car pulling into the driveway froze him mid-motion. Headlights swept across the wall through the blinds. Keys jingled at the front door.

"Hurry up, sweetie," Claire's voice carried through the door as she unlocked it. "It's getting cold out here."

Jackson slipped into the hallway, scanning for exits. The front door was opening. He ducked into the master bedroom, leaving the office door slightly ajar.

"But I thought Daddy would be home," Emma's voice whined as they entered.

"He must be working late again. Go put your backpack away and you can play in your room until dinner."

Jackson crouched behind the bedroom door, listening to small footsteps padding down the hall toward Emma's room. He needed to move—now.

"Mommy, was Daddy's door open before?" Emma called out.

Claire paused in the entryway, frowning. "I don't think so, honey. Why?"

"It's open now."

Claire's heart skipped. "Emma, go to your room and close the door. Play with your dolls until I call you."

"But Mom—"

"Now, Emma." Her voice left no room for argument.

Small footsteps retreated, followed by the soft click of a door closing. Claire stood motionless in the hallway, listening. The house felt wrong—the air disturbed in ways she couldn't articulate. Her eyes drifted to the office door, slightly ajar when they always kept it closed.

Claire moved to the kitchen, fingers wrapping around the handle of a heavy cast iron skillet. She crept back toward the office, straining to hear any sound that didn't belong.

A floorboard creaked somewhere down the hall—not from Emma's room, but from her and Ethan's bedroom.

Claire tightened her grip on the skillet and moved toward the sound.

Claire pushed the bedroom door open with trembling fingers, the heavy iron skillet raised like a shield. Her breath caught in her throat as a large, shadowy figure emerged from the darkness of the room.

Jackson's eyes narrowed, calculating his next move. He stepped forward, his imposing silhouette filling the doorway, and Claire's world tilted dangerously on its axis.

"Who are you?" Her voice wavered, a crack in her composure. "What do you want?"

Jackson's gaze flicked to the skillet. "Just a friendly visit, Mrs. Miller," he said, his tone anything but friendly.

The sight of him—a stranger invading her sanctuary—ignited a spark in Claire's memory, and suddenly she was back in that dimly lit fraternity house room, the air thick with the stench of stale beer and cheap cologne.

Claire's grip on the skillet tightened, her knuckles turning white. The sight of the intruder—his presence in her home, her sanctuary—ripped open the fabric of her carefully constructed reality. Suddenly, she was no longer standing in her bedroom, facing a man who radiated menace. She was back in college, in that room filled with laughter and the clink of beer bottles, the air heavy with testosterone and the metallic tang of fear.

The flashback hit her with the force of a physical blow. She remembered the dizzying sensation of too much alcohol, the way her college boyfriend's face had blurred at the edges, becoming something grotesque and predatory. She remembered the weight of bodies pressing her into the mattress, the cruel hands gripping her shoulders, her hips, her thighs, refusing to let her move. She remembered the sound of her own voice, screaming until it cracked and faded into nothingness, as the laughter around her grew louder and more mocking.

The memories crashed over her in nauseating waves. The smell of cheap aftershave mingling with the sour scent of beer. The feeling of fabric tearing, the cold air against her bare skin. The sharp, searing pain as each of them took what they wanted, leaving her broken and bleeding on the bed.

The room spun. Claire's grip on the skillet faltered as her body stiffened, the weight of her past crushing her chest until she couldn't draw breath. Her vision tunneling, she was no longer in her bedroom but trapped in that moment of terror, the sensation of hands tearing at her clothes, the pain and humiliation flooding back as if it were yesterday.

Jackson watched as Claire's eyes glazed over, her face going slack. He'd seen fear before, but this—this was different. It was as if she'd left her body, leaving behind an empty vessel. The skillet clattered to the floor, its echo a stark reminder of the intrusion.

Uncertain and impatient, Jackson took a step back, then another, slipping past Claire's immobile form and through the bedroom door. He moved swiftly down the hallway, past the closed door of Emma's room, and out the back door, leaving no trace of his presence but the lingering scent of cigarette smoke and the echo of Claire's unspoken trauma.

The sound of the skillet hitting the floor jolted Emma from her play. Dropping her dolls, she crept out of her room, drawn by the noise. She found her mother standing frozen in the hallway, tears streaming silently down her cheeks.

"Mommy?" Emma's voice trembled, confusion and fear mingling in her wide eyes.

Claire didn't respond, her gaze fixed on some distant horror only she could see.

Panic clawed at Emma's chest.

She ran to the living room, fumbling with the cordless phone. Her small fingers pressed the buttons with practiced precision. "911, what's your emergency?" the voice on the other end asked.

"My mommy won't move," Emma sobbed into the receiver. "Please help her."

The emergency rooms' fluorescent lights cast harsh shadows across Claire's face as she lay motionless on the hospital bed. Monitors beeped in steady rhythm, tracking her vital signs. Physically, she was stable—but mentally, she had retreated somewhere unreachable.

"Dissociative state triggered by severe trauma," the doctor explained to Ethan, who stood at the foot of Claire's bed, his face drained of color. "Has she experienced anything like this before?"

Ethan shook his head, unable to tear his gaze from his wife's vacant expression. "No, never this bad. She's had... difficult moments, but nothing where she completely shut down."

The doctor made notes on her clipboard. "The police mentioned there was an intruder in your home?"

"That's what my daughter told the emergency responders." Ethan's voice cracked. "I wasn't there. I should have been there."

In the waiting area, Emma sat with a hospital social worker, clutching a stuffed bear someone had given her. Her small fingers traced patterns on the bear's fur as she answered questions in a trembling voice.

"Did you see the man who was in your house?" the social worker asked gently.

Emma shook her head. "I just heard a noise. Then Mommy wouldn't talk anymore."

Back in Claire's room, the psychiatrist who had been called in studied her chart. "Your wife's history of sexual trauma makes her particularly vulnerable to this kind of psychological shutdown. The home invasion likely triggered a severe flashback, essentially trapping her in that traumatic memory."

"Will she... come back?" Ethan's question hung in the air.

"Most patients do, but the timeline varies. Hours, days, sometimes longer." The psychiatrist's eyes softened with compassion. "Has she been in therapy?"

Ethan nodded, the irony of his wife's secret therapy sessions now revealed through this crisis not lost on him. "Yes, for years apparently. I only found out recently."

Night fell outside the hospital windows. Nurses moved efficiently through their rounds. Claire remained unresponsive, her eyes open but unseeing, locked in a prison of her own memories.

Ethan sat beside her bed, holding her limp hand, drowning in guilt. The security cameras he'd installed had captured Jackson leaving their home—evidence that would eventually reach Detective Marlowe—but they had failed in their primary purpose: to protect his family.

CHAPTER THIRTY-FOUR

Rebecca's Dilemma

R ebecca shifted in her car seat, the cramping in her legs a testament to hours of surveillance. Her camera lens tracked Jackson as he moved with practiced stealth around the perimeter of Ethan's home. The soft click of the shutter captured his methodical reconnaissance—checking windows, testing the front door.

"What are you up to?" she whispered, zooming in as Jackson disappeared around the rear of the house.

The unmistakable sound of a car pulling into the driveway drew her attention. Through her viewfinder, she captured Claire exiting the vehicle, her face tired but smiling as she helped Emma gather her backpack and lunch box. The little girl skipped toward the front door, pink backpack bouncing with each step, unaware of the danger lurking behind their home.

Rebecca's finger hovered over her phone. One call to 911 could prevent whatever Jackson planned. But the writer in her brain calculated the narrative impact—this confrontation could be the climactic chapter her book needed.

"Shit," she muttered, gripping her phone tighter. Her journalistic detachment warred with basic human decency. Claire and Emma were innocent bystanders in this dangerous game between Richard and Ethan.

She watched Claire unlock the front door, Emma chattering animatedly beside her. They disappeared inside, the door closing behind them with terrible finality.

"Just getting material for the book," Rebecca reminded herself, the justification sounding hollow even to her own ears.

Moments later, Jackson burst from the back door, moving with greater urgency than before. Rebecca's camera captured his hasty retreat, the slight bulge of a weapon visible beneath his jacket. His face betrayed neither triumph nor failure—just cold professionalism.

Rebecca's stomach clenched. What had he done inside?

The wail of sirens soon shattered the quiet. Rebecca ducked lower in her seat as police cruisers and an ambulance screeched to a halt in front of Ethan's house. EMTs rushed inside with equipment while officers secured the perimeter.

Through her telephoto lens, she captured the gurney being wheeled out, Claire's pale, unresponsive form strapped to it. Emma followed, clutching a police officer's hand, her small face contorted with terror.

Rebecca lowered her camera, nausea rising in her throat. She'd chosen her book over a child's mother, her career over basic humanity. Starting her car, she pulled away from the curb, the weight of her choice crushing her chest.

* * *

Rebecca's hands trembled as she laid the photographs across Detective Marlowe's desk. The images formed a damning timeline—Jackson circling Ethan's house, testing windows, disappearing around back, emerging just minutes before Claire was found catatonic.

"I was there." Rebecca's voice cracked. "I watched him break in. I saw Claire and Emma arrive. I did nothing."

Marlowe's face hardened as she examined each photograph. Her eyes, cold and precise, moved from the evidence to Rebecca's face.

"You watched a man break into a home where a woman and child were about to enter, and you took pictures instead of calling 911?" Marlowe's voice cut like steel.

Rebecca stared at her hands. "I'm not proud of it, Detective."

"Pride has nothing to do with it. Your inaction could have cost Claire Miller her life. That little girl could have lost her mother."

"I know." Rebecca's shoulders slumped. "I convinced myself I was just gathering material for my book. But I crossed a line."

Marlowe gathered the photographs, her movements sharp with disgust. "Yes, you did."

Back at her desk, Marlowe pinned the new evidence to her case board.

Marlowe stood before her evidence board, arms crossed, jaw tight. The photographs Rebecca had provided formed a visual timeline of Jackson's movements—methodical, practiced, predatory. She tapped one showing him testing Ethan's window, remembering Officer Daniels' report from yesterday.

"Lost him near Oakwood and Third," Daniels had said, frustration evident in his voice. "One minute he was three cars ahead, the next—gone."

Marlowe had been annoyed then. Now that annoyance crystallized into something sharper.

"He didn't just give you the slip," she murmured to herself. "He had a job to do."

The break-in last night was not some random attempted burglary, it now appeared in its true light—an attempt at intimidation? Was he looking for something? Possibly even murder by Richard's hired muscle? He could have easily murdered Claire if he'd wanted to. Claire obviously wasn't the target, perhaps Ethan was. The photographs connected Jackson to Richard through their documented meetings, and now to the attack on Claire.

She stepped back, reassessing everything. The prowler reports, Erika's murder, the financial crimes, the intimidation—all connected in ways she hadn't initially seen.

"This isn't just about a murder anymore," she muttered to her partner. "It's about silencing witnesses."

Across town, Rebecca sat in her apartment, staring at her manuscript. The words blurred before her eyes. Her laptop contained chapters of meticulously documented surveillance, psychological profiles, and narrative tension—all built on her willingness to watch rather than act.

She closed the file and opened a new document. If she couldn't undo her choices, she could at least ensure justice was served.

Marlowe stood before Judge Keller, her evidence organized with precision.

"Your Honor, we have photographic evidence connecting Richard Langford to Jackson Mercer, who we now have evidence of breaking into Ethan Miller's house yesterday. The financial audit has uncovered significant embezzlement. We believe Erika Matthews was killed to prevent her from exposing these crimes."

The judge took his time as he reviewed the documentation meticulously. "Detective Marlowe, you have your warrant. Mr. Langford's home and office. Immediate execution."

CHAPTER THIRTY-FIVE

Bedside Confession

Ethan's eyes remained fixed on Claire's pale face, her chest rising and falling. The sterile hum of the hospital room filled the void left by the silence of his wife. Her parents had just left with Emma, the little girl's confusion and fear momentarily eclipsed by the promise of grandparental comfort. Ethan had thanked them, his voice a hollow echo, as he hugged Emma tightly, inhaling the scent of her hair, a mixture of innocence and childhood that seemed so out of place in this chasm of despair.

Now, as he sat alone by Claire's side, the gravity of the situation pressed down on him with a palpable weight. His gaze drifted over the contours of her face, the soft curve of her cheek, the gentle slope of her nose—features he had memorized through years of shared intimacy, now rendered lifeless.

The door to the room opened with a soft creak, and Ethan looked up to see Vanessa standing there, her eyes brimming with empathy. She had become an unexpected pillar of support amidst the chaos, her presence offering a semblance of solace in the midst of the storm. Without a word, she approached, her steps slow and deliberate, as if not to disturb the fragile peace that draped over Claire's motionless form.

Vanessa's hand reached out, touching Ethan's shoulder lightly, a gesture that spoke volumes in its silent compassion. He turned towards her, his eyes glistening with unshed tears, the facade of composure crumbling away to reveal the raw vulnerability beneath. Her arms enveloped him, pulling him into an embrace that seemed to absorb some of his pain, if only for a fleeting moment.

Ethan's body shook as he succumbed to the sobs that had been building inside him, the release of emotion a painful catharsis that left him feeling both drained and strangely relieved. Vanessa held him, her hand stroking his back in soothing circles, her presence a balm to his fractured spirit.

As his sobs subsided, Vanessa knelt before him, her face level with his. Her eyes held his, communicating without words a depth of understanding that he had not realized he so desperately needed. In the quiet of the hospital room, with only the steady beat of Claire's heart monitor punctuating the silence, Vanessa's hand found Ethan's. She offered him a small, reassuring smile, and then her attention shifted, her gaze focused on the zipper of his pants.

With deft, tender movements, Vanessa began to unburden Ethan in more ways than one. Her mouth moved with a reverence that was both humbling and arousing, the warmth and wetness of her tongue contrasting sharply with the clinical chill of the room. Each stroke, each gentle suction was a wordless encouragement, an invitation for Ethan to release not just his physical tension but his emotional turmoil as well.

And as the pleasure built within him, a dam within Ethan broke. The words began to spill forth as Vanessa's ministrations continued, each revelation syncing with the waves of sensation coursing through his body. He confessed his nightly walks, his compulsion to watch the intimate lives of others, his obsession with Erika—watching her night after night until the lines between fantasy and reality blurred.

The truth about Erika's murder poured out of him, the horror of witnessing her final moments and his own paralyzing fear. His voice, barely above a whisper, was thick with shame as he admitted his fascination with Erika, his guilt for his inaction, and the twisted mix of arousal and terror he had felt as he watched her die.

The intensity of his confession grew alongside the physical pleasure Vanessa was so skillfully administering. His breaths came faster, his words tumbling out in a rush as he neared the precipice of his climax. "I should have done something... I could have stopped it... I'm sorry... I'm so sorry," he gasped.

And as he reached the peak of his physical and emotional release, his body tensed, and with a final, shuddering moan, he found his release, the final words of his confession spilling out as his body convulsed with the force of his climax.

Spent and exposed, Ethan slumped back in the chair, his breaths ragged and uneven. Vanessa sat back on her heels, her gaze lingering on his face, offering silent support and understanding.

As the room descended into a hushed stillness, a subtle movement caught Ethan's eye. Claire's fingers, previously motionless at her side, now fluttered gently against the crisp white sheets. The barely perceptible motion was like the first ripple on a once-still pond, a sign that somewhere beneath the surface, Claire was fighting her way back to consciousness.

Ethan's heart skipped a beat. Had she heard everything? Had his confession reached her in the depths of her unconscious state? The implications of what she might have overheard sent a jolt of fear through him, but he quickly pushed it aside. For now, the only thing that mattered was that Claire was showing signs of waking up.

Vanessa's eyes widened as she caught the subtle movement of Claire's fingers against the sheets. In an instant, her expression transformed from intimate compassion to calculated efficiency. Without a word, she rose from her kneeling position, smoothing her skirt with practiced precision.

Ethan remained transfixed by his wife's stirring fingers, missing the rapid change in Vanessa's demeanor. When he finally tore his gaze away to look at her, she was already backing toward the door, her movements fluid and silent.

Their eyes met for a fleeting moment – hers cool and assessing, his confused and vulnerable. Something passed between them, an unspoken acknowledgment that transcended the intimacy they had just shared. Vanessa's lips parted slightly as if to speak, but instead, she simply gave a nearly imperceptible nod.

With the practiced ease of someone accustomed to slipping in and out of rooms unnoticed, Vanessa reached behind her for the door handle. She pulled it open just enough to create a gap she could slide through, her body turning sideways to minimize her presence. Not a sound escaped as she extracted herself from the scene, the door closing with barely a click behind her.

The space where she had stood moments before now empty, Ethan was left alone with the weight of his confession hanging in the air and the stirring form of his wife on the hospital bed.

He reached out, taking her hand in his, the warmth of her skin a small but significant reassurance. "Claire," he whispered, his voice thick with emotion, "I'm here, my love. I'm here."

CHAPTER THIRTY-SIX

Richard's Cornered

Detective Marlowe's team moved with practiced efficiency through Richard's meticulously organized home office. The warrant, still warm from the printer, had granted them access to both his residence and corporate workspace simultaneously.

"Document everything," Marlowe instructed, her voice clipped as she surveyed the room. "Every file, every note, every flash drive."

A junior detective carefully photographed the contents of Richard's desk before removing items. Another officer methodically emptied the safe hidden behind Richard's framed Harvard MBA diploma a predictable hiding spot that had taken them all of three minutes to locate.

The front door slammed downstairs, followed by raised voices. Marlowe didn't flinch, continuing her inspection of a leather-bound ledger.

Richard burst into the office doorway, face flushed with rage. "What the hell is going on here? This is my private residence!"

"Mr. Langford." Marlowe didn't look up from the document she was examining. "We have warrants for both your home and office. Your wife has already been shown the paperwork."

Richard's gaze darted around the room, cataloging what the officers had already discovered. His eyes widened at the open safe.

"This is outrageous. I'll have your badge for this invasion of privacy."

Sophia appeared behind him, her judicial demeanor firmly in place. She stood in the doorway, arms crossed, watching the scene unfold with detached interest.

"Richard." Her voice cut through his bluster. "Don't make this worse than it already is."

He spun to face her. "You let them in? Without calling me first?"

"They had a warrant." Her expression remained impassive. "Signed by Judge Keller. Everything is in order."

As Richard continued his protests, Marlowe's phone buzzed. She checked the message and allowed herself a small, satisfied nod.

"Mr. Langford, the team at your office has just located documents relating to the Decker offshore account. I suggest you save your explanations for your attorney."

Richard's face drained of color. He staggered slightly, reaching for the doorframe to steady himself.

Sophia observed his crumbling composure with cold, calculating eyes.

Hours later, after the police had departed with boxes of evidence, Sophia poured herself a generous glass of scotch in their now-silent living room. Richard sat across from her, shoulders slumped in defeat.

"How long have you known?" he asked finally.

"About the embezzlement? Months." She took a measured sip. "I found the transfer records when I was looking for our tax documents in February."

Richard stood, his fists clenched, a vein pulsing at his temple. "You think you're so clever, don't you? Finding those records like some kind of amateur sleuth."

Sophia met his anger with an icy glare. "I didn't need to be clever. You've always underestimated me, Richard. That's been your fatal flaw."

He advanced on her, his presence imposing as he loomed over her petite frame. "You're my wife. You're supposed to stand by me, not plot against me."

Sophia didn't back down. "I stood by you through enough. But this? This is too much, even for me."

Their argument escalated, words thrown like daggers, each striking deep, old wounds reopened, bleeding fresh. The tension in the room was palpable, a living thing that threatened to consume them both.

And then, with a suddenness that shocked them both, the argument turned physical. Richard's hand shot out, grip tight around Sophia's wrist, a bruising hold. She responded with a stinging slap across his face, the sound echoing through the room like a gunshot.

A twisted, primal need took over, and their hate-filled encounter became a frenzy of torn clothing and aggressive, punishing touches. Richard pinned Sophia against the wall, his body a weapon, his actions a clear assertion of dominance. But Sophia was far from submissive; she fought back with a ferocity that matched his own.

Their final sexual encounter was a performance of their fractured power dynamics. Every thrust was a statement, every gasp a battle cry. It was violent and ugly, a perverse dance between two people who had once loved each other. Richard's grip on her hair was punishing, Sophia's nails clawing at his back hard enough to draw blood.

When it was over, they lay tangled in a heap of limbs and torn fabric, the evidence of their animosity strewn across the room.

Sophia was the first to rise, her movements sharp and efficient as she collected her clothes. She dressed with cold precision, each motion deliberate and controlled. Richard watched her, his own nakedness a vulnerability he had never shown before.

"Get out," Sophia said, her voice steady and calm. "Get out of our home."

Richard sat up slowly, the gravity of the situation settling over him like a shroud. "This is my house, too."

Sophia laughed, a sound devoid of humor. "Not anymore. You're no longer welcome here."

He made a move toward her, a reflexive gesture of defiance. "And if I refuse?"

Sophia's eyes hardened, her threat slicing through the air between them. "Then I'll make sure you're charged with rape along with all the other charges you're facing, Richard. After all, I didn't consent to any of that."

The fight went out of him then, replaced by a heavy resignation. He realized with crushing clarity that his marriage, his life, was over. Sophia had outmaneuvered him, and there was nothing he could do to salvage the wreckage.

Richard dressed slowly, each article of clothing a reminder of the power he had lost. Sophia watched him, her expression one of contempt and relief.

As he walked out the front door, Richard Langford left behind everything he had ever worked for—his wealth, his status, his home, and his marriage. The empire he had built was crumbling, and there was no one left to catch him when he fell.

CHAPTER THIRTY-SEVEN

Awakening

Claire awoke to the sterile glow of fluorescent lighting, her head throbbing with a dull ache. The room was unfamiliar, all crisp white sheets and antiseptic smells—a hospital room. She turned her head slowly, the motion sending waves of pain rippling through her skull. There, sitting beside her bed, was Ethan.

His face was a mask of concern, but his eyes betrayed him. They were hollow, haunted by secrets and lies. Claire's memory returned in a rush—the argument at home, the receipts, the confrontation, and then... Ethan's confession, the sounds of betrayal echoing through the walls.

She tried to sit up, her voice hoarse as she spoke. "You don't have to pretend anymore, Ethan."

His facade crumbled, replaced by a look of raw vulnerability. "Claire, I—"

She cut him off, her words laced with the bitter sting of betrayal. "I heard everything. Your confession. The... sounds."

Ethan recoiled as if slapped, his face a canvas of shock and shame. "Claire, no—it's not what you think," he stammered, reaching for her hand, but she pulled away, the mere thought of his touch repulsive.

"Not what I think?" Claire's voice rose, a blend of disbelief and fury. "I know what I heard, Ethan. The moans, the rhythmic... squelching. The sound of you... finishing. In the very room where I lay, unconscious and vulnerable."

Ethan's eyes darted around the room, landing on anything but Claire's piercing gaze. "It was a mistake," he said, his words hollow against the sterile walls. "I was weak, and I let my... compulsion take over."

Claire laughed, a harsh, mirthless sound that cut through the tension. "A compulsion? You mean your inability to control your predatory instincts? Your need to objectify and use women, even when your wife is lying next to you, fighting for her life?"

Ethan's silence was her confirmation. Claire's heart shattered into a thousand pieces, each one reflecting a fragment of the life they had built together—a life now revealed as a facade.

"I don't even know who you are," Claire whispered, her voice breaking. "You're a stranger to me. A sick, twisted stranger."

Ethan sank into the chair beside the bed, his head in his hands. "I never wanted you to find out like this," he mumbled through his fingers. "I wanted to stop. I wanted to be the man you deserved."

Claire turned her head away, unable to bear the sight of him. "But you're not, Ethan. And I don't think you ever will be."

For a long time, the only sound in the room was the steady beep of the heart monitor—a stark contrast to the chaos of emotions swirling between them.

Ethan's eyes dropped to the floor, the weight of his actions pressing down on him.

Claire's anger simmered just below the surface, a pot ready to boil over. But alongside the rage was a strange sense of relief. The not knowing, the wondering, the doubt—it had all been stripped away, leaving her with the stark, ugly truth.

"How could you?" she whispered, the question hanging heavy in the silence.

His shoulders shook as he fought back tears. "I don't know. I'm so sorry, Claire. I—"

"No," she interrupted, her voice firm despite the pain. "You don't get to apologize. Not for this."

Ethan reached for her hand, but she pulled away, the contact too much to bear.

"Our marriage is over," Claire said, the finality of her words settling over them like a shroud. "But we will need to co-parent Emma. She deserves better than this—better than us."

Tears streamed down Ethan's face, each one a testament to the love he had lost, the trust he had shattered. He nodded, accepting the terms of their new reality.

"I'll do whatever it takes, Claire," he said through his sobs. "I'll go to therapy, I'll move out, I'll—"

She held up a hand, stopping him mid-sentence. "It's too late for that, Ethan."

The room fell silent once more, the hum of the hospital machines a stark reminder of the life they had once shared, now fractured beyond repair.

Ethan stood, his movements sluggish, as if he were walking through quicksand. He lingered by the door, his gaze locked on Claire, a silent plea for forgiveness in his eyes. But she had none left to give.

With a heavy heart, he stepped out of the room, leaving behind the wreckage of their marriage. Claire watched him go, her own heart aching with the loss of what might have been.

But as the door swung shut, Claire felt a flicker of resolve. She had survived worse than this—much worse. She would heal, she would move forward, and she would make sure their daughter never suffered the same pain she had endured.

For Emma's sake, she would find the strength to face whatever came next. Alone.

* * *

Richard slammed his car door, the sound echoing through the empty driveway of what had been his home just hours before. Sophia's words still rang in his ears: "Get out. I don't know you anymore." Twenty years of marriage, dissolved in an instant, or had it been dissolving for far longer?

He checked his phone again—still nothing from Jackson. The man had vanished completely after their last meeting, likely cutting his losses. Smart move. Richard's lips curled into a bitter smile. Everyone was abandoning the sinking ship.

"Cowards," he muttered, starting the engine.

His hotel room felt sterile and impersonal, much like his future prospects. The walls seemed to close in as he paced, mind racing. The police had enough to charge him with financial crimes, but murder? That still hinged on circumstantial evidence.

If he was going down, Ethan Miller would join him.

The Miller house stood quiet and unassuming. Richard slipped on latex gloves before using the skills Jackson had taught him to pick the lock. Inside, he moved methodically through rooms, searching for anything connecting Ethan to Erika.

In the master bedroom, Richard rifled through drawers until he found a leather-bound journal hidden beneath Claire's sweaters. Expecting financial records or evidence of an affair, he instead found something far more valuable.

"Session 145: Dr. Chen says I'm making progress, but the flashbacks persist," Richard read, skimming entries detailing Claire's sexual trauma. "Still haven't told Ethan the specifics. Can't bear to see the pity in his eyes."

Richard's pulse quickened. Page after page documented Claire's therapy journey—her struggles with intimacy, her husband's growing frustration, her guilt over their failing marriage.

"Perfect," he whispered.

The journal revealed Ethan's growing resentment, his nocturnal disappearances, Claire's suspicions. It painted the picture of a man with secret compulsions—a man who might snap under pressure.

Richard flipped to the journal's final entries, his pulse quickening as he read Claire's most private thoughts.

Ethan came home late again. When I asked where he'd been, he gave the same vague answer about "clearing his head." The news about that woman from his office was on TV again. I caught him staring at her photo with an expression I couldn't read.

He called out her name last night. "Erika." Not once, but twice. He was having a nightmare, thrashing in bed. When I woke him, he looked terrified. Said he couldn't remember what he was dreaming about. He's lying.

Richard's hands trembled with excitement as he turned to the final page.

I found receipts from restaurants near her apartment building. Multiple nights, including the night she died. The timing matches his "walks." God, how could I be so blind? He was having an affair with her. But there's something else... something worse I can barely bring myself to write. The way he's been since her death—the panic attacks, the nightmares, checking the locks three times every night. He jumps whenever there's a police car on the news.

What if it wasn't just an affair? What if he... No. I can't even think it. But could Ethan be capable of murder? The man I married wouldn't be. But I don't know who he is anymore.

"Bingo," Richard whispered, a smile spreading across his face. "This is a gold mine."

He carefully closed the journal, tucking it inside his jacket. This was exactly what he needed—reasonable doubt, another suspect, a man with motive and opportunity. A man whose own wife suspected him of murder.

Richard left as quietly as he had entered, making sure to lock the door behind him.

His phone buzzed—Marlowe requesting he come in for additional questioning tomorrow morning.

Perfect, he thought. This will give Marlowe all she needs to go after Ethan.

Richard placed the journal on the passenger seat, tapping his fingers against the steering wheel as he considered his next move. The hotel room felt too confining, too quiet with just his thoughts. He needed to act while momentum was on his side.

He pulled out his phone and composed a text to Detective Marlowe: "I've discovered something relevant to your investigation. Can we meet tonight instead of tomorrow?"

Her response came quickly: "Police station. 9PM."

Richard smiled. The urgency in her reply told him everything he needed to know—she was hungry for a break in the case. And he was about to serve Ethan Miller on a silver platter.

He drove carefully, precisely at the speed limit. No mistakes now. The journal sat beside him like a ticking bomb, Claire's private thoughts weaponized against her husband. The irony wasn't lost on him—Ethan's voyeuristic tendencies had made him vulnerable, and now his wife's private journal would finish the job.

At a red light, Richard flipped through the pages again, mentally cataloging the most damning entries. Claire's suspicions about Ethan's whereabouts on the night of the murder. The nightmares where he called out Erika's name. The receipts placing him near her apartment. His erratic behavior since her death.

Richard checked his watch—8:30 PM. He had just enough time to grab coffee and rehearse his concerned colleague routine. He would appear reluctant, even pained, to share such personal information about a coworker. "I just couldn't keep this to myself," he would tell Marlowe. "Not when a woman's killer is still out there."

The light turned green. Richard accelerated, already imagining the look on Ethan's face when the police showed up at his door. By morning, the focus of the investigation would shift dramatically. By tomorrow night, Richard might even be free to leave town while the police built their case against Ethan.

CHAPTER THIRTY-EIGHT

Collision Course

Ethan's key trembled in the lock. The house stood silent, empty—just like his future. He pushed the door open, stepping into the hollow space that had once been his home. Their home.

Claire's slippers still sat by the couch. Emma's drawings still decorated the refrigerator. But Claire wouldn't be coming back. Not after what he'd done.

The hospital scene replayed in his mind with sickening clarity.

"How could I be so stupid?" he whispered to the empty kitchen.

It had been a moment of madness. Vanessa's mouth sliding up and down on his manhood. Her fingers expertly working him while Claire lay unconscious. The rush of being watched without watching—a perverse inversion of his compulsion.

Ethan slumped onto the couch, burying his face in his hands. He'd lost everything—his wife, his daughter, his identity. The careful compartmentalization of his life had collapsed. The man who watched others had finally been seen for what he truly was.

The soft rap on the door startled Ethan from his self-recriminations. He wasn't expecting anyone. Wearily, he rose from the couch, each step an effort against the gravity of his grief.

He opened the door to find Vanessa, her face etched with concern. "Vanessa? What are you doing here?" Ethan's voice was a hollow echo of himself.

"I had to know what happened at the hospital, after I left." she said softly. "I wanted to make sure you were okay."

Ethan's eyes betrayed him, the pain of his confession to Claire, her horrified awakening, still raw and bleeding.

Vanessa stepped inside, her presence a warm breeze in the cold stillness of the house. "Ethan, I'm so sorry," she whispered, her arms wrapping around him.

Ethan allowed himself to be held, the comfort of another human being a balm to his open wounds. "Claire... she heard everything. She knows about... us."

Vanessa pulled back, her eyes searching his. "And how do you feel about that?"

"Lost," Ethan admitted. "I've lost my family, Vanessa. Everything I've ever cared about."

She took his hand, leading him to the couch. "Ethan, I came here seeking answers for Erika's death, but somehow, I found... you."

"When I heard she was murdered, I knew it had to be connected to her job. I applied for the position to find out who killed her."

Ethan's body went rigid. "And now you know it was Richard."

"I know everything, Ethan." Her hand found his, squeezing gently. "I heard what you said at the hospital when you thought Claire couldn't hear. The voyeurism, the obsession with my sister... seeing her murdered."

Ethan pulled away, shame burning through him. "Then why are you here? Why comfort me?"

"Ethan, there was nothing you could have done," Vanessa said softly. "It was Richard that killed her, not you. I don't blame you." She moved closer, her hand returning to his. "I just feel closer to you. You were there with her in her final moments when I couldn't be."

Her fingers traced the veins on the back of his hand. "You saw her. You know her secrets. In some strange way, it's like... you're my last connection to her."

Their eyes locked, a silent understanding flowing between them. The air grew thick with an unspoken yearning, a need for connection, for solace in the storm of their lives.

Before either could speak again, their lips met in a desperate, hungry kiss. Clothes abandoned, they moved to the bedroom—Claire's scent still lingering in the air—and fell onto the bed.

Vanessa straddled Ethan, her hips rocking against his, her fingers entwined with his. Their lovemaking was fierce, a wildfire consuming the remnants of their past lives. Every touch, every moan was a testament to their shared brokenness, their raw vulnerability laid bare.

Ethan's hands explored Vanessa's body, her curves yielding under his touch. She arched her back, her breath hitching as he entered her. They moved together, a dance as old as time, each thrust a declaration of their need for each other.

Vanessa's breath quickened as she rode Ethan, her body tensing with each movement. The knowledge that this was Claire's bed—the same sheets, the same pillows—sent an unexpected thrill through her. She ran her fingers over the headboard, imagining Claire's hands gripping the same spot.

"This is where you sleep with her," Vanessa whispered, her voice husky with desire. "Where you lie next to her every night."

Ethan's eyes widened slightly, but his rhythm didn't falter. Vanessa leaned down, her lips brushing his ear.

"Does it excite you? Having me here where she should be?"

Her fingers traced the wrinkles in the pillowcase—Claire's pillowcase—as a perverse satisfaction bloomed inside her. She was claiming something that belonged to another woman, inserting herself into the most intimate space of Ethan and Claire's marriage.

"Her scent is still here," Vanessa murmured, inhaling deeply. The faint traces of Claire's perfume mingled with the musk of their lovemaking. "I can smell her."

She pressed her palms flat against the mattress, feeling the impression where Claire's body had lain countless nights. The thought of Claire returning to this bed—unknowingly sleeping where Vanessa had been—sent a shudder of pleasure through her body.

Vanessa's movements grew more urgent, more demanding. She wasn't just making love to Ethan; she was conquering territory, marking what didn't belong to her. The forbidden nature of their act intensified every sensation, every touch.

"She'll never know," Vanessa whispered, arching her back. "This will be our secret."

The bed creaked beneath them—the same sounds it made when Ethan was with Claire. Vanessa closed her eyes, imagining Claire's face if she could see them now, in her sacred space. The thought pushed her closer to the edge.

Vanessa's climax came in waves, her body shuddering with the intensity of her release. Ethan followed, the sensation of Vanessa's body tightening around him pushing him over the edge.

Afterward, they lay entwined, the sweat cooling on their skin. Vanessa propped herself up on one elbow, her hair falling in a curtain around her face.

"Ethan," she began, her voice a whisper, "I never expected to feel this way about you. But I am. I'm falling in love with you."

Ethan's heart, still reeling from the aftershocks of their love-making, stuttered in his chest. "Vanessa, I—"

She placed a finger against his lips, silencing him. "You don't have to say it back. I know you're still grieving your marriage. I just needed you to know how I feel."

Ethan reached up, tracing the line of her jaw with his finger-tips. "Maybe that's why I feel the same," he said, his voice hoarse with emotion. "You understand me so completely... it's unlike anything I've ever known."

Their eyes met, a silent vow passing between them. In the quiet aftermath of their passion, they found a moment of peace, a sanctuary from the chaos of their lives. And for the first time in a long time, Ethan didn't feel quite so alone.

* * *

While Ethan and Vanessa explored their newfound intimacy, Richard Langford sat across from Detective Marlowe in an in-terview room at the police station. Despite the pending charges against him, he maintained his composure, hands folded neatly on the metal table.

"I appreciate you meeting with me, Detective." Richard's wedding ring—still on his finger despite his marriage trou-bles—caught the fluorescent light as he slid a leather journal across the table. "I believe this information will be of significant interest to your investigation."

Marlowe's expression remained neutral as she opened the journal.

"Claire Miller's journal," Richard explained. "A concerned colleague provided these to me. They detail her suspicions about her husband's... proclivities."

Marlowe scanned the pages, her sharp eyes noting dates and key phrases. The entries described a husband who disappeared at night, who came home aroused after these "walks," who had searched for information about voyeurism.

"Mrs. Miller writes about finding receipts from restaurants near Erika's apartment," Richard continued. "About Ethan's strange behavior after Erika's death. About his obsession with security and being watched."

"And how exactly did you come by this?" Marlowe asked, her voice clipped.

Richard's smile didn't reach his eyes. "As I said, a concerned colleague. Someone who witnessed Ethan's... inappropriate interest in Erika while she was alive."

"I see." Marlowe's tone revealed nothing.

"The evidence is compelling, Detective. Ethan Miller was stalking Erika. He watched her for months. When she discovered him, confronted him perhaps, things escalated." Richard leaned forward. "I'm being framed for a crime that Ethan Miller committed."

Marlowe closed the book. "These accusations are serious, Mr. Langford."

"They're the truth."

"I'll follow up on this information," she said, standing. "But I should remind you that fabricating evidence is a serious offense."

"I would never," Richard replied, his face a mask of sincerity.

Thirty minutes later, Detective Marlowe's unmarked car pulled up outside the Miller residence. The house was quiet, with no signs of activity.

She approached the front door and rang the bell, listening to it echo through the house. After a moment, she heard hurried movements inside—footsteps, hushed voices, the sound of a door closing.

Marlowe waited patiently, one hand resting near her service weapon.

Finally, the door swung open to reveal a disheveled Ethan Miller, hastily dressed in sweatpants and a t-shirt. His hair was mussed, his face flushed.

"Mr. Miller," Marlowe said, her observant eyes noting everything from his bare feet to the fresh scratch marks visible at the collar of his shirt. "I need to ask you some questions about your relationship with Erika Jensen."

From somewhere inside the house came the soft sound of a floorboard creaking.

CHAPTER THIRTY-NINE

Truth and Consequences

E than stepped back, gesturing Marlowe inside. "Detective, I can explain—"

"Can you explain why your car was repeatedly seen near Erika Jensen's apartment in the weeks leading to her murder?" Marlowe's gaze was penetrating. "Or why multiple witnesses reported seeing a man matching your description watching her building?"

Ethan's face drained of color. "I—"

"Or perhaps you'd like to explain these?" Marlowe produced several printed pages. "Searches for 'how to stop compulsive voyeurism' from your home computer. Receipts from establishments near Ms. Jensen's residence on nights when neighbors reported a prowler."

"That's not—" Ethan stammered.

"Richard Langford provided evidence suggesting you've been watching women without their consent for years, Mr. Miller. Including Erika Jensen."

Before Ethan could respond, footsteps sounded from the hallway. Vanessa Carter emerged, fully dressed and composed despite the interruption.

"Detective Marlowe, I believe I can shed some light on this situation." Her voice was steady, professional—nothing like the marketing associate persona she'd cultivated.

"Ms. Carter?" Marlowe's eyebrow raised slightly.

Marlowe's expression shifted as Vanessa retrieved a briefcase from beside the sofa.

"Richard Langford is attempting to frame Ethan because he discovered these." Vanessa opened the case, revealing organized files and a USB drive. "The complete contents of Erika Jensen's safe deposit box.

She handed Marlowe a folder. "Erika documented every-thing—Richard's embezzlement through the Decker account, his violent tendencies, even his previous assault that Judge Sophia helped cover up. She was blackmailing him."

"And how did you obtain these?" Marlowe asked.

"We found some of Erika's journal entries," Vanessa ex-plained, gesturing to the files in Marlowe's hands. "There are copies of those in the files I just gave you. In those entries, she mentioned a key to a safe deposit box. We followed up and what you have there is what was contained in that box."

Marlowe flipped through the documents with practiced efficiency, her expression remaining neutral even as her eyes widened slightly at certain passages.

"This contradicts your department's previous statement that Ms. Jensen had no personal documentation at work," Marlowe said, looking up sharply.

"Because Richard had IT scrub her work computer," Vanessa replied. "But he didn't know about her physical backup system."

Marlowe's gaze snapped to Vanessa's face, studying her features with new intensity.

"There's something else you should know, Detective." Vanessa's voice softened slightly. "I am Erika's half-sister. We share the same mother. I only learned about her existence less than a year ago. When I heard of her murder, I came here looking for answers."

"You intentionally applied for a position at the company where your sister worked without disclosing this relationship?" Marlowe's tone sharpened.

"Would you have hired the grieving sister of your murdered employee?" Vanessa countered. "I needed to understand who she was, who might have wanted her dead."

Marlowe stared at Vanessa studying her resemblance to Erika.

"I couldn't risk anyone knowing. Not until I found what I needed." Vanessa turned to Marlowe. "Our mother left when Erika was very young. She started a new life—then had me. I found letters in my mother's belongings after she died last year. That's how I discovered I had a sister, a half sister."

Marlowe's expression remained carefully neutral. "And you chose not to come forward with this information during the investigation?"

"I was afraid it would compromise my position here. I needed access." Vanessa's composure cracked slightly. "She was black-mailing Richard, but she was also documenting everything as insurance. She was smarter than anyone gave her credit for."

"And your expertise in financial fraud detection?" Marlowe asked.

"That's genuine. My previous employer was investigated for similar schemes. I recognized the patterns in Richard's work immediately."

Marlowe sat silent, thinking. "This information changes things significantly, Ms. Carter. Or is that even your real name?"

"It is. Different fathers." Vanessa's eyes held steady. "Everything else I've told you is true. I came here for justice for my sister."

Marlowe examined the documents, her trained eyes quickly recognizing their significance, before finally closing the box. "I need to make a call. Richard Langford won't be walking away this time."

* * *

Marlowe strode from Ethan's house, phone already pressed to her ear. "This is Detective Marlowe. I need an immediate arrest warrant for Richard Langford on charges of first-degree

murder, embezzlement, witness intimidation, and conspiracy."
She paused, listening. "Yes, I have compelling new evidence. The
safe deposit box contents confirm everything. Send units to his
residence and office immediately."

Three hours later, Richard paced the confines of a mid-range
hotel room, bourbon in hand, watching breaking news coverage
of his own manhunt. His phone buzzed with a text from his
fixer Jackson: "Police everywhere. Can't help. On my own now."

Richard hurled the phone against the wall.

A sharp knock at the door froze him mid-stride.

"Richard Langford, this is Detective Marlowe with the police
department. We have a warrant for your arrest. Come out with
your hands visible."

Richard grabbed a pistol from his overnight bag. "I'm armed!
Stay back!"

"Mr. Langford, there's no way out. The building is surrounded."

Through the peephole, Richard saw tactical officers positioning in the hallway. He backed away, gun pressed to his temple. "I'm not going to prison! You understand? I'll end this right
now!"

"Richard." A familiar voice—Sophia's—came through the
door. "It's me."

"Sophia?" His voice cracked. "What are you doing here?"

"Let me in, Richard. Just me."

After a tense negotiation, the door opened just enough for Sophia to slip inside. She stood before him in her judicial robes, her expression a mixture of disgust and pity.

"Put the gun down," she said calmly.

"You're still in your robes." Richard's hand trembled. "Court today?"

"I was presiding when they found you." Her voice was ice. "I signed your arrest warrant myself."

Richard's face contorted. "You what?"

"I've spent years protecting you, Richard. Covering for your indiscretions, your violence. I won't do it anymore." She stepped closer. "You killed that woman in cold blood."

"She was blackmailing me! She would have ruined everything!"

"And now you've done that yourself." Sophia's eyes hardened. "The evidence is overwhelming. Your offshore accounts have been frozen. Your intimidation tactics documented. It's over."

Richard's shoulders slumped, the fight draining from him visibly. The gun lowered inch by inch until it dangled uselessly at his side.

"I want to see my lawyer," he whispered.

Outside, camera crews from every major network jostled for position. The financial director's arrest was already national news—a scandal involving murder, embezzlement, and a judge's husband too juicy to ignore.

CHAPTER FORTY

Full Circle

Six months later, Ethan unlocked the door to his two-bed-room apartment in the west side of town. The place was modest but meticulously organized—everything in its place, everything visible from any vantage point. No hiding spots, no secrets. That had been his therapist's suggestion.

He set down a bag of groceries and checked his watch. Emma would arrive in an hour for their weekend visit. The custody arrangement gave him every other weekend and Wednesday dinners—not what he wanted, but more than he deserved.

His phone buzzed with a text from Claire: "Emma packed her science project. Don't let her forget to bring it back Sunday."

Ethan smiled and texted back a thumbs-up emoji. Their communication had evolved into something functional, if not warm. The divorce papers had been finalized three months ago, shortly after Richard's guilty plea had made national headlines.

His new marketing position at a small agency paid less than Horizon Financial but offered something more valuable—anonymity. Nobody there knew about his connection to the "Financial Murder" case that had dominated cable news for weeks. Rebecca's book, "A View to Die For," had become a bestseller, though she'd kept her promise to change names and details enough to protect him.

Ethan opened his refrigerator and arranged Emma's favorite snacks on the middle shelf where she could reach them. He'd child-proofed the apartment and decorated her small bedroom with space-themed wallpaper that matched her current obsession with astronomy.

His twice-weekly therapy sessions had given him tools to manage his compulsions. The urge to watch others hadn't disappeared, but he'd learned to recognize the triggers and redirect his attention. The ankle monitor he'd worn for the first three months after his confession to voyeurism charges—a plea deal that kept him off the sex offender registry—had been removed last week.

Detective Marlowe had attended his final court appearance, watching with those knowing eyes as the judge declared his probation terms satisfied. She'd nodded to him in the hallway afterward—not forgiveness, but acknowledgment of his efforts.

As Ethan arranged Emma's favorite board games on the coffee table, he felt the familiar tightness in his chest ease slightly.

He still woke sometimes from dreams of Erika's final moments, still caught himself scanning windows when walking at dusk. But for the first time in years, he wasn't living a double life.

The doorbell rang at exactly 6:30 PM. Ethan checked his watch—Emma had been picked up by Claire two hours ago, right on schedule.

He opened the door to find Vanessa, her blonde hair pulled back in a simple ponytail, wearing jeans and a soft blue sweater that made her eyes more green than brown.

"You're exactly on time," he said.

"Always am." She stepped inside, her familiar scent—something citrusy and clean—filling his entryway. "How was your weekend with Emma?"

"Good. We built a model solar system for her science project. Jupiter's rings are a little lopsided."

"Saturn," Vanessa corrected with a small smile. "Jupiter doesn't have rings."

This was their rhythm—comfortable, intellectual, charged with something neither of them fully acknowledged. Since the Richard investigation had concluded, they'd fallen into a pattern that defied conventional labels. Not quite dating, not merely friends.

"I brought dinner." She held up a bag from their favorite Thai place. "And that documentary about deep sea creatures you mentioned."

In the kitchen, they moved around each other with practiced ease, reaching for plates and glasses without colliding. Vanessa somehow felt she belonged in this space.

"The audit committee finalized the last of the recovery procedures," she said, spooning curry onto her plate. "The company's finally moving past the Richard scandal."

Ethan nodded. "That's good."

"I saw Rebecca's book at the airport. End cap display."

"She sent me a signed copy. I haven't read it yet."

Vanessa's fingers brushed his as she reached for the water pitcher. The contact sent electricity through him—always did. She met his eyes, neither pulling away nor leaning in.

"We should talk about this," she said quietly.

"This?"

"Us. Whatever this is." She gestured between them. "Six months of dinner and documentaries and..."

"And nothing else," Ethan finished.

"Is it because of what you know I know? About you? About what you used to do?"

He looked at her—really looked at her. Unlike Erika, whose beauty had been a weapon, Vanessa's intelligence shone through her eyes. She knew his darkest parts and hadn't run.

"Partly," he admitted. "But also because I'm still learning how to be honest. With myself. With others."

Vanessa set down her fork, her eyes never leaving his. "Ethan, I know everything about your past, and I'm still here. Does that tell you anything?"

The words hung between them, heavy with meaning. She knew about his voyeurism, his witness to murder, his lies to Claire. She'd seen the court documents, the therapy reports, everything.

"I..." he started, then stopped.

"Ethan, I love you and I want more."

The declaration hit him like a physical force. Six months of careful distance, of friendship that simmered with unacknowledged tension—all of it collapsed in those eight words.

"I want more too," he said, his voice barely above a whisper. "I love you too. I'm just so confused as to where to go next."

He hadn't planned to say it, but the truth had escaped before he could catch it. Love. The word he'd used so carelessly with Claire, thinking possession was the same as devotion.

Vanessa reached across the table and took his hand. Her palm was warm against his.

"Quit overthinking it Ethan, just go with your heart. I know what you were, what you are and it doesn't matter to me as much as it matters to you." Her voice grew softer, more intense. "I'm all in Ethan. I pray to God you are as well."

* * *

The evening air was crisp, the sky a tapestry of deepening blues as twilight surrendered to night. Vanessa stood in Ethan's backyard, the soft glow from the kitchen window casting her silhouette in a warm halo. She turned to face him, her eyes reflecting the moonlight.

"Tonight, we're going to try something different," she said, her voice steady, her gaze unwavering.

Ethan's heart pounded in his chest. The old compulsion stirred within him, a serpent uncoiling in the pit of his stomach. "What do you mean?"

"I mean, I want you to watch me."

He swallowed hard, the implications of her words setting off a cascade of conflicting emotions. Desire mingled with fear, excitement with trepidation. "Vanessa, I don't know if that's a good idea."

"It's okay, Ethan. I trust you." She stepped closer, her hand reaching out to touch his arm. "And I think this could be good for you. Controlled. Safe."

He searched her face for any sign of hesitation, but found none. Instead, there was a strength in her eyes, a conviction that told him she had thought this through.

"Alright," he agreed, his voice a hoarse whisper.

Vanessa nodded and walked toward the house. She paused at the edge of the patio, her fingers toying with the hem of her sweater. Then, with a deliberate slowness, she lifted the fabric over her head and let it drop to the ground.

Ethan's breath caught in his throat as she continued to undress, each piece of clothing a deliberate unveiling. He was acutely aware of the cool air on his skin, the rustle of leaves in the breeze, the distant hum of the city. His senses were heightened, attuned to every detail— every movement of her body under the soft light.

Vanessa turned and made her way to the window, her bare skin bathed in the golden glow from inside the house. She leaned against the sill, her profile etched against the translucent curtains. She was framed like a piece of art, and Ethan was utterly captivated.

He watched as she closed her eyes and tilted her head back, her chest rising and falling with each steady breath. She was the embodiment of tranquility, of controlled abandon. This was her gift to him—acceptance, trust, and the permission to indulge in his compulsion in a way that harmed no one.

Ethan felt the chains of his old life loosen slightly. This was different. This was consensual, a shared experience. He was not a voyeur preying on the unaware; he was a participant in a deeply intimate act.

With each passing moment, the tension between them built—a taut wire vibrating with anticipation. Vanessa's eyes fluttered open, and she looked directly at him, a subtle nod beckoning him to join her.

Ethan crossed the lawn, his steps measured and deliberate. He approached the window, his gaze locked with hers as he closed the distance between them.

He reached out and traced the outline of her face through the glass, his fingers shaking slightly. The barrier between them was thin, a mere pane of glass, yet it represented a chasm that they were bridging together.

Vanessa smiled, her lips parting as she mouthed the words, "Come inside."

Ethan nodded, a silent vow passing between them. This was a new beginning, a chance to redefine his compulsion—to transform it from a solitary vice into a shared exploration of trust and desire.

He moved away from the window, his heart racing with the knowledge of what was to come. As he walked toward the back door, he felt the weight of his past begin to lift, replaced by a budding hope for the future.

* * *

Claire sat across from Michael in the dimly lit restaurant, her fingers toying with the stem of her wine glass. She'd met him at an art exhibit three weeks ago—a fellow teacher with kind eyes and a quiet laugh that didn't demand anything from her.

"You seem different tonight," Michael said, his voice gentle. "More relaxed."

Claire smiled, feeling the truth of his words. "I am." She took a sip of her wine, savoring the warmth that spread through her chest. "It's been a long journey."

Long didn't begin to cover it. Three years of therapy, of unpacking trauma, of learning to inhabit her body again. Dr. Chen had encouraged her to start dating six months ago, but Claire had resisted until now.

"I'm glad you suggested dinner," Michael said, his eyes crinkling at the corners.

Claire nodded, feeling a flutter of anticipation rather than the familiar dread. "Me too."

When his hand brushed hers across the table, she didn't flinch away. Instead, she turned her palm upward, allowing their fingers to intertwine. The contact sent a pleasant shiver up her arm—not fear, but possibility.

Later, as they stood on her porch, Michael leaned in slowly, giving her time to pull away. Claire closed her eyes and met him halfway, their lips touching in a kiss that was tender and unhurried.

"I'd like to see you again," he whispered against her mouth.

"I'd like that too," Claire replied, surprised by how much she meant it.

Inside her empty house, Claire leaned against the door, her heart beating steadily in her chest. She pulled out her phone and sent a quick text to Dr. Chen: "You were right. I was ready."

The reply came moments later: "Proud of you, Claire. Remember, baby steps."

Baby steps indeed. Claire touched her lips, still feeling the ghost of Michael's kiss. For the first time in years, she felt a spark of desire that wasn't tangled with fear—a clean, bright feeling that belonged solely to her.

She was reclaiming pieces of herself, slowly but surely. Not for Ethan, not for anyone else. For herself.

* * *

Ethan left his therapist's office as dusk settled over the city. Six months since Richard's arrest. Six months of weekly sessions unpacking his "compulsive tendencies," as Dr. Winters diplomatically called them. Progress had been slow but steady—fewer urges, better control.

He cut through Madison Park, taking the long way home. The evening air carried the scent of rain-washed concrete and distant cooking. Street lights flickered on one by one, casting pools of amber light across his path.

That's when he saw her.

In a ground-floor apartment across from the park, a window stood open, curtains drawn back. A woman moved through the room, completely naked. The familiar rush hit him—that electric current of forbidden witnessing.

She was tall, willowy, with honey-blonde hair cascading down her back. Her skin glowed in the warm light of her bedroom as she stretched, arms reaching skyward, the movement lifting her small, perfect breasts. Her waist curved inward before flaring to rounded hips. She turned, giving him a profile view as she bent to pick something up from her bed.

Ethan's mouth went dry. His heart hammered against his ribs. He felt the old hunger rising, demanding to be fed.

Keep walking. Just keep walking.

He forced his feet forward, one step, then another. His therapist's voice echoed in his mind: "Recognize the trigger. Acknowledge the urge. Choose a different response."

Three more steps. Four. His body felt heavy, as if wading through mud. Sweat beaded on his forehead despite the cool evening air.

You're better than this now. A life you're rebuilding.

Five steps. Six. The woman was still visible in his peripheral vision. She was applying lotion now, hands sliding over her thighs, up her stomach, across her breasts.

Ethan stopped. His breathing came in shallow bursts. The world narrowed to that illuminated window, to the private ritual unfolding inside.

He turned back, stepping into the shadow of a large oak tree. From here, no one would see him watching. Just this once. Just for a moment.

Some demons, Ethan realized, you never truly escape—you just learn to live with them.

CHAPTER FORTY-ONE

Epilogue

Detective Marlowe closed the manila folder labeled "Jensen, Erika – Homicide" and ran her thumb along the edge of the case file. Six months since Richard's conviction, three since the sentencing. Justice served, by most definitions.

She slid open her desk drawer and extracted a photograph—Ethan Miller at the company memorial service, his face a mask of careful neutrality while his eyes told a different story. She'd printed it from security footage, keeping it separate from the official file.

"Still think you were there that night," she murmured, studying his features. "Still think you saw something you're not telling me."

She tapped the photo against her desk twice before slipping it into her personal drawer beneath a stack of unrelated files. Not evidence, just intuition—the kind that kept her awake some nights.

"Some cases never really close," she said to the empty office.

Vanessa Carter knelt before the simple granite headstone, placing a bouquet of white lilies against the cool stone. ERIKA JENSEN, the inscription read, followed by dates that spanned too few years.

"Hello, sister," she whispered.

"I came to Horizon looking for you," she said, brushing fallen leaves from the grave. "Found your killer instead."

She traced the engraved letters with her fingertip. "We never got to meet, but I finished what you started. Richard's locked away, the company's cleaned up its finances." A sad smile crossed her face. "I'm sorry I couldn't save you. I was too late."

The wind rustled through nearby trees as Vanessa sat in silence, mourning the connection they'd never have.

Rebecca Sanders stared at her laptop screen, cursor blinking at the end of her new book proposal. "The Watchers: A True Crime Study of Voyeurism and Murder" had landed her a substantial advance and a two-book deal.

Her publisher wanted more of the same—another voyeur, another crime.

She glanced at her camera equipment on the desk—the telephoto lens, the night vision attachment, the small directional microphone. Tools of her trade.

"Research or obsession?" she muttered, closing her laptop.

Rebecca moved to her window, raising binoculars to her eyes. Across the street, a man argued with his wife, gesturing wildly. Three floors up, a teenager danced alone to music only she could hear. Two buildings over, an elderly man fed his cats.

She lowered the binoculars, suddenly uncomfortable with the familiar thrill of watching unseen.

The line between researcher and voyeur had never seemed thinner.

Ethan adjusted the telescope on his balcony, the cool metal smooth beneath his fingertips. The night sky stretched above him, vast and glittering. He'd taken up astronomy three months ago—a suggestion from his therapist to find healthier outlets for his observational tendencies.

"Look up, not across," Dr. Winters had said with pointed emphasis during their last session.

He focused on Jupiter, its pale orange glow distinct among the stars. Emma had been fascinated when he'd shown her the planet and its moons last weekend, her eyes wide with wonder. That moment—sharing something beautiful with his daughter—had felt pure in a way few things did anymore.

The telescope's eyepiece was cool against his skin as he tracked the constellations. Cassiopeia. The Big Dipper. Familiar patterns in the darkness.

His hand drifted to the adjustment knob, lowering the telescope's angle ever so slightly.

The rooftop of the building across the street came into view. Then the top floor windows. His breath quickened.

"Just checking the alignment," he whispered to himself, a lie so practiced it almost sounded true.

The telescope continued its downward journey, past empty offices, past darkened apartments, until it settled on a window with lights still burning. A woman moved through the frame, phone pressed to her ear, gesturing animatedly.

Ethan's fingers tightened around the telescope. The familiar rush returned—the heightened awareness, the quickening pulse, the sense of power that came with seeing without being seen.

He watched her pace, talking, laughing at something said on the other end of the call. She was a stranger, unaware of his presence across the void between buildings.

His phone buzzed in his pocket. Claire's name flashed on the screen.

"How was therapy today?" her text read.

The woman across the street moved to her window now, gazing out at the night, her expression pensive.

For a moment, their eyes seemed to meet across the distance, though logic told him she couldn't possibly see him in the darkness.

Ethan's hand trembled as he slowly raised the telescope back toward the stars.

In a third-floor apartment three blocks from Ethan's building, Sharon Reeves adjusted her binoculars, focusing on the man with the telescope. The lenses brought Ethan's features into sharp clarity—the tension in his jaw, the hesitation in his movements as he redirected his telescope toward the stars.

"That's it," Sharon whispered. "The struggle is the interesting part."

She'd been watching Ethan for six weeks now, ever since noticing the man's suspicious behavior during her own evening observations of the neighborhood. At first, Sharon had assumed Ethan was simply another amateur astronomer. Then she'd noticed the pattern—how the telescope inevitably drifted downward from the stars to windows, how Ethan's posture changed when he found something of interest.

Sharon recognized a kindred spirit.

A professor of behavioral psychology specializing in compulsive disorders, Sharon had started watching neighborhood residents as research for a paper on urban isolation. Somewhere along the way, the academic distance had collapsed. The notes became personal. The observations, nightly.

"We're not so different, you and I," Sharon murmured, tracking Ethan's movements. "Just degrees of the same condition."

She lowered her binoculars for just a moment, then raised them again to find Ethan had disappeared from the balcony. Sharon panned across the apartment windows until she located him inside, now sitting beside a beautiful blonde woman on the couch, his face animated in conversation.

Sharon felt a twinge of something—envy, perhaps—at the scene of domestic normalcy.

From somewhere behind her, a floorboard creaked. Sharon froze, suddenly aware of the irony—that she might not be the final link in this chain of observation. That someone else might be watching her watch Ethan watch others.

She turned slowly, scanning her darkened apartment, finding nothing but shadows.

Yet the feeling persisted—of being observed, catalogued, understood.

Perhaps we're all watchers.....Perhaps we're all being watched.

About Julie Freebush

Passionate and Dedicated

Ever wondered what it's like to live a life filled with passion, desire, and forbidden love?

Meet Julie Freebush, the author who knows no bounds when it comes to exploring the realms of *eroticism*.

Julie has had an intense fascination with *seduction* and *temptation* since her childhood, when an innocent skinny dipping experience sparked something deep inside her.

Her stories are filled with *seduction*, *temptation*, and *illicit encounters* that will leave you *breathless*.

Julie spends her days *writing* and her nights "*Researching*".

As an author who knows no bounds.

Julie's experiences range from the *scandalous* to the downright *explicit*, and her writing is a testament to her *insatiable appetite for pleasure*.

Julie's works are filled with *secrets, lust, and explicit encounters* that will leave your heart racing. So, if you're ready to embark on a journey of *sensuality* and *illicit pleasure*, join *Julie Freebush* in her world of *Short & Steamy Tales of Erotica.*

For all the latest releases and current happenings with Julie, stop by her website.   JulieFreeb ush.com

Also by Julie Freebush

Private Pages: The Descent of Erika Lawrence

(Neglected Wives Series)

Savage Tides: Survival and Desire

Julie's Unabridged ADULT Research Stories Series

Short and Steamy Tales of Erotica:

Volumes One & Two

Home From the Army: Book One An Erotic Tale of Passion, Seduction, Family and Forbidden Desires